BORN IN SIN

KINLEY MacGREGOR

BORN IN SIN

An Avon Romantic Treasure

AVON BOOKS
An Imprint of HarperCollinsPublishers

AVON BOOKS
An Imprint of HarperCollins*Publishers*
10 East 53rd Street
New York, New York 10022-5299

Copyright © 2003 by Sherrilyn Kenyon
ISBN: 0-7394-3164-1

Printed in the U.S.A.

For Lyssa and all her wonderful insights that help so incredibly much, and for Nancy, who keeps me sane. For my dearest friends, Janet, Lo, Rickey and Cathy.

But mostly for my husband, who has always been and will always be the greatest love of my life. You keep me sanest of all and allow me to pursue my dreams. I may not always say it or show it, but deep down where it counts, I keep a running tally of just how much I do owe you. You're the best, hon, and I love you.

Prologue

Outremer

The cold night wind carried laughter on it as it blew against Sin's desert-blistered cheeks and dry, cracked lips. Unused to such a sound, he crouched down low in the shadows on the outskirts of the English camp and listened. It had been a long time since he had heard such.

But his hesitation cost him, as Marr rammed a barbed stick into his spine. "Why do you stop, maggot? Go!"

Sin turned to his Saracen master with a look so feral that for once Marr shrank back.

Barely ten-and-eight years old, Sin had spent the last four and a half years of his life beneath the harsh hand of his trainers. Four and a half long years of being beaten, tortured and cursed. Of having his morals, his language and his identity stripped from him.

At long last he had become the animal they called

him. There was nothing left inside him. No pain, no past.

Nothing but an emptiness so vast that he wondered if anything could ever make him feel again.

He *was* death, in every sense of the word.

Rad handed him the long, curved dagger. "You know what to do."

Aye, he did. Sin took the dagger in his hand and stared at it. His hand was one of a youth just barely entering his manhood, and yet he had committed sins and crimes that had aged him into an ancient.

Marr urged him forward. "Finish quickly and tonight you will eat well and have a bed for your comfort."

Sin looked back at Marr as his stomach rumbled from hunger. Day to day, they fed him only enough to keep him barely alive. He had to kill for anything more than a crust of rotten bread and stale water. They knew he would do anything for a decent meal to lessen the hunger cramps in his belly. Anything for a night free of torture and pain.

From the shadows, Sin watched the English knights sitting in their camp. Some of them ate, while others played games and passed wartime stories. Their tents were bright even in the darkness. The colors were faded by the night, but still evident.

Again he heard their music and songs.

It had been so long since he'd last heard Norman French spoken, let alone sung. It took him a few minutes to remember and understand the foreign words they used.

On his hands and knees like the animal they had trained him to be, Sin crept toward the camp. He was a shadow. An unseen phantom who had but one purpose.

Destruction.

He slipped easily through the English guards until he reached the largest and grandest of the tents. Here was the target for the night.

Lifting the bottom of the tent, he looked inside.

A gold brazier stood in the center of the tent, the coals from it casting shadows on the linen canvas. In one corner was a bed so large and golden that for a minute Sin thought he was dreaming the sight. But it was real. The carved dragon heads were regal and bespoke the high station of the man who slept in blissful ignorance, clutching at covers made from snow leopards and lions.

A man who had no idea his life was about to end.

Sin focused his gaze on the target. One quick cut and he would be dining on figs and roasted lamb. Drinking wine and sleeping on a feather tick instead of scratchy sand where he had to be vigilant against scorpions and asps and other things that scavenged in the night.

Suddenly a new idea came to him while the wounds and welts on his back throbbed. He looked about the tent again, noting the wealth and power of the man on the bed. This was a king. A fierce king who made the Saracens tremble with fear. One who might be able to free him from his owners.

Freedom.

The word rang in his head. If he had any soul left, he would gladly trade it for a night's sleep in which chains didn't hold him down. Trade it for a life where no one ruled him. No one tortured him.

He curled his lip at the thought. When had he ever known anything else? Even in England he had known nothing but torment. Nothing but ridicule.

He had never belonged anywhere.

Kill him and be done with it. Eat well tonight and worry about the morrow when it comes.

That was all he knew. That basic philosophy was what had gotten him through his short, hard life.

Determined to eat again, Sin crept forward.

Henry came awake the instant he felt a hand on his throat. Then he felt a cold, sharp blade pressing against his Adam's apple.

"One word and you die." The cold, harsh words were tinged in an accent that was a strange blend of Scottish, noble Norman French and Saracen.

Terrified, he looked to see what sort of man could infiltrate his guard and . . .

Henry blinked in disbelief as he caught sight of his killer. It was a scrawny, frail boy dressed in Saracen rags. Reeking of hunger and with black eyes devoid of emotions, the boy stared at him as if he were weighing the value of Henry's life.

"What do you want?" Henry asked.

"Freedom."

He frowned at the child and the peculiar, thick accent he spoke in. "Freedom?"

The boy nodded, his eyes burning eerily in the darkness. Those eyes didn't belong to a child. They belonged to a demon who had seen hell firsthand.

One half of the boy's face was swollen and blackened from a beating and his lips were split and cracked. His neck was red, raw and bleeding as if he normally wore a steel collar around it that he fought against. Henry looked down to see similar injuries on both of his wrists. Aye, someone made a habit of chaining the child like an animal. And the boy had made a habit of fighting his manacles.

When the child spoke, his words stunned him even more than the boy's ragged appearance. "If you will give me my freedom, I will give you my loyalty until the day I die."

If those words had come from anyone else, Henry would have laughed. But there was something about this child that let him know gaining this boy's loyalty was quite a feat and that, once given, it was truly valuable.

"If I say no?"

"I will kill you."

"My guard will capture you if you do and they will kill you."

The boy shook his head slowly. "They will not capture me."

Henry didn't doubt that in the least. It had been quite a feat for the child to get this far already.

He looked at the boy's long, black hair and black eyes. Still, his sun-blistered skin was fairer than most of those born to this region. "Are you Saracen?"

"I am . . ." He paused. The sharpness faded from his eyes and revealed a pain so profound that it made Henry ache from the intensity of it. "I am not Saracen. I was squire to an English knight, who sold me to the Saracens so that he could buy passage home."

Henry lay stunned at the news. Now he understood the poor shape of the boy. There was no telling what abuse and depravity the Saracens had heaped on him. What kind of monster would sell a child into the hands of an enemy? The cruelty of it overwhelmed him.

"I will see you free," Henry said.

The boy narrowed his eyes suspiciously. "This had best not be a trick."

"It's not."

The boy released him and moved away from the bed.

Henry watched as the child went to squat by a wall with one hand on the canvas, no doubt ready to flee should Henry make a sudden move. Slowly, so as not to frighten him, Henry got up and left the bed.

The boy looked about nervously. "They will be coming for me."

"Who will?"

"My masters. They always find me when I escape. They find me and they . . ."

Henry saw the horror on the boy's face, as if he were reliving whatever they had put him through. The boy began to pant in panic.

"I have to kill you," he said, rising to his feet. He drew his dagger again and moved toward Henry. "If I don't, they will come for me."

Henry grabbed the boy's hand before he could sink the dagger into his chest. "I can protect you from them."

"No one protects me. I have only myself."

They wrestled for the dagger.

Someone drew back the tent flap. "Majesty, we found—" The guard's voice died as he caught sight of their struggle.

The guard shouted for reinforcements.

The boy let go of the dagger as guards swarmed into the tent. Henry watched in awe as the scrawny child fought like a cornered lion. Had the boy possessed any strength on his starved bones, he would have easily defeated the twelve-man guard. But as it was, they brought him down hard on the floor.

Still the boy fought so furiously that it took five guards to keep him there.

"Release him."

All twelve of his guards looked at him as if he were crazed.

"Majesty?" his captain asked hesitantly.

"Do it."

It wasn't until they let go that Henry realized the boy's arm had been broken during the fight. His nose was bleeding and he had a cut on his forehead. Still, the child made no sound as he pushed himself to his feet. He merely held the broken arm to his side while he watched them warily as if expecting the absolute worst from them.

The child neither begged nor pleaded, and that told Henry much about what horrors the boy must have lived through. He stood strong and defiant before all of them.

His guards regained their feet and the captain came forward to address Henry, but he still kept a jaundiced eye on the youth. "We found two Saracens on the edge of camp, Sire. I am sure he is one of them."

"We are sure as well," Henry said. "Boy, what is your name?"

The youth dropped his gaze to the floor. When he spoke, his voice was barely audible. "My masters call me Kurt."

Henry frowned at the foreign term he'd learned the first few weeks they had been in this land. It was used to mean either maggot or worm. "What is your Christian name?"

"When I served the Earl of Ravenswood, I was called Sin."

Henry's breath caught at the name, for he knew who this child was. "You're the MacAllister's son?"

Again, the emptiness returned to the boy's eyes. "I am no man's son."

Indeed. When Henry had offered to return this boy home to his father in Scotland, the old laird had said as much. Sin was the only one of the Scottish boys whose father had refused to have him.

Not knowing what do to about the matter and having little time to deal with it, Henry had left the boy in Harold of Ravenswood's custody.

Obviously, that had been a mistake.

It wasn't often Henry felt guilt. But he felt it now. It gripped his heart with unfamiliar pain and burned in his soul. This poor, unwanted boy had been his ward and he had left him to a fate no child should ever know.

"Fetch a surgeon," Henry said to his captain. "And bring food and wine for the boy."

Sin looked up in shock at the order. Part of him still expected the king to hang him. At the very least beat him. That was all he was fit for. That and killing.

"Don't looked so surprised, boy," Henry said. "Come the morrow, we shall see you home."

Home. The vague, elusive dream of that word had haunted him all his life. It was all he'd ever wanted. A home where he could be welcomed, a people who would accept him.

His father had thrown him out of Scotland, where no one had ever wanted him, and the Saracens had spurned and spat on him in Outremer, but maybe this time, when he went to England, the people there would want him.

Maybe this time, he would at last find the home he had ached for.

Aye, in England he would find peace.

Chapter 1

London
Twelve years later

"I would sooner geld myself. Drunk. With a dull knife." Sin spoke with a slow, deadly emphasis on each word.

King Henry II stood a few feet away from him without the protection of a bodyguard or other courtier. They were alone in the throne room, and no doubt any other man would be cowering before his monarch. But Sin had never cowered in his life, and Henry knew better than to expect such behavior from him now.

Henry's face hardened. "I could command it of you."

Sin cocked one arrogant brow and asked, "Then why don't you?"

Henry smiled at that, and the tension left his body as he closed the distance between them.

Their friendship had been forged years ago, in the

dark of night, and at the end of a blade pressed deep against Henry's throat. Sin had spared the king's life and since that day, Henry had treasured the only man who had never been awed by his power or authority.

Sin answered to no man, be he king, pope, sultan or beggar. But then, there was nothing in life that awed Sin. Nothing in life that commanded him, or touched him. He was completely alone.

And he preferred it that way.

"I didn't gain this throne by being a fool, Sin. Should I command you to it, I know precisely what you'd do. You'd turn your back on me and head straight for yon door."

Henry looked sincere. "God's truth, you are the only man alive I never wish to make my enemy. 'Tis why I ask this as a friend."

"Damn you."

Henry laughed. "If I am damned, it is certainly for more serious offenses than this matter." The humor left Henry's face and he stared straight into Sin's eyes. "Now then, *as a friend,* I ask again. Will you marry the Scotswoman?"

Sin didn't answer. He clenched his teeth so tightly that he could feel the angry tic starting in his jaw.

"Come now, Sin," Henry said with an almost pleading note in his voice. "I need you in this matter. You know the Scots. You are one of them."

"I am not a Scot," Sin snarled. "Not now. Not ever."

Henry ignored his rebuff. "You know how they think, you know their language. You alone are capable of this. Should I send another, those bloodthirsty savages would no doubt cut his throat and send his head back to me."

"And you think they wouldn't do that to me?"

Henry laughed. "I doubt if the Archangel Michael could cut your throat unless you consented to it."

Truer words had never been spoken. Still, this favor sat ill in Sin's gut. The last thing on earth he desired was to be shackled to the Scots. He hated everything to do with Scotland and its people, and would sooner rot with pestilence than ever put one piece of his body in Scotland again.

"I promise, my reward will be great," Henry said.

"I have no need of your money or rewards."

Henry nodded. "I know. 'Tis why I trust you so much. You're the only man I have ever known who is truly above bribery. You are also a man of honor, and I know you would never walk away from a friend who needed you."

Sin met his gaze without flinching. "Henry, *as a friend,* I ask you not to ask this of me."

"I wish I didn't have to. I don't relish the thought of my only true ally so far from me, but I need a man I can trust, one who knows the soul of the Scots people, to lead them. The only other subject who could possibly end this matter is your brother Braden. Since he is now married . . ."

Sin ground his teeth together. He had been glad to see his brother wed, but how he wished Braden were a bachelor once more. Braden was the one who knew how to please a woman.

Sin knew war. His home the battlefield, all he had ever trusted in life not to betray him were his sword, his shield and his horse.

And he wasn't any too sure about his horse.

He knew nothing of women and their softness, and he had no wish to know aught of them.

"If it is of any consolation," Henry added, "she is a fetching wench. You will have no trouble siring a child on her."

Sin narrowed his eyes. He balked at the thought of siring a child, especially one simply for the purpose of passing on titles and lands that meant nothing to him. "I am not a stallion, Henry."

" 'Tis not what the rumors that circulate through my court say. I've heard you're quite—"

"Does this woman know what you have planned?" Sin asked, cutting him off. He didn't like discussing anything personal. And most especially not with Henry.

"Of course not. She knows nothing of you. 'Tis not her concern. She is my hostage and she will do as she's told or I will see her executed."

Sin rubbed his hand over his face. He had no doubt Henry would do just that. He also knew who would be asked to fulfill that decree. "Henry, you know how I feel about a wife."

"Aye, I do. But in all honesty, I truly wish to see you wed. I have valued your service, but it has always concerned me that you have nothing in life you value. I have given you lands, wealth and titles, and you spurn them as if they're poison. All the years I have known you, you have lived with one foot already in the grave."

"And you think a wife would bring me back over the threshold?"

"Aye."

Sin snorted. "Then I shall remind you of that the next time you complain of Eleanor."

Henry laughed so hard he choked. "Were you any other man, you would be dead for such audacity."

"And I would say the same of you."

At least it succeeded in checking Henry's mirth.

Henry paced a small path in front of Sin and fell quiet. By his face, Sin could tell he was thinking of something long ago.

When the king spoke, his voice was thick with nostalgia. "I remember well the night you held that dagger to my throat. Do you remember what you said?"

"Aye, I offered you my loyalty if you would grant me my freedom."

"Yea, you did. And I need your loyalty now. Philippe is on my heels trying to wrench Normandy and Aquitaine from my hands, my sons are yapping for their own slices of power, and now this Highland clan attacks the few Englishmen I have guarding my northern borders. I cannot continue to be attacked from all sides. Even a raging bull can be brought low by a pack of hungry dogs. And I am tired of it. I need peace before they kill me. Will you help me?"

Inwardly, Sin cringed as he heard the four words he had never been able to deny. Damn his blackened soul for it. It was the one piece of his conscience that hadn't been destroyed, and Henry knew it.

Sin growled low in his throat. Surely there had to be a means to escape this wretched event. And surely he . . .

Sin almost smiled as the thought occurred to him.

'Twas perfect, and as insidious as he himself was.

"Aye, I'll marry the wench, but only if you can find a priest who will sanction it."

Henry's face blanched.

Sin smiled evilly. In the last nine years, he had been excommunicated five times. The most recent one carried a papal ban so severe that it should have him roasting out eternity right by the devil's side.

The pope himself referred to Sin as Satan's Most Favored Spawn.

Henry would never find a priest who would dare allow Sin to take part in a sacrament.

"You think you have me, don't you?" Henry asked.

"I think nothing of the sort, Henry. As you said, I know the Scots and know they would accept nothing less than a sanctified marriage. I have merely given you the conditions of our union."

"Very well, then. I accept your terms and intend to hold you to them."

Chapter 2

"**A**re we going to escape this time, Callie?" Caledonia of the Clan MacNeely pulled her baby brother to a stop in the narrow corridor where they were making their way out of King Henry's castle.

She knelt beside his little body. "If you'll be keeping your words to yourself we just might," she whispered.

Callie smiled to soften her harsh words, and straightened the brown Phrygian cap on his small head. His face still held the baby-fat cheeks and bright, trusting blue eyes of the toddler he had been not all that long ago. "Now, remember, we're English servants, which means if you open your mouth, they'll know we're Highlanders for sure."

He nodded.

Callie tucked Jamie's orangish red curls back under his cap. His hair was the same shade as her own. But that was all they shared, for Callie looked like her dearly departed mother and Jamie favored his own mother, Morna.

He looked at her now with blue eyes steeled by determination, and with a sagacity no lad of his tender age should possess. At six years, the boy had seen more than his fair share of tragedy. God willing, he would see no more of it.

She kissed the lovable little demon lightly on the brow and rose to her feet. Her stomach knotted with nerves, she led him slowly down the lone corridor toward the spiral stairs that should exit by the rear of the castle.

At least that was what she'd been told by the maid who had been helping them plot their escape. How she prayed her newfound friend hadn't lied to her or betrayed her.

They had to get out of this place. Callie could stand no more. If she had to stomach another Sassenach leering at her or making crude comments about her wild Scottish heritage, she would have his tongue for it.

But it was what they did to Jamie that truly made her blood boil. The son of a laird, he was equal to the highest-born of the English. And those beasts made him serve them like the lowliest of peasants while they mocked and belittled him. She could stand no more of her brother's tears; no more of watching the knights rough-handle the young lad and cuff his ears.

The English were animals!

Ever since King Henry's men had killed her guards and captured the two of them as they traveled to visit her sickly aunt, Callie had been trying to find a way for them to escape and make their way home.

Yet, for all her careful cunning, these wretched English beasts were truly spawns of the devil. No matter what she tried, it seemed one of them always saw through her escape and stopped her.

But this time—this time, she would succeed.

She knew it.

Tightening her grip on Jamie's hand, she paused at the top of the stairs. She pulled back the corner of her linen veil and cocked her head to listen.

Nothing.

It appeared no one was about to challenge them. They were free!

The maid, Aelfa, had promised her that once they left the stairs, the back door opened just a few feet from the postern gate that the servants used during daylight hours to travel from the castle into London. The maid had sworn to her that no one would stop her once she reached it.

Callie's heart pounded in sweet expectation. She rushed down the dark spiral steps at a breakneck speed, with Jamie one step behind.

Freedom!

She could taste it. She could smell it. She could . . .

Callie's thoughts scattered as she tripped and fell over something on the stairs.

She felt her body pitch forward and all she could do was extend her arms in hopes of catching herself. But instead of falling, she felt strong arms wrap about her and pull her against a chest as hard as the dark stone walls surrounding her.

Faster than she could blink, the man released her to stand on the stair above him.

"God's blood, woman, watch where you're going."

Jamie opened his mouth to speak.

Callie quickly covered his mouth with her hand and did her best English accent. "Forgive me, milord."

It was only then she dared look at him.

Being on the tall side, she was used to standing eye level with most men. But where she expected to see his head, she saw only wide, muscular shoulders encased by darkness.

Her heart pounded. For those were very large shoulders indeed.

Callie frowned at his black clothes. Never before had she seen a man not of the Church dressed all in black. And this man was definitely no priest.

His mail, coif and surcoat, which were darker than pitch, bore no markings on them whatsoever.

How very odd.

She tried to take a step back, but Jamie on the stair behind her and her narrow perch on the step prevented it.

She felt trapped all of a sudden, trapped by the knight's powerful presence, which seemed to seep into her very bones. This was a dangerous man. A deadly one. She felt it with every instinct she possessed.

She dared to look up his tanned, strong neck, which bore a deep scar, then over his handsome face, to see the eyes of the devil himself. Those midnight-black eyes burned with intelligence and fire. They seared her with an eerie light that made her tremble.

Callie swallowed.

Never had she seen such a man. Without a doubt, he was the fairest of face and form she'd ever beheld. His features were well defined and sculpted, his jaw strong and perfect and dusted by just a hint of manly stubble.

Hair as black as his clothes fell past his shoulders in the style of her Highland brethren. And as she stared at him, she saw the tiniest of flaws on his face. An almost invisible scar above his left eyebrow.

But it was those black eyes that held her captive. Those deadly eyes, so dark that she couldn't even see the pupil in them, which terrified her. For they were cold and empty. And worse, they were narrowed on her with far too much interest.

Remembering that she was garbed as a servant and that the man before her was obviously a lord of some standing, Callie decided she had best make a hasty retreat.

She bobbed a quick curtsy to him, grabbed Jamie's hand and ran down the last few steps and out the door.

Sin frowned at the door as it slammed shut. There had been something very strange about what had just happened. And it wasn't the powerful, unexpected lust he had felt the moment those green eyes had met his gaze.

Nay, his instincts had been honed from years of training. They were trying to tell him something.

But all he could focus on was the image of the woman's Cupid's-bow mouth, and the strange disappointment he felt over not knowing the color of her hair.

Indeed, her light blue veil was an abomination that did nothing for the green of her eyes or the fresh sunkissed skin of her face.

She had been beguiling.

Captivating.

And refreshingly tall.

Standing well over six feet, he had seldom met a woman so close to his own height. Though she had been a bit too slender for his tastes, her breasts had appeared ample enough to satisfy even his lustful brother Braden.

And her eyes . . .

Vibrant and warm, they had sparkled with vitality and intelligence. They had . . .

They had been too bold, he realized with a start. No servant met a lord's gaze, and most especially not his, with such pride and unyielding directness. She hadn't cringed from him, which meant she obviously didn't know who he was.

There could only be one person at King Henry's court who wouldn't recognize him.

The Scotswoman.

And she was headed for the back gate.

Cursing, Sin bolted after her.

Callie stopped abruptly as a group of knights came between her and the gate. There were six of the demons, to be sure. Six of them armed from training and on their way into the castle.

Of all her unfortunate luck!

Jamie's hand trembled in her own. She gave a gentle squeeze to comfort him.

They would simply have to try and brazen it out. Aye, with any good fortune at all, the knights would pay her no heed and would let her pass without thought.

Lowering her gaze, she skirted the men and made for the gate.

"Well, well," one of the men said as she drew near. "What have we here?"

"A fine serving wench," another responded. "One to serve our needs finely."

The others laughed. "Ah, Roger, you truly have a way with words and with the peasants."

Callie quickened her steps.

One of the men cut her off.

She stopped dead in her tracks and dared a quick look to see the hunger burning in the man's brown eyes.

"Forgive me, milord," she said, the title sticking in her throat. It was not in her nature to grovel or cower, and if not for her brother, she wouldn't deign to do so now.

But she had to get them out of here.

"I've work to be aboot." Callie cringed as she heard her brogue slip.

"Aye, that you do," he said, his voice low and husky. "And I definitely have a need for you to tend." He reached down with one hand to adjust the sudden bump in his chausses.

Callie clenched her teeth in frustration. She was caught now. Still, she wouldn't give up without a fight.

The knight grabbed her and pulled her close for a kiss.

Before his lips could make contact with her own, she kicked him hard in the little bulge he seemed so very proud of.

He let go of her with a curse.

Her only thought survival, Callie seized the hilt of his sword and pulled it free of the scabbard.

The men laughed at her. "You'd best be putting that down before you hurt yourself, little one."

Callie rotated her wrist and spun the sword expertly around her body. "The only thing I'll be hurting is one of you." This time, she didn't bother disguising her accent. "Now I suggest you remove yourselves from me path."

The humor left their faces.

One of the braver men unsheathed his sword. They stared at one another for several seconds and she knew the thought in his mind. He assumed her weak. Ineffectual.

Well, she was all woman, to be sure, but her father had seen her well schooled in the art of swordplay. There wasn't a knight born who would touch a Scot when it came to war. Not even when the Scot was a woman.

"Get her, Roger," the knight she'd kicked said as he limped his way to the others.

Roger smiled evilly. "Believe me, I intend to." He licked his lips as he raked a lecherous look over her. "In more than one way."

He attacked.

With the flair of a seasoned warrior, Callie parried his thrust. If the man wanted a fight, she was definitely the one to give it to him.

"Run, Jamie!" she said to her brother.

He didn't go far before one of the other knights grabbed him.

Cursing her ill fortune, Callie engaged her enemy. She was one move away from disarming him when a cold, familiar voice gave her pause.

"Drop your sword, milady."

Out of the corner of her eye, she saw the man from the stairs. Yet what stunned her most was the way the other knights reacted to his presence.

They actually shrank away from him.

Roger looked to the black knight and sneered, "Stay out of this. 'Tis no concern of yours."

The black knight arched a brow. "Given how the lady just humiliated you with the fact she's the better swordsman, I seriously doubt you want to test my steel." He gave the man a goading stare. "Or do you?"

She saw the indecision on Roger's face.

"Let it be, Roger," one of the knights said. "You know he'd love a chance to kill you."

Roger nodded slowly, then lowered his sword and stalked off.

Callie turned to face the man who terrified the others. He stood as still as a statue and watched her with a guarded look that betrayed nothing as to his thoughts or mood. The light breeze stirred the tendrils of his black hair and he stared unblinkingly at her.

Aye, he was a deadly one, to be sure. She doubted if old demon Red Cap himself would be more fierce to face.

She held her sword steady.

The black knight smiled coldly. "I see you know how to handle a man's tool."

Several of the men snickered.

Her face flushed bright red at his crude comment. "I don't take kindly to your insults."

"No insult intended, milady, I assure you. I admire a woman who can hold her own."

She couldn't tell if he was sincere or mocking. His body and tone gave her no indication.

"Now drop the sword."

"Nay," she said firmly. "Not until my brother and I are free."

"Milady?" Callie recognized the voice of the maid who had helped her with their disguises. The lass stepped out of the shadow of the castle's doorway to look at her. "Do as his lordship says, milady. Please, I beg you. You've no idea who he is, but take me word for it. The last thing ye be wanting to do is cross his lordship."

The black knight held his hand out. "The sword."

For some unknown reason, she almost complied. But one look at Jamie and she knew she couldn't cede their best chance. She took a step toward the black knight.

She angled her blade straight for his throat, and to her amazement he didn't budge or flinch. He merely stared at her with those black, soulless eyes. Calm. Patient. Like an adder waiting for its prey to come close enough for it to strike.

She paused.

Then, before she could blink, he stepped forward with an amazing speed, caught the tip of the blade between his forearms, and flipped her sword out of her hands. It arced high into the air, spinning as it fell. He caught the hilt easily in his hand, then twirled it about once before burying the blade deep in the ground beside him.

His smile was even colder than before. "Didn't your mother ever tell you not to tempt the devil unless you were willing to pay his fee?"

Callie's fingers stung from having the hilt torn from her grasp, but she said nothing. In truth, she didn't know how to respond. All she knew was that he had defeated her. No one had ever disarmed her before.

And he hadn't even drawn his own weapon. The humiliation of it stung her deeply.

"Now, what do you think we should do with this scamp?" the knight holding Jamie asked.

"A good whipping should suffice, followed by cleaning out a cesspit or two."

"Nay!" she shouted, but they paid her no heed.

All the knights laughed except the black knight. His eyes blazed furiously at the others. "Release the boy," he said with that same calm tone.

"Come now, my lord. Can we not have a bit of fun with him?"

He turned his fearsome, obsidian stare to the knight who had spoken. "My idea of amusement is disemboweling those who contradict and annoy me. What say you that you and I have a bit of fun?"

The knight paled, then instantly released Jamie. He ran to Callie's side and balled his fists into the coarse material of her skirt.

"Did you see what he did?" Jamie asked in a loud whisper. "Aster would die to know you let an unarmed Sassenach take your sword away."

"Shhh," Callie said softly, holding him to her side with one arm as she faced the black knight.

The man's gaze never wavered. "I think 'tis time you return to your room, milady."

Callie lifted her chin in a worthless sign of defiance. He knew as well as she did that he had bested her. This time.

But next time, she would find a way to beat these Englishmen, and get the two of them home where they belonged.

Holding her head as high as she could, she turned and headed back toward the castle, with Jamie still clutching her skirt.

The maid held the door open for her and actually flinched as the black knight drew near.

He followed them back up the stairs. And even worse than the strange hot and cold feeling running through her body was the way Jamie kept glancing back at the knight with worshipful awe showing clearly on his young face.

"Tell me," Callie said over her shoulder as she neared the top of the stairs, "why is everyone so afraid of you?"

For the first time, she heard just a hint of bitterness in the black knight's voice. "Everyone fears the devil. Don't you?"

Callie scoffed at his words. "You are a man, sir. Not the devil."

"You think so?"

"I know so."

"Truly?" he asked, his voice edged by humor. "Are you a witch, then, to be on such familiar terms with the devil?"

Callie paused at the top of the stairs and whirled to face him, angered over such a question. People had been burned and hanged for less. No doubt these English would love to see her executed as a witch. "I am God-fearing."

He stood so close to her, she could smell the warm, clean scent of his skin. Those black eyes seared her with their probing intensity, and when he spoke his tone was low. Lethal. "I am not."

She trembled at that. For there was no doubt he meant it.

To her dismay, he reached out and touched her cheek. The warmth of his hand surprised her, and it raised chills over her entire body as he traced one finger near her ear. She couldn't believe the tenderness of his touch, the way his fingers felt feather-light against her skin. It did the strangest things to her body. Made her throb and ache with a need she'd never before encountered.

Then he gently pushed back her veil to run his hand just along her hairline, where she felt him crook his finger around one of her curls and pull it free of the linen.

His gaze narrowed on his hand, and one corner of his mouth curled in disgust.

"Red," he said, his voice scarcely more than a growl. "I should have known."

"I beg your pardon?" she asked, confused as to why something as simple as her hair color would elicit such a heated response from him when nothing else had.

A shuttered look came over him as he dropped his hand from her face and took a step back.

"Aelfa," he said to the maid. "Take her to her room and see to it she stays there."

"Aye, milord," the maid said, dropping to a low curtsy.

Sin didn't move until after he saw the Scotswoman enter her room.

You should have let her escape.

In truth, it had been his momentary intent. Only his loyalty to Henry had prevented it.

Well, that and the small fact that he knew he'd never have to marry her. Not even Henry possessed that much power or money.

Still . . .

Sin felt just a tiny stirring of regret as he recalled the way she had disarmed Roger.

The wench had spirit. He'd give her that much. But that kind of spirit before one's enemies was more curse than virtue.

He should know.

Shaking his head at the dismal memories he refused to think about, he headed down the narrow corridor to his own room, which turned out to be next to hers.

Sin clenched his jaw at Henry's audacity. No wonder the man had become king. His tenacity would rival a mule's. Still, it was no match for Sin's.

He opened the door to his room and moved toward the spartan bed by the window. He spent a large amount of his time at Henry's court and, unlike the other courtiers who lived in Henry's hall, he'd never cared how luxurious his bed was. So long as it had a frame big enough to hold him and came with a blanket, it was enough for him.

As carefully as he could, Sin pulled his surcoat and mail hauberk from his body and placed them over the small trunk at the foot of his bed. Then he inspected the damage her sword had wrought on his forearms.

Oblivious to the pain, Sin unlaced the sleeves of his aketon as he headed toward the washstand. After draping the padded garment over a simple wooden chair, he poured water into the bowl and washed the blood from his forearms.

Reaching for a cloth, he heard a commotion outside in the hallway.

His wounds forgotten, Sin grabbed his sword from the bed and threw open the door.

Three of the royal guards were dragging the boy from the Scotswoman's room, while a fourth guard held the woman back. The boy wailed like a dying harpy and the woman fought like a feral cat.

"What goes here?" Sin demanded.

The guard closest to him blanched, then said hastily, "His Majesty wants the boy moved to another location."

"Nay!" the Scotswoman snarled. "You'll not take him from me for them to abuse. Haven't you done enough to the lad?"

"Please!" the boy wailed as he kicked and fought against the knights so fiercely that one of his shoes was thrown off. "Don't let them take me. I don't want to be beaten or hit anymore."

Anger welled inside Sin at the boy's words.

The woman struggled even more furiously against the guard holding her. If she continued, she'd end up bruised and bloody. As would the boy.

"Release him," Sin ordered.

Everyone froze at his words.

"Milord," the guard holding the woman said, "we are acting on the king's orders."

Sin directed a cutting glare to the man, who shrank back a full two steps. "Tell Henry I said it would be fine."

"And if she escapes with the boy?" another guard asked.

"I will take custody of them. Think you she will escape *me*?"

Sin saw the indecision in the guard's eyes as he weighed whose wrath he feared more—Sin's or Henry's.

In the end, the man released the boy, who ran quickly to his sister.

"I will tell the king what you said," the guard responded, his resentful words weakened by the note of fear in his voice.

"Yea," Sin said dryly, "tell him."

As the guards left, Callie looked up at the black knight who had saved her brother from being taken. His kindness to them was beyond measure.

It had been on her mind to thank him, but as her gaze darted over his body, she couldn't speak.

Indeed, 'twas all she could do not to gape.

His bare, tawny shoulders were as wide as they had appeared beneath his mail. His body was hard and well defined, the muscles flexing with every breath he took.

But what held her gaze captive were the numerous deep and angry scars crisscrossing the bare flesh. He looked as if he had survived untold battles and attacks. The sight wrenched her heart.

And it was then she saw his bleeding forearms. "You're hurt."

He glanced down at the blood. "So it appears."

"Have you someone to tend it?"

"I have myself."

He started back to his room, but Callie followed. "Would you like for me to send in my maid?"

"Nay," he said in that emotionless tone as he paused in the doorway and glanced from her to Jamie, then back to her. He gave her a meaningful glare that was no doubt meant to intimidate her into cowering like the others. Though it did send a tremor down her back, she was a long way from cowering. Much like he must have been, she'd been taught to let no man see her fear of him.

The knight stepped back. "My only wish is to be alone."

"But your wounds—"

"Will heal," he snapped.

Och, but the man was insufferable. Fine, then, let him rot.

Callie turned about, retrieved Jamie from the hallway, and returned to her room.

But she didn't stay there. How could she? There was no doubt in her mind where the black knight had gotten his wounds.

Her sword.

Of course, he wouldn't have been hurt had he not stopped her from escaping. Still, he had saved her and Jamie from the others. Whether she liked it or not, she owed him.

And Callie had never been one to remain indebted to anyone. Gathering her sewing kit and a small bag of herbs from her trunk, she ordered Jamie to stay with Aelfa, then opened the door.

Determined to owe him no more, she went to face the devil in his own lair. She only hoped he didn't gobble her up.

Chapter 3

Sin heard the latch on his door rattle. Instinctively, he pulled the dagger from his boot and balanced it between his thumb and forefinger, waiting to see if it needed to fly into the chest of whomever was trespassing.

The door opened a hair to show him a pert little nose, followed by the profile of an angel. An angel who paused while she stared at the wall opposite him.

"Sir? Sir Bl . . . Knight? Are you in here?"

Sin tucked the knife back into his boot. "Given how this is my room, where else would I be?"

She still hadn't looked inside, and she chose to ignore his sarcasm. "Are you decent?"

Sin snorted. "There are many, milady, who say I haven't a decent bone in my entire body."

"And there are many who say it's drafty here in the hallway. What I want to know is, are you dressed?"

"I'm as dressed as I was the last time you saw me,

which means you should go back to your room, posthaste."

She didn't. Instead, she opened the door wider and, to his immediate dismay, stepped inside.

Her gaze scanned the room until she found him, sitting on the bed. And when those light green eyes focused on his bare chest, Sin could swear he felt a riveting shock from the bottom of his feet to the top of his head. His groin drew tight and hot with a need so profound that he actually ached from it.

What the devil was the matter with him? He wasn't some callow youth, to swell at the sight of some winsome maid. He had conquered his body and his lust long ago.

But for some reason, his control slipped every time she came near him. Worse was the knowledge that she could be his. All he had to do was go to Henry and he could have her.

If he dared such. . . .

Oblivious to the havoc she caused him, she crossed the floor to stand in front of the bed.

"What are you doing here?" he asked sharply.

She took his words in stride. "I'm here to tend the wounds I caused."

Sin fingered the makeshift bandage on his left arm. It was far from a perfect wrap, but it would suffice.

Besides, the last thing he needed was for her to come any closer to him than she already was.

"Then you have no fear, milady. You weren't the cause of my wounds."

She frowned. "You didn't get them when you disarmed me?"

"Aye, but it wasn't your actions that caused them so much as my own."

She waved his words away with her hand as she set a dark brown leather bag and a small basket on the bed beside him next to the piece of white linen he had been using for bandages.

"You are arguing just for the sake of it, and I shan't listen anymore. Now stop your fussing and let me see about those wounds before they fester and rot your arms off."

Sin stared at her incredulously. He couldn't remember the last time someone had dismissed him so flippantly, but he was relatively sure he must have been in swaddling when it happened.

She reached for his right arm. He quickly moved it out of her grasp.

"Why would you care whether or not my arms rotted off?" he asked as she again tried to capture his arm. "I should think you would be wishing for it as opposed to trying to prevent it."

She paused and gave him a peeved glare because he wouldn't hold still. "Because you saved Jamie."

"And you think you owe me?"

"Aye."

He snorted again. The foolishness women could get into their heads. Still, it was the first time in his life anyone had ever *wanted* to tend a wound of his.

He found it strangely comforting, and that thought made him angry.

He didn't need comfort. Ever.

He shot to his feet and sought to put some distance between them.

She pursued him across the room like a herding lioness.

"My lady, if you had any idea who and what I was, you'd know better than to be alone with me in my room."

Her eyes fluttered to his face and for the first time he saw a bit of trepidation. Then she reached again for his arm.

Sin groaned as he realized she wouldn't leave him alone until he submitted to her treatments. Fine, then, the sooner she wrapped his arm, the sooner he could return to peace.

Ever a reluctant patient, he made a grand showing of stretching his right arm out to her.

Thank you was evident in her eyes as she gingerly pressed her fingertips to the wound.

"I do know who you are," she said softly as she examined the cut. "Aelfa told me all about you."

"And what did she say?"

To his dismay, she held his fist in one hand while the long, graceful fingers of her right hand glided over his hot skin with a soothing coolness that seemed to reach far deeper than just his flesh. Worse, it sent a rush of heat straight to his groin, which burned and throbbed with need.

Sin held his breath as strange and foreign sensations swept through his entire body. No one had ever touched him so gently. So kindly.

But the most terrifying of all was the sudden need he felt to reach out, cup her head in his hands, and pull her lips to his own.

By the very saints, what was wrong with him?

All he could do was stare at her like some besotted ape as he struggled to keep his breathing even and normal.

She bent her head ever so slightly down as she studied the cut. "This one is not so deep, but it still needs a poultice if it's to heal without festering." Her long, tapered fingers continued to brand his skin with unfamiliar kindness. "This burn scar looks fairly new. Is it from battle?"

Sin shook his head, but didn't elaborate. There was no need to go into the events that had caused that particular injury.

Besides, it was all he could do just to stand there calmly and not pull her into his arms as an image of her lying beneath him tore through his mind.

She turned to head back to his bed, where she had left her accoutrements.

He stared at her trim back, but it was her hips that held the most appeal for him. Well shaped and round, they beckoned a man in a way most carnal. Indeed, he could easily imagine walking up behind her, lifting the hem of her dress and burying himself deep inside her until he fully sated the fire in his groin.

"My wounds are fine," Sin snapped, wanting her out of his room immediately.

She looked over her shoulder, glared at him, then looked back down and continued digging out some noxious-smelling plant as if she didn't care one fig for what he'd said.

The woman was mad. Insane! Completely and utterly moonstruck. No one disregarded him when he spoke. No one.

So rare was this that Sin had no idea how to deal with it.

After a few seconds, she straightened from the bed. "I need wine. Have you any?"

"Nay," he lied.

It didn't work. She spied a flagon on the table by the hearth.

Going to it, she quickly learned it was far from empty and Sin wished he had drunk the whole of it the night before.

She gave him a smarting stare, then poured a goblet of it.

Sin narrowed his eyes.

"I wish you would stop scowling at me," she said as she returned the lid to the flagon. " 'Tis unnerving."

"The devil is oft—"

"And stop with the devil nonsense. I told you I know who you are and I'm not afraid of you."

"Then you, milady, are a fool."

"I'm not a fool," she said with a meaningful look as she wrapped her long, sensuous fingers around the bowl of the goblet and brought it toward him. "But I do know demons when I see them."

"Obviously not."

She pulled leaves from the plant and dropped them into the wine. "Demons feed on children, they don't stop them from being hurt."

"And what would you know of demons?"

She met his gaze levelly. "Quite a bit, actually."

She added more herbs and bits to the wine until it formed a thick paste. Then she took the paste and smeared it over his skin, her touch searing him with heat.

"Do you have a name?" she asked.

"Since you claim to know me so well, you tell me."

She paused. "Well, I'm rather sure your mother didn't name you Demon Butcher, Satan's Spawn, or King's Executioner."

Sin suppressed a smile at her cheekiness. Aye, she was a brave lady, with the heart of a lioness. "My mother gave me no name at all," he said as he watched her wrap a bandage over his arm.

Those light green eyes flashed as she met his gaze. "You have to be called something."

She stood so close that her breath fell softly against his skin as she spoke and the warm, floral scent of her filled his head.

He became acutely aware of the fact that all he wore was a pair of chausses and she was dressed in naught save a thin servant's dress. One that would be easy to divest her of.

His mouth watered.

The woman was beguiling, and for some reason he couldn't fathom, he wanted to hear his name on her lips.

"Those who dare speak to me directly call me Sin."

She nodded. "Cyn? Short for Cynric?"

"Nay," he said, recovering his stoicism as he remembered who and what he was. "S-I-N. As in conceived, born in, and am currently living happily in."

He felt her hand tremble for the first time.

"You like to frighten people, don't you?" she asked.

"Aye."

"Why?"

"Why not?"

To his surprise, she laughed. It was a wondrous, musical sound that came from deep within her. Sin stared at her, entranced by the way her face softened.

By the saints, she was a beauty. And right then he wanted desperately to taste those lips. To feel her breath mingling with his own as he claimed her. To allow Henry to see them wed so that he could enjoy her for the rest of his life.

He froze at the thought.

Nay, he would never allow himself such comfort. Even though she touched him gently now, she would curse and fear him as all others did if she knew the truth of him and what lay in his past.

It was not for him to feel comfort or solace. He had crushed and banished that delusion long ago.

She opened up his other bandage, and gasped as she saw the blood that had already soaked the cloth.

"I am sorry for this," she said. "I never meant for you to be hurt."

He cocked a chiding brow at her. "Might I point out, milady, that when one picks up a sword in offense or defense, it can pretty much be determined that someone *will* get hurt."

That rose blush returned to her cheeks as she reached for her needle. "This needs to be stitched."

"It will heal on its own."

"It will leave a scar."

Sin looked down at the multitude of scars marring his bare chest and arms. "Think you it matters?"

Callie looked up at his words. Even now she couldn't read the emotions buried in those deep, dark eyes. What agony he must have suffered, to be able to shield himself so completely.

Normally she could read even the most careful of souls. But this man was a complete enigma to her.

"It matters to me," she said, wondering why it was so. Yet it was.

As gently as she could, she made four short, tiny stitches in his arm. It amazed her that he didn't cry out or tense. It was almost as if he didn't even feel what she was doing; but then, given the severity of some of his larger scars, she could deduce he had been hurt so much that this tiny wound meant nothing to him.

But it meant a lot to her conscience, for she had never been one to cause pain in others. Though her father had been a mighty warrior, her mother had been a healer, and it was her mother's love of life to which she subscribed.

She cut a fresh bandage from the linen and wrapped it over her stitchery.

Lord Sin remained silent as she worked, and yet she could feel his eyes on her. Searching.

There was something different about this man, though she couldn't say what. And it wasn't just the fact that he seemed to delight in making people fear him.

He's the devil's own, Aelfa's voice whispered in her ear. *They say he has murdered over one hundred people just for the pleasure of it, and killed thousands more in battle. When he was first brought to court, he was wearing the robes of a heathen and spoke in tongues no one knew.*

They say he sold his soul to the devil to make him invincible.

Callie didn't know how much of that was true, but from the looks of his body, she would say he was far from invincible.

Even so, he possessed a strength and power that was undeniable. Never had she seen his equal.

For the first time in her life, she felt herself drawn toward an Englishman.

What are you thinking?

She blinked. Indeed, what *was* she thinking? She was the daughter of a laird who had spent his entire life trying to rid their precious lands of the English! Her father had died while fighting them, and she would never betray his memory.

Looking at Lord Sin's chest, Callie wondered how many of the scars on his body he had received while fighting her own race. And how many of those thousands killed in battle had been Scots?

"There," she said as she finished wrapping his arm.

Sin frowned at the sudden veil that came over her face. He didn't know what thought had descended, but he grieved the way it had robbed her of her serenity.

She gathered her supplies, mumbled a good-bye and quickly left the room.

His frown deepened. He should be thrilled she had finally gone, and yet . . .

Why, all of a sudden, did the room seem colder?

Shaking his head, he banned the thought. He had more important things to do than to dwell on a woman who wasn't his concern.

Henry would just have to find another of his men to marry her.

* * *

The next morning, Sin had finally succeeded in pushing the wench from his thoughts.

Of course, it had taken a cold bath to help and he had spent an agonizing night tormented by dreams of rose-red lips and sweet green eyes.

After he broke his fast, he stubbed his toe so severely he feared the digit broken. The pain of it had driven the woman right out of his mind.

Now he was heading toward the stable, where he intended to take a brisk ride to further keep his mind and body under heel.

"Sin?"

He paused midstride. The voice sounded strangely familiar, and yet he couldn't place it.

Looking over his shoulder, he spied a man with dark auburn hair who stood a few inches shorter than him. Again, there was something familiar about the face, but it wasn't until the stranger smiled that Sin knew his name.

"Little Simon of Ravenswood," Sin said, extending his arm to Simon as he stopped by his side. "How long has it been?"

Simon shook his arm and patted his sore forearm with brotherly affection. "Nearly a score of years, I think."

Aye, it had been. The last time Sin had seen Simon was on the day Simon's father had ridden to Ravenswood to claim his son from Harold, the former Earl of Ravenswood.

"Your brother?" Sin asked, thinking of Draven of Ravenswood. The two of them had often been partners in their protection of Simon from the old earl's malice. "I trust he is well?"

Simon nodded. "Aye, he married Emily of War-wick two years past."

Sin almost smiled at the news. "Old Hugh finally allowed one of his daughters to marry?"

"Aye, can you believe it?"

Sin shook his head. "Nay, I can't. I'm sure there's quite a story to that."

"Join me in a drink and I'll tell you of it. But what of you? Are you marri—"

"Shh," Sin said, interrupting him. "Don't even breathe that word, lest you jinx me."

Simon frowned. "Jinx you? How so?"

"Henry has been making matrimonial threats. As yet, I've avoided it. My hope is to stay the execution."

Simon laughed at his words. "Then may you continue to elude the noose."

"So tell me, Simon, what has you here in Henry's court?"

Simon smiled devilishly. "I came seeking adventure, but what I've found is nothing more than a few kegs of ale, some wenches needing comfort and many a boastful knight reliving glorious events that never happened." He sighed wistfully. "Who knew court could be so boring?"

"Give it time, little brother. Court intrigue abounds."

"Aye, for you I imagine so. I've already encountered several of your enemies."

Sin nodded. "Just make sure you don't encounter them in darkened corners, especially if they see us speaking together."

Simon's look turned hopeful. "Now, *that* would give me something interesting to do."

Before Sin could respond, something flashed in the corner of his eye. Turning his head, he tried to see what it was that had attracted his notice.

Courtiers and servants moved freely about the yard, attending their pleasure and duties. There was nothing unusual.

Nothing, that is, except for a strangely shaped man who was hobbling near the far wall of the inner bailey. No one seemed to pay any heed to the fellow, but something about him didn't seem quite right.

Sin held his hand up to Simon in signal that he'd be right back, then took a step forward to catch a better look at the man, whose cloak was just a bit too thick for the unusually warm day.

And as he closed the distance, Sin noticed the strangest thing of all.

The old man had four legs.

Arching a brow in disbelief, he watched as the four-legged man made his way, unchallenged, toward the stable.

"Tell me, Simon," Sin said as his friend drew near. "Have you ever seen a four-legged beggar?"

"Is this a riddle?"

"Not a riddle, but a puzzle. A puzzle to see just how far she can get before someone stops her."

"She?"

Sin pointed toward the dark figure entering the stable, then quickened his steps to catch up.

He told Simon to wait outside an instant before he slipped into the darkness of the stable to see the figure separate into two halves.

In spite of himself, he smiled as he snuck along the

stalls to watch the Scotswoman lead the boy to a cart and cover him with hay.

"Are you sure this is going to work?" the boy asked.

"Aye," she assured him. "I overheard the lad saying he'll ready the cart for the carter to get extra supplies in town. We'll just lie quietly until he stops and then we'll disappear into the city."

She climbed up and covered herself.

A few minutes later, an older boy entered and started hitching a team to the cart.

The woman had ingenuity, Sin would certainly give her that. And if not for the fact that he had assumed responsibility for the boy and woman, he would allow her to flee.

But he couldn't do that.

The only question was, should he thwart her now or wait?

He decided to wait. He wanted to see how far she could get on her own.

Leaving the shadows, he quickly saddled two horses, then led them to where Simon waited outside.

"Feel up to a bit of adventure now?" he asked Simon.

"Always."

They mounted their horses, then waited until the carter entered the stable. A few minutes later, he took the cart out.

"What are we doing?" Simon asked as they followed the cart across the castle's bailey and into London.

"We're following yon wagon," Sin answered.

"Why?"

"Because it is in front of us."

"Well, that certainly answers that. 'Twould be difficult to follow the cart if it were behind us."

Sin smiled. "Be patient, Simon, and you will see why we follow it."

The carter headed into the merchant district, which was thick with activity and people. When the carter stopped outside a small cluster of shops, Sin spied a straw-covered head peeping over the side of the wagon. Once the man disappeared from sight, the woman scrambled from the cart, with the boy one step behind.

No one seemed to notice her peculiar activity, or if they did, they ignored it.

She took a moment to dust the straw off them, but somehow she missed a piece that hung in the midst of one coppery curl. It bobbed as she moved.

Simon laughed as she took the boy's hand and led him through the crowd. "Why was she hiding?"

"She seeks to escape royal custody."

The mirth faded from Simon's eyes. "Should we notify the guards?"

"Nay, I think we can manage to retake her."

"Then what are we waiting for?"

"I have no idea. I simply like watching her maneuver."

From his horse, Sin could follow her easily through the crowded streets as she wended her way through the town. She kept her head lowered, with one hand on her brother the entire way. Every few steps, the boy would pause and get distracted, slowing her down, and all the while he chattered away about everything and everyone they passed.

No doubt she would be free if not for him.

"Halt!"

Sin jerked his head to see Roger of Warrington in the crowd. The knight was staring straight at the Scotswoman.

She met Roger's gaze over the heads of those surrounding her, then grabbed her brother's hand and started running through the crowd in the opposite direction.

"Halt, I say!" Roger shouted louder.

"Oh, that's effective," Sin said sarcastically. "Halt or I shall say halt again."

Roger's orders didn't even slow her down, so Roger attempted to run after her, but the crowd prevented him. Sin saw the frustration on Roger's face a moment before he shouted, "Twenty silver marks to the person who stops that woman and child!"

Sin cursed Roger's stupidity as every person on the street stopped what they were doing and started after the woman and boy.

"That was unwise." Simon voiced Sin's thoughts with a much more polite choice of words than those in Sin's mind.

Sin reined in his horse as Shitan grew nervous from all the sudden activity. His warhorse had been trained to kill and the last thing he wanted was innocent blood spilled because Roger was an idiot.

"We'll never catch her now," Simon said.

"Aye, but we will."

Turning his horse about, Sin headed away from the

crowd and into a side street. When it came to the streets of London, he knew them well.

Not to mention he could follow the woman's path by the screams and shouts of the mob. He spurred his horse forward. He would have to catch her before the raging mob tore her apart.

Callie trembled as she ran pell-mell through the streets. Her sides ached as she struggled to breathe.

"I can't keep up," Jamie wailed.

"You have to, sweeting. If we stop now, they'll have us for sure."

She didn't dare tell him that the mob would most likely tear them apart in an effort to claim the twenty silver marks. 'Twas a fortune the knight had offered.

Jamie stumbled.

Callie turned around to help him up, but it was too late. The frenzied mob surrounded them instantly.

"I have them, milord!" a grimy man shouted as he grabbed her arm.

"Nay, ye don't, ye ugly bugger, I have her."

The cry went up from every direction as a thousand hands pulled at her, ripped her clothes and hair. Callie cried out in pain, but no one seemed to care.

"Jamie!"

She could neither see nor hear her brother through the crowd.

Then, out of nowhere, a huge black stallion appeared. The crowd scattered as the horse reared, flashing hooves and driving them away from her.

Her heart pounding, Callie looked up to see Lord Sin.

He brought his horse under control with the ease of

a seasoned warrior. And when he extended his hand to her, she didn't hesitate to accept it.

He pulled her up to sit before him and she quickly looked to see Jamie being rescued by an auburn-haired knight on a light gray horse. Breathing in relief, she crossed herself and whispered a quick thank-you to the Lord and His saints.

But her relief didn't last long, as she became acutely aware of the man holding her. The strength of him surrounded her, making her strangely hot. English though he might be, there was something about Lord Sin that she found greatly appealing. Something about him that made her body burn with a lustful throb that stunned her.

At a score-and-six in age, Callie was a far cry from an uninformed maid who knew nothing of the relationships between men and women. Even though she had never been touched by a man, her married friends had seen her well schooled in the mechanics of wifely duties. She'd always found the idea of what they described a bit messy and undignified. At least until she had seen Lord Sin's bare chest.

In that moment, her thoughts had taken a sharp turnaround.

For some reason, the thought of being so intimate with him seemed anything but disgusting or crude. Indeed, she'd been much occupied with the sudden question of how his lips would taste. Of how his large, tanned hands would feel on her body while she ran her fingers through his silken hair.

"It appears, milady, that you are ever out of the clutches of Scylla and into the hands of Charybdis."

She blinked at his deep baritone as she dragged her

thoughts away from their course and focused them on what was happening to her. "My uncle claims 'tis a special talent I possess."

Lord Sin smiled at that, causing a strange weakness to sweep through her. He was simply breathtaking when he smiled.

He wheeled his horse about and started for the castle.

"I don't suppose I could bribe you into setting us free?" she asked hopefully.

"You know better."

Her throat tightened as she blinked back tears at the harsh insistence in his voice. "All I want is to go home. Can you not understand that?"

A strange emotion darkened his eyes as if her words had pricked at some sad memory. "Aye, milady," he said quietly. "I can well understand your feelings."

"Then why can't you let me go?"

"Because Henry needs you here to see to it that your people leave his alone."

"You mean leave *your* people alone."

His gaze turned dull at that. "I have no people," he said solemnly.

She paused, and her gaze dipped to his chest, where English knights wore their family or lord's arms. His was bare and suddenly she understood why. "If you don't owe your allegiance to the English, then let—"

"I owe my allegiance to Henry, and Henry wants you to stay."

She went rigid in frustration. "Fine," she breathed. "But I won't stop trying."

"And I won't stop catching you."

Callie crossed her arms over her chest as she tried her best not to touch any part of him. But it was difficult. Especially since his arms surrounded her like bands of steel, keeping her locked onto his saddle.

The scent of elderberries and sandalwood clung to him. It was a warm, intoxicating smell. She could feel his strong heart thumping against her shoulder blade as they made their way back into the inner bailey of the castle.

He was so handsome, this stranger, and though he denied it repeatedly and the courtiers constantly assured her otherwise, she suspected he was not the devil he pretended to be. If he were the monster of legend, he wouldn't be capable of such kindness. Nor would he have cared what happened to her or her brother.

As they drew near the stable, she saw the English king waiting with two of his guards standing behind him. There was also a small group of noblemen and -women who eyed them and the king curiously. No doubt they were seeking gossip fodder.

The look on King Henry's face was not a happy one.

"What happened?" the king demanded as they stopped before him. "I was just told of her disappearance and was preparing a search party."

Lord Sin helped her down, then slung one long leg over his horse and dismounted.

"Nothing," he said, then added belatedly, "Sire. The lady merely felt the need to get a breath of fresh air. I had my eye on her the entire time."

Henry narrowed his gaze on her suspiciously while Simon and Jamie dismounted from their horse. Simon held her brother back with a gentle hand. For once

Jamie remained silent, awed by the presence of the English king their uncle had made out to be Lucifer incarnate. No doubt the lad feared to move, lest Henry make his next supper from the lad's flesh.

When the king glanced back to Lord Sin, she noted the way his gaze softened ever so slightly. "Well, 'tis glad we are to see you two together. 'Tis our hope to see the two of you well suited."

Callie frowned as an uneasy feeling came over her. "I beg your pardon, Majesty?"

Henry ignored her as he took a step toward Sin and said in a tone for only the two of them to hear, "I have found that priest, Sin, and on the morrow I shall see the two of you wed."

Chapter 4

"I beg your pardon?" Callie repeated, her heart stopping. "What did you say?"

Sin paid her no heed as the king's eyes turned sly, devious.

"Have we been remiss?" Henry asked in a tone that feigned innocence. He knew she had no knowledge of what he spoke and it angered her for him to toy with her like this. "Caledonia of the MacNeelys, meet your soon-to-be husband, Sin."

She saw the fury smoldering in Sin's black eyes. Fury that sparked and built at the mention of her name. "What is her name?"

"Caledonia," Henry repeated.

Sin cursed, though why her name should cause him such distress, she couldn't imagine. Not that it mattered to her; she wasn't about to be married to an Englishman.

"I will not marry him."

Henry arched a brow in warning of her tone. "If you wish to return home, you will."

"My people will kill him."

Henry laughed. "They might try, but we assure you, they won't succeed."

She turned her gaze to Sin. "You knew of this?"

"I have yet to consent."

Henry scoffed. "You gave your word. Should we find a priest for the event, you would adhere to our agreement."

Sin narrowed a suspicious glare on Henry and crossed his arms over his chest. If her future didn't hinge on the victor of this confrontation, she might have found their behavior enjoyable. It wasn't often a woman got to see two such powerful men clash.

"First," Sin said slowly, "I want to meet this priest of yours and make sure he's not some peasant dressed in monk's robes."

The king managed to look both offended and amused. "Think you we would do such?"

"I have no doubt."

Henry laughed again. "Sin, my boy, you know us too well. But in this, there is no trickery. 'Tis the will of Our Savior that we should find you a spouse."

" 'Tis the will of Lucifer that you should torment me until the day he can take over."

"Perhaps."

Callie glared at each of the men in turn. She had no intention whatsoever of honoring any agreement forged by two Englishmen without her consent. Especially since such an agreement would be to the extreme detriment of her clan. "Whatever bargain the two of you hatched, it doesn't concern me. I will not marry an Englishman."

Henry looked thoughtful as he stroked the reddish beard on his chin. "Very well, then, you leave us no choice. We shall march our army into your lands and put down every man and male child to ensure peace. We shall start on the morrow with the death of your young brother."

Jamie gasped and stepped back, stumbling over Simon.

His face horrified, Simon scooped the lad up and held him close. He patted Jamie on the back comfortingly.

Callie's heart stopped as terror consumed her over Henry's cold-blooded threat. "You wouldn't dare such."

Her words of defiance were over the line of acceptance and they all knew it. Henry gave her a stare that made her tremble. Even so, she wouldn't cower. Not over something this important, especially while he threatened Jamie. If he even attempted to carry out that threat, she would see to it herself that he paid for his crime with his life.

"We would counsel you to watch your tongue," Henry said, his voice thick with malice. "Of royal Scots lineage you might be; *he* most certainly is not. Now, do you honestly think you could stop us from doing what we must to ensure the prosperity of England?"

She locked gazes with Sin and saw the warning in his eyes. Aye, Henry could be that ruthless. They both knew it.

"This is preposterous," she insisted to the king.

"Preposterous or not, come morning you two shall marry or our army marches into Scotland. The choice is entirely yours."

Callie met Henry's gaze as an equal. She wasn't going to let him see her fear, or her shivering. If she were a man, he'd never dare this, and it angered her that these Englishmen thought so little of their women.

How she wished this were a bluff. But she knew better.

The rebels in her clan, led by an unidentified man known simply as the Raider, had been unmerciful to the English who had dared settle in Scotland. She was sure the only reason Henry had refrained thus far from marching on her clan was the rather large matter of her kinship with King Malcolm of Scotland. It was also what had kept her safe in his hands.

As cousin to the Scottish king, she had spent much of her early life at his court and knew of the royal way of life and the way kings thought.

And she knew that if she dared take Sin into Scotland, those rebels who had been attacking the English would no doubt attack him and his men as well. It would be open warfare in a matter of days.

This had all the trappings of a disaster.

In her mind's eye she could see it clearly. Sin's army marching in and his soldiers wreaking havoc with the men of her clan, who hated all things English. Neither side would back down nor be reasonable. Her clansmen would never stomach an English army on their lands.

Whatever was she to do?

"What size army will you lead into my home?" she asked Sin, terrified of his answer.

"None. I will go alone."

Henry laughed out loud until he realized Lord Sin was in earnest. "You can't be serious."

Sin shrugged nonchalantly. "Even as few as ten English knights living among the Scots would invite the kind of conflict you're trying to avoid. The only chance for peace is one man against them."

Sin's knowledge of her people surprised her. As did his courage. But it was beyond foolishness to walk alone into enemy territory and expect them to surrender and bow. The day would never come when the Scots would do such.

Henry's face turned dark, his eyes angry as he regarded Sin. "They'll kill you."

"You said they couldn't," Sin reminded him.

Henry's face darkened even more from the weight of his rage, and the heads of the courtiers came together as they gossiped, reminding Callie that this entire discussion was being witnessed and noted.

Henry shook his head. "That was when we thought you'd have your men with you. What kind of fool—"

"I'll go with him."

Callie turned to see Simon still holding on to Jamie. Jamie's eyes were larger than saucers and the lad chewed his fist nervously.

Henry cursed. "Simon, we would have thought better of your sense than to entangle yourself with this."

Simon appeared to consider that. "Nay, Majesty, I appear to be rather suicidal in such matters. Besides, I've always wanted to see Scotland."

Sin scoffed. "Who says I shall allow it?"

A taunting, irreverent smile played on the edges of Simon's lips. "Allow it or not, I will be there. I figure it would be easier traveling with you, but either way, I will make for Scotland. You need someone at your back."

His words seemed to bitterly amuse Lord Sin. "I assure you, my back is *well* protected."

Something unspoken passed between them. Something that obviously bound these two men together on the level of brothers. Something that seemed sinister and cold, judging by the tormented looks in both their eyes.

"Well I know it," Simon concurred. "But even the strongest of us can use a friend now and again."

"I appreciate the thought, Simon; however, I have yet to agree to the marriage."

"You agreed," Henry insisted.

Callie wanted to argue, but she knew better. There was only one hope for her.

Escape.

There was no way to argue with these men who didn't care one whit about her or her opinions. She was nothing to Henry except a political pawn to be used as he saw fit.

As for Sin, she didn't know what he would gain from their union. But then, she didn't intend to stay around long enough to find out. Let him find an English heiress to marry. Or some other lass who caught his fancy.

She had to get away from here. From these men and this horrible country, or else all was lost.

"Well," she said slowly, backing away from them.

"If I am to marry on the morrow, I'd best be returning to my room, where I can make preparations for it."

"You're going to marry a devil?" Jamie asked, curling his lip at the thought of it. "Bet you grow horns if you do."

She ignored him and took him from Simon's arms.

Jamie shook his head like an old man chastising a child. "I wonder if you'll get a tail, too."

Callie sighed. Well, at least the lad had found his tongue again. She shushed him and still he rattled on and on about the consequences of marrying into the devil's royal family.

"Bet your children will be born with the tongues of snakes. Scales, too. Think you they'll have poison in their teeth if they bite me? You remember that time, don't you, when Robbie's baby bit me? I think I still have the bruise. Dermot said it went bone-deep, though it just looked kind of purple to me."

Sin watched the two of them head back to the castle all the while the boy prattled.

The woman had reversed herself just a little too quickly and he knew her mind, could see her thoughts plainly. She was plotting a new escape.

He motioned Simon to him. "Watch her while I speak to Henry."

"Should she escape custody, you won't have to marry her."

"I know. Watch her just the same. She has an incredible knack for getting herself into trouble."

Callie felt Lord Sin's gaze on her as she made her way with Jamie toward the castle. At the door, she stopped to look back and found Simon a few feet behind her.

Oh, cursed toads, Sin must have sent the knight to watch over them.

No matter. It merely made her escape more challenging. It by no means made her plans impossible. In her youth, she had often thwarted her intuitive nurse to slip out of the castle so that she could swim naked in the pond. If she could fluster Torna, who was part fey with her abilities to read Callie's mind, she could easily bypass a mere Englishman.

As Simon approached, she noted the black raven on his green surcoat. By the cut and cloth of the stylish piece and pride of the knight, she surmised he was a man of some standing and wealth. No doubt a great nobleman. "What are you lord of?" she asked politely.

He opened the door for her. "Only myself, milady. I am a landless knight."

"Friend to Lord Sin?"

He hedged a bit as she walked past him. "I suppose I'm as close as he gets to a friend."

"Meaning?"

"He only has enemies and those who would curry his favor to reach the king's ear." He shut the door behind her and Jamie, then led her through the bright hallway, splashed with color from the stained-glass windows, toward the stairs.

"Can I play with your sword?" Jamie asked.

Simon's eyes were gentle and kind as he ruffled the boy's red curls. "When you're older."

Jamie stuck his tongue out and Simon laughed at the imp. "You know, they say every time a boy sticks his tongue out, it sends a message to the night ogres where the boy sleeps."

"It does not." Jamie looked quickly to Callie. "Does it?"

She shrugged. "I know nothing of these night ogres."

Jamie ran up ahead of them, but kept his tongue in his mouth.

"Into which category do you fall?" she asked Simon, returning to their conversation. "Do you curry his favor or are you an enemy?"

"I fit into a third category that seems exclusive to myself, my brother and the king." He paused and pierced her with a sincere stare. "I owe Sin my life and quite probably my sanity as well. He did things for me no child should ever have to do, and I thank God every night for that man's loyalty to me at a time when any other boy would have been protecting himself and cowering in a corner somewhere."

"For that you would travel to Scotland to die with him?"

The sincerity in his eyes was scorching. "You have no idea."

A chill went up her spine at his words. Whatever had happened to them, it must have been horrible indeed.

Simon glanced to where Jamie was waiting for them at the top of the stairs, near her door.

He lowered his voice to keep Jamie from overhearing him. "I was scarce your brother's age when Sin laid his body over mine to keep me safe. He almost lost his own life that day because of it. The night my mother was killed, it was Sin who hid me from her murderer's wrath. From the wall where I was hidden, I could hear the beating he took rather than reveal my location. There are times at night when I can still hear and see the blows he received defending me not just that night, but for all the years we lived at Ravenswood.

"The last image I have of him as a child is with a hand wrapped around his throat by a man who swore Sin would be sorry for helping me. I shudder to think what was done to him over it. But knowing Harold as I do, I am quite certain he made good on that promise."

She shivered at what he was describing. But it went a long way in explaining the man she knew Sin to be.

Once they reached the top of the stairs, Callie gathered Jamie to her and opened the door to her room. Lord Sin was a fascination for her, but that was all he would ever be. She couldn't give him anything more than that.

Not while she had an escape to plan.

Sin spent hours trying to dissuade Henry from his madness. The man would not be swayed.

Damn.

A wife. The mere thought made his stomach queasy. What would he do with a wife?

He wasn't the kind of man who needed, let alone *wanted,* comfort. Hearth. Home. And, God forbid, love.

All he wanted was to be left alone.

Unbidden, an image of his brother Braden and sister-in-law Maggie drifted through his mind. Whenever his sister-in-law looked to his brother, a light so bright came into her eyes that it was blinding.

No one had ever given him such a look.

Less than a handful of people had ever looked at him with anything other than scorn or hatred. Not that he needed any tenderness in his life. He'd lived quite well without it. Why would he want it to change now?

Still . . .

Sin shook his head. No more thoughts on the matter. He would do as Henry wished, but there were ways yet to thwart him. An unconsummated marriage was easy enough to dissolve. He would go to Scotland, find this Raider who had been harassing Henry's people, put a stop to him, then regain his freedom.

Henry would be happy, and he was quite sure Caledonia would as well. . . .

Caledonia.

He cursed at the irony of her name. *I hate everything to do with Scotland and its people, and would sooner rot with pestilence than ever put one piece of my body in Scotland again.* Sin's vow echoed in his mind.

Disgusted, he made his way up the stairs toward his room.

When he first reached the landing, he thought nothing odd about the hallway outside of his and Caledonia's room being empty. Not until he heard a rhythmic thumping that echoed from the other side of her door.

With one hand on the hilt of his sword, he paused with a frown to listen.

Thump, thump . . . thump, thump . . . thump, thump . . . He cocked his head and moved closer to the dark oak door and splayed his hand over the wood.

It sounded much like a bed hammering against the wall while two people . . .

A stab of rage went through him. Especially when he heard the muffled grunts. He curled his hand into a fist. Nay! Surely Simon knew better than that.

Sin pressed his ear to the door.

There was no mistaking the sound. It was definitely a bed striking the stone wall with a tremendous amount of force. And the rhythm could be nothing other than a man thrusting.

"Simon," he hissed under his breath, "you're a dead man."

Unsheathing his sword, Sin narrowed his eyes and flung open the door to see two lumps beneath the covers, writhing in unison on the bed.

Sin couldn't remember the last time anything had made him this angry. But for some reason, the thought of Simon deflowering Caledonia made him want blood. Simon's blood.

Every last tiny drop of it.

His wrath barely leashed, he approached the bed silently, then angled his sword to the small of the largest lump's back.

Both lumps froze.

"This best not be what I think it is." Sin tore the blanket from the bed.

Shock rooted him to the floor as he took in the full sight before him.

Simon lay on his side, fully clothed, tied both to the bed and to a lump of pillows with a rope. A gag of linen was stuffed into his mouth. Simon's hair was tousled all about his head. His surcoat was soaking wet and his eyes were swollen and red, and they burned with a rage that was tangible.

Sin sheathed his sword, then pulled out his dagger to cut away the gag.

"It isn't what you *were* thinking," Simon said. "But it's what you're thinking now."

"What the devil happened?" Sin set about cutting him free of the lump and bed.

Simon's face flushed with anger. "She told me she had woman troubles. Then, when I came to check on her to see if I needed to fetch a physician, she blew some witch's brew into my eyes."

"Why are you wet?"

"After they tied me down, the wench tried to drown me."

Sin would have laughed had he not been trying to decide who to strangle first, Caledonia or Simon.

"I should leave you tied up here."

"If it'll keep me safe from that she-witch, then please do so."

Sin cut the last rope. "Any idea where she was bound for?"

"None whatsoever."

"How long since she fled?"

"At least an hour."

Sin cursed. With that amount of time, she could be anywhere in London.

Caledonia paused as she glanced around the streets of London. The afternoon crowd that bustled in between the large buildings was fairly thick. None of them should recognize her or Jamie.

With her brother's hand held tightly in hers, she wended her way north toward an inn where she remembered stopping on her way into London. The keeper had owned a stable with horses to be bought. If she could get to those horses, she would buy one for each of them with the money she had managed to hide from Henry. He'd had no idea when he'd taken her that she'd possessed a small fortune in her bodice.

Once they were safely away from the inn, they would don the robes of a leper and no one, not even thieves, would dare stop them then.

They would be home in no time.

"Are we to walk all the way home?" Jamie asked.

Callie smiled. "Just a little farther, sweeting."

"But my legs are so tired, Callie. Can we not stop for a rest? Just a little one? A minute or two before my legs fall off and then I'll never be able to run again."

She didn't dare stop. Not when they were so close to leaving this place behind.

Lifting Jamie up in her arms, she held him to her side and continued on. "Och, lad, you've gotten heavy," she said as she skirted women carrying baskets of market goods. "Why, I remember when you scarce weighed as much as a loaf of bread."

"Did Da sing to me then?"

Callie's heart clenched at his question. Poor Jamie barely remembered their father, who had died almost three years ago. "Aye," she said, squeezing him. "He sang to you every night when your mother would put you to bed."

"Was he a big man like Dermot?"

Callie smiled at the mention of their brother. At

ten-and-six, Dermot stood a good three inches taller than she. "Bigger than Dermot." Indeed, her father was closer to Lord Sin's height.

"Do you think he'll be happy to see my mother while he's in heaven with yours?"

Callie arched a brow at the odd question. "Mercy, imp, wherever do you think up these questions?"

"Well, I was just wondering. One of the king's knights told me that poor servants can't go to heaven, only noble people can. I was thinking then that God wouldn't want my mother there with yours."

Callie took a deep breath at the nonsense. Her mother may have been of royal blood and Jamie's mother a simple shepherdess, but only a fool would spout off such rampant stupidity. And to a wee bairn, no less.

"He was being mean to you, Jamie. God loves all people equally. Your mother is a good soul who loves us, and the Lord in His mercy will see her in heaven along with the rest of us when, God forbid, she dies."

"Well, what—"

"Jamie, please," she begged. "I'm needing every breath to carry you. Please, no more questions."

"Very well." He wrapped his thin arms around her neck and laid his head on her shoulder.

Callie walked on for as long as she could, but after a time her arms and back ached. "Lad, I need for you to walk on your own for a bit."

Jamie got down and held on to her skirts as they headed along another crowded street.

"How many days do you think it'll take us to walk through London? A hundred? Two hundred?"

It felt like two thousand. "We'll get out eventually.

Try not to think about that. Think about being home again."

"Can I think about my mother's mincemeat tarts?"

"Sure."

"Can I think about Uncle Aster's horse?"

"Fine."

"Can I think—"

"Jamie, my love, can you please think to yourself?"

He heaved a weary sigh, as if the burden of thinking to himself were more than he could bear.

Callie pulled him to a stop as she spied a group of mounted knights riding through the city. She let go of Jamie's hand to pull her veil around her face in case they should glance her way.

Laughing, the mounted knights paid no heed to her. But it wasn't until they had ridden past that her heart stopped thudding and she found her wobbly legs able to continue on.

"That was close," she breathed. She reached to re-take Jamie's hand, only to realize he wasn't there.

Oh, Lord, nay!

"Jamie!" she called, scanning the crowd around her. "Jamie!" Her panic gripped her anew. She saw no sight of his brown cap. No sight of his red curls.

Where could the wee lad be?

"Jamie!"

Terror consumed her. Where was he? Where could he have gone to? He'd been right beside her only an instant before, and she had told him a thousand and one times not to wander off. Especially not in un-known places where strangers were about.

Oh, Lord, anything could happen to him!

Callie scanned the crowd again, seeing several

small children, but none that bore any resemblance to her imp.

Could he be in trouble? Her heart hammering, she searched all around her as fast as she could.

"Blessed Sainted Mary, where could you be, lad?" she whispered over and over as she searched. "Please, Lord, give me my brother back. I swear I'll never again ask him to be quiet and I'll answer every single question he asks. I'll never ever lose patience with him again. Just please, God, please let me find him before something happens to him." Tears welled in her eyes.

He could have fallen in the river or he could have gotten run over by a cart. He could have been kidnapped by thieves or some horrid such! Her mind played through numerous horrific scenarios, and all of them culminated with Jamie needing her and she not being there to protect him.

If anything happened to him, she would never be able to live with herself.

The pain in her chest was excruciating. It tore through her lungs, making it hard to breathe.

She had no idea where to look. No idea how to find him in this foreign city.

Through her panic only one clear thought emerged.

Lord Sin.

He would find Jamie. She was sure of it.

Now she just had to find him.

Sin scanned the crowd around him while he rode through the streets. He'd cornered poor Aelfa, and with little provocation the maid had confessed Cale-

donia's plan. Now he just had to get to the inn before
the wench bought her horses.

With Simon behind him, they were making good
time.

Out of the crowd, Sin spied a light blue veil on a
woman so tall she stood head and shoulders above
those around her. Even though she appeared frantic
and hurried, he recognized her instantly.

"Caledonia!" he called.

She stopped immediately.

Instead of running away as he expected, she rushed
to his side. "Blessed saints and glory," she said, her
face streaked by tears as she placed her hands against
his right leg. Her desperate touch shouldn't have af-
fected him at all, and yet it burned his skin with a
throbbing heat that pulsed straight to his groin. "I am
so glad to see you."

Her words set him back. Never in his life had anyone said such a thing to him, let alone held such a sincere look about it.

Something bad must surely have happened, for her
to want to see the likes of him.

It was then he realized the boy wasn't with her.
Sliding from his horse, he held her by her arms.
"What has happened?"

"It's Jamie." She shrugged his touch away, grabbed
his arm and started pulling him down the street with
her as she looked all about. "He's gone and we have
to find him. He was here a few minutes ago and then
he vanished. Jamie!" she shouted his name.

Several people looked at them, but no one answered.

"Simon," he called. "The boy is missing. Can you see him from up there?"

Simon shook his head and moved his horse to stand beside them. "Where were you when he disappeared?"

She wiped her eyes with her hands and looked up at Simon. "Not very far from where we were yesterday. Maybe one street over."

"By the baker's shop with the stuffed squirrel in the window?" Simon asked.

"Aye. I believe so."

Sin arched a brow at the expression on Simon's face. "You think you know where he might have gone?"

"Aye."

Caledonia took a deep breath and her grip on Sin's arm tightened.

"But," Simon said, his voice sour, "I'll take you there provided neither one of you ever mentions the bed incident to me or anyone else. Ever."

Caledonia blushed. "I am so sorry for that. But I did wash your eyes out. Do they still burn?"

Simon's face turned the color of Caledonia's hair, though whether from anger or embarrassment, Sin couldn't tell.

When Simon spoke, his voice was colder than a snowstorm in January. "They are fine. Thank you, milady, for your kindness."

Sin mounted his horse, then reached his hand down to Caledonia. Her eyes relieved, she grabbed on to him and he noticed the tiny bones of her hand. The softness of her touch. He'd never felt anything like her delicate hand in his.

He pulled her up to ride before him and turned his attention to Simon. "Where are we bound for?"

"On the way back yesterday, I was telling the boy about the sweets at the Unicorn Maiden. I even showed him where the shop was located and he said he would give anything to see the pastries and cockapies. I have a feeling he might have gone there. Though why I should bother rescuing *him* I'll never know. I swear my head still throbs from the little demon."

Callie felt heat sting her face. "He didn't mean to hit you, Simon. I swear that part of it was an accident."

He gave her a droll glare that told her he didn't believe a word of it.

Callie didn't say anything as they rode toward the bakery. Jamie knew better than to leave her side. He'd never done anything this foolish in his life and she couldn't imagine what had possessed him.

And the lad had best be in trouble when they found him. If not, she was going to throttle his young life right out of him.

It didn't take long to retrace her steps to the corner where Jamie had vanished. Simon led them a few yards over to a small bake shop, where an old woman was leaving with a basket full of bread.

As they approached the store, Callie saw the squirrel Simon had mentioned and she recognized the small face staring out the window, scanning the passersby, and noted the smile of extreme jubilation as its large blue eyes focused on her. He was obviously as glad to see her as she was to see him.

"Oh, Blessed be St. Mary," she whispered.

Relief tore through her as she slid from the horse and ran inside the store to her brother. He'd been close by the entire time, but without the men, she'd never have known to look here.

Tears ran down her cheeks again as she swept him into her arms. "Little runt," she breathed. "You scared me."

"I'm sorry, Callie." He pulled back and showed her the honey bread in his hand. "I thought we'd be needing something to eat for the journey. You've had nothing all day."

Her hand trembled as she took the bread from him. "I would much rather starve than lose you."

"I'm sorry, Callie. I never meant to scare you. I was just hungry."

Sin swallowed at the sight of their reunion. At the love the two of them had for each other.

The boy looked up at Simon. "I wanted to buy the swan pastries you told me about, but the baker's wife said I didn't have enough coin for that." He looked back at his sister. "You like pastries."

While she kissed his cheek and assured herself the demon was hale, Sin paid for enough swan pastries to make the rapscallion's belly ache.

Callie looked up as Lord Sin handed her brother his purchase. "Thank you for your kindness."

By the expression on his face, she could tell her words made the knight terribly uncomfortable.

As they left the shop and headed back to the castle, Callie realized she wasn't going to make it home. At least not alone. She'd been fooling herself even to think it. Worse, she'd almost lost the one person who meant the most to her in the world.

Dear saints what if they hadn't found Jamie? What if he had gotten hurt or killed or . . .

It would have been all her fault. She closed her eyes as pain swept through her. The last thing she wanted was to tell Morna she'd let something happen to Jamie. It would be the death of the poor woman who had been a mother to her as well.

Nay, she'd take no more chances with his safety.

But then what was she to do?

Her thoughts turned to the man who would be her husband. Could she trust him?

For an Englishman, he seemed reasonable enough. As did Simon.

Perhaps, if she allowed them to go home with her, her clan might see that not all Englishmen were beasts. Perhaps they could win them over. . . .

What are you? Daft? Get your head out of the dream world, lass, and put it on earth where it belongs. There's little to no chance of the MacNeelys ever accepting an Englishman into their midst.

It was a long shot, no doubt, but it was the only one she could see.

If she married Sin, they could go home safely.

Like it or not, she would submit to this marriage and trust in the Lord above to see her through it and to know what was best. Surely it must be His will, otherwise she and Jamie would have succeeded by now and been on their way home. This day had been an omen, and Callie believed wholeheartedly in omens.

Tomorrow Sin would be her husband.

She watched Sin mount his horse. He slid gracefully into the saddle like the born warrior he was and sat proudly on the back of his horse with his long hair shining in the daylight. He was a fine sight there, handsome, strong. The kind of man a woman dreamed about at night and hoped to see just once in the flesh.

And he could be hers. . . .

The hand he extended to her was both powerful and tender. He might not be her first choice for husband, but there was kindness in him. Fairness, too.

If only he were of Scots blood.

Still, there were far worse men to be married to.

"Milord?" she asked as he settled her before him. "What will you do to my people when you take me home?"

Sin clenched his teeth at her question. The very idea of returning to Scotland made him ill. If he had his way about it, he'd never again venture there.

Of course, he did have his brothers there, and while he was with her, he would make a point of seeing them. They alone made the idea of leaving England tolerable.

"I will ensure Henry's peace is kept," he told her. "So long as your men refrain from raiding his people, I will do naught." What he didn't tell her was that he intended to find the so-called Raider, put an end to the man's mischief, then get himself out of their marriage as quickly as possible.

But even as the thought swept through his mind, he became aware of the woman before him. The way she smelled and felt in his arms. She was warm and soft, a gentle balm to soothe him.

He'd never held a woman like this. Never even dared hope for any kind of comfort in his life.

Comfort. He sneered at the word. Comfort was for

weak-minded fools. He didn't need it and he damn sure didn't want it.

He would do what he had to for Henry's sake and then he would be back to fulfill his oath of loyalty. That was his life and he had no desire for it to change. He had fought too long and hard for his peace of mind to let this little bit of baggage in his lap come along and rattle him.

"So," he said quietly as he looked down at her. She had her head tilted to study his hands. "You're going through with this marriage, then?"

She glanced at him over her shoulder and he caught a whiff of her light lavender scent. The smell of her stirred him furiously. His arms were pressed against her rib cage and her red lips were parted just enough so that he could easily claim her mouth for a passionate kiss.

The thought fired his body even more. The devil preserve him, he wanted this woman in a way most desperate.

She stared at his lips as if she felt the heat between them. As if she, too, were dreaming of the kiss he longed to give her.

"I see no way to avoid it," she said quietly. "Do you?"

He smiled at the hopeful note in her voice. "Nay, lady, I don't. But I am working on it."

The smile on her face bedazzled him. "In that case, good luck. I wish you much success."

Sin shook his head at her. She was a rare treat. One he would love to take a bite of and see if she was as saucy in his mouth as she was in his lap.

Strangely enough, he couldn't resist playing with her. "Should I be offended?"

Callie bit her lower lip. He was teasing her. The light in his eyes said as much. Charmed by his uncharacteristic behavior, she teased back. "Nay, no offense intended. You're actually very nice when you're not trying to be frightening."

"Nice?" He asked in disbelief. "That is probably the only title no one has ever heaped upon my head."

"No one?"

"No one."

Callie pulled back to look up at him. "It must scare you, then, to know I know the truth of you when no one else does."

Lord Sin arched a brow at her. "Who says that is the truth of me?"

"I do, and unless you have a horn to pull out and show me otherwise, I shall never believe anything else of you."

Sin cleared his throat at her words. The woman need do no more than glance down and she would see proof enough of a horn that desired only to be naughty with the nymph in his lap.

Oh, the spirit of this wench and the education he would kill to give her. He could just imagine her lying naked in his arms, her breasts pressed up against him. The taste of her flesh on his tongue.

She was a temptress without equal.

"Tell me," he whispered, "why it is you alone hold no fear of me?"

"I can't imagine. Surely I am foolish. Aelfa assures me you eat small children every morn to break your fast. Do you?"

"Nay, I find them to be too harsh on the belly. All

that moving around once they're swallowed. Not worth the effort, really."

She laughed, and it was a truly enchanting sound. This had to be the most peculiar conversation he'd ever had in his life.

She pushed a stray piece of copper hair back beneath her veil. "Does anyone other than me know you can be playful?"

Sin scoffed. "Playful? Milady, your fire is missing a few logs if you think that of me."

"More's the pity, then."

"How so?"

"We all need to play from time to time. Is that not right, Simon?"

Sin glanced over to see Simon eavesdropping. The man nodded. "Indeed it is, milady. But I can attest, Sin has never known a moment's worth of it. Not even as a child."

A deep frown crossed her brow as she regarded Sin. "Is that true?"

"Not entirely. I did have a few years of fun with my brothers and a moment or two with Simon in our youth."

Her frown lightened, putting a sudden glow into her light green eyes. "You have brothers?"

"Aye. I had four of them."

"Had?"

"One died a few years back."

The joy left her face, and to his amazement, she gently patted his arm in sympathy. "I'm very sorry for the loss. You must miss him much."

In truth, he did. Though he hadn't seen Kieran since Kieran was Jamie's age, Sin still held fond memories of his younger brother. The knowledge that his brothers had all been home and were being cared for was the only thing that had made his hell bearable growing up. As he had suffered at the hands of Harold and the others, he had reminded himself that if not for him, one of his brothers would have been tortured in his place.

Better he should be beaten and humiliated than any of them. They were good and decent, and they deserved only the best that life could provide for them.

"We have a brother, too," Jamie said. "Dermot the doormat."

"Jamie!" Caledonia snapped. "He would have your head for that."

"It's better than what he calls me."

"Your older brother?" Sin asked her.

"Nay. I am the eldest."

He nodded. "That explains much."

"Much of what?"

"The way you treat Jamie. The way you're so determined to get home even when you know you stand no chance."

Callie frowned at him. "You are the eldest?"

He gave a subtle nod.

They reined to a stop just before the stable. Simon slid down with Jamie while Sin helped her down.

"Simon, can you see her back to her room without—"

Simon cleared his throat loudly. "Remember, there will be no mention of *that*."

Sin smiled wryly. "Fine. Can you get her back without any more of that-which-will-remain unmentioned happening again? Or do I need to hire a bodyguard for you as well?"

Callie bit her lip impishly. "We will play nicely with Simon, won't we, Jamie?"

"If you say so, Callie."

She watched as Sin left them. Then she reached for Jamie's hand and walked back to the castle, with Simon by her side. "Simon, how long have you known Lord Sin?"

"He was nine when King Stephen sent him to foster with my stepfather."

So, he had known him for quite some time. That was good. Mayhap this knight could help her better understand the man who would be her husband.

As they entered the castle, Jamie pulled away from her and bounded up the stairs ahead of them.

"Know you why he is so sad?" she asked.

Simon gave her a suspicious stare. "How did you—"

"His eyes. He hides it well, but every now and again I see it."

Simon took a deep breath as they climbed the dark stairs. A muscle worked in his jaw, as if he were warring within himself over whether or not he should tell her anything about his friend. Finally he spoke. "He has many reasons, milady."

"Such as?"

"I was just a boy when Sin was brought to us, but I remember that night vividly. King Stephen's men had been unkind to him on his long journey to our home, and when he entered the great hall, his eyes were blackened from punches. His nose was still bleeding and his lips and jaw swollen. It looked as if they had dragged him the whole way to Ravenswood over the roughest roads they could find.

"They had shackled him in irons about his neck and hands. Still, he stood erect and faced Harold of Ravenswood with a strength and dignity few *men* possessed. The old earl was renowned only for his cruelty and love of all things brutal, and as such even the stoutest of heart was known to grow a bit pale when they looked upon him. And yet here was a boy who stood without flinching. One who met the earl with his lips curled and his eyes narrowed in hatred. Harold asked him how it came to be that he held such courage before him."

Simon dropped his voice and whispered in her ear so that Jamie wouldn't overhear his words. "Sin said he was hell-spawned from the loins of a whore and sired by a heartless bastard."

She sucked in her breath at such horrendous words. She could barely imagine a child saying such.

"He told Harold that he had no soul and there was nothing Harold could ever do to hurt him." His eyes bleak, Simon sighed. "All I can say to that is that Harold took up that challenge and did everything he could to make Sin bow down to him in fear."

Her chest drew tight at the words. She slid her gaze to Jamie as the lad swept into their room, and tried to imagine him in such a state. All little Jamie had ever known was loving arms and a doting family. She didn't even want to think what it would take to make a child like the one Simon described. Just how much had Sin suffered? And why? Why would anyone do such a thing to a mere lad?

Everyone deserved love. It was what her mother, God rest her soul, had always taught her.

"Why was he in chains?" she asked as they joined Jamie in the room.

Talking loudly to himself, her brother knelt before their trunk and started digging out the toys Aelfa had brought for him. He lined the knights up and catapulted them with his shoes while she and Simon went to stand by the window.

"Sin was a political hostage. Sent as a guarantee that his father would no longer oppose King Stephen."

Callie grew quiet as she remembered the story one of the courtiers had told her of William the Marshal after she had met William her first day at King Henry's court. Like Sin, William had once been handed over to King Stephen in guarantee of his father's good behavior. When William's father returned to warring against the king, Stephen had almost killed the lad.

What she remembered most were the cruel words John Fitz Gilbert had shouted down to Stephen when the king reminded him of his son William, who would bear the punishment of his father's actions: *Go ahead and kill him. I have hammer and anvil with which to forge even stronger sons.*

It was obvious Sin's father had been of like mind. How horrible for Sin. Her own father would have killed any man who even looked askance at one of his children.

Simon caught one of the toy knights as it flew through the air and handed it back to Jamie, who whooped and howled at his game.

"Tell me, Simon, is there a lady Lord Sin fancies?"

Simon shook his head as he returned to her side. "He keeps his own company. He learned long ago to trust no one. Not even a woman."

"Meaning?"

"He has many enemies at court. Including some who would gladly kill him if the opportunity ever presented itself. Women as well as men."

Callie couldn't imagine living a life in which no one could be trusted. "And he has no friends?"

"He has me and King Henry."

"Nay, Simon. He just has you."

Simon frowned. "I don't understand."

"If Henry were really his friend, he wouldn't ask Sin to venture into an unfriendly country where he would be even less welcome than he is here."

Simon gave her an appreciative look. "True enough, milady."

Simon excused himself and took Jamie out to play before the lad destroyed the room.

Seating herself at her dressing table, Callie tried to think what she should do. Part of her knew it was the worst sort of foolishness to bring an Englishman into her clan, and yet another part of her was fascinated by Lord Sin and the possibility that he could be the bridge between her clan and the English.

She was well past the age of marriage. Years ago, she'd been promised to a man who had died of illness mere months before their wedding. She'd spent two years mourning him. Just as she reached the end of that period, her father had died. Since then, she had been too occupied with the problems of her clan and the unknown rebels to think about a husband.

How she wished Morna was here. Jamie's mother was good at thinking through matters such as these. She would help her decide what was best.

But then, Callie knew the answer in her heart. She had to get home before the rebels or her uncle attacked the English to get her back. Her Uncle Aster wouldn't rest until she and Jamie were home, and there was no telling how many of her clan would perish in that foolishness.

If Sin kept his word and left his men behind, then perhaps there could be peace. Perhaps the men of her clan could see the English weren't so terribly bad. Of course, from what she'd seen, some of them were demons incarnate; but then, even some of her precious Scots could be a bit bloodthirsty as well.

Oh, what was she to do?

Her head ached as thoughts and doubts chased each other around.

The door to her room opened. Callie looked up to find Aelfa standing pale in the doorway, wringing her hands. Though they hadn't known each other long, the lass had come to mean a great deal to Callie. Aelfa had been her only friend and confidante these weeks past, and had aided her in ways that would have the tiny woman beaten if anyone ever learned of it.

Now the dear soul looked as if she'd seen the devil himself on her heels. "Aelfa, what is it?"

She moved forward, biting her lip and twisting her wide sleeve in her hands. "Oh, milady, I just be hearing something awful, I have, and I know not who to tell or what to do about it. Maybe I should just forget what I heard. Aye, forget it." She looked around a bit wildly as she nodded in silent agreement with whatever words were in her head.

Aelfa froze and her large brown eyes widened even more. "But if I do and he dies, then I would be responsible. God might not forgive that. Would it make me an accomplice? Aye, I think it would. The king himself might want me dead for that one. Oh, Lord, I'm too young to die. I haven't even a husband yet, nor children. I don't want to die yet. Nay!"

Callie pressed her fingers to her temple in an effort to follow the woman's prattle. She took Aelfa's arm in a gentle grasp and tried to get the lass to calm a bit and explain what had her so distraught. "Aelfa, what exactly did you hear?"

"Men talking in a room down the stairs."

Now, that, unlike her previous monologue, made sense. "What were they saying?"

The lass crossed herself, her eyes turning wild again. "They said they were going to kill Lord Sin tonight so that one of them could marry you for your lands. He said he'd be teaching them—beg your pardon, milady—them Highland dogs how to mind their betters, and that he would train the—beg pardon again—Scots bitch to heel."

Callie's heart froze at the words as disbelief tore through her. It was quickly followed by rage and indignation. Just who would dare say such?

"Have you told his lordship?" she asked the young maid.

"Nay. He scares me too much."

Callie patted her on the arm in gratitude. "Thank you, Aelfa. I'll tell him myself."

When she reached the door, Aelfa's voice stopped her. "Milady, you realize that should they kill him, you won't have to marry him?"

The thought had never entered her mind. And even now that it had, her choice was clear.

She couldn't stand by and see a man slaughtered. Especially one to whom she owed so much. Regardless of what others thought, she knew the heart of the black knight, and it wasn't so dark or forbidding.

Without another word, she left the room in search of Lord Sin.

Chapter 5

Sin stood in the center of Henry's throne room, waiting for the king's return. Why he bothered, he couldn't imagine.

Henry had made his decision clear. Sin was to find the Scots rebel leader and kill him.

There was nothing unusual about the order. He'd murdered more than once at Henry's command. It was what made him anathema to the court. An abomination to the pope.

It was also what had saved his life as a boy.

He'd only been ten-and-four when he'd taken his first life. He'd never forget that moment. Scared and shaking, he had followed his orders and gone into the man's room at a local inn. The man had been nothing more than a poor pilgrim who had come to Outremer to pray. The Old Man of the Mountain, the leader of the Saracens who had bought and trained him, had ordered the pilgrim slain and Sin knew that had he failed, they would have taken him out and . . .

He shook his head to banish the memory.

He didn't like to remember the past. There were no happy memories of childhood or of anything else.

All he remembered was the wanting.

Yearning for a mother's kindness. A father's gentle hand. What he had gotten was innumerable insults and beatings. Torture at times so cruel and severe that he wondered how he had managed to survive it with his mind and body intact. Then again, maybe his mind wasn't so sound after all. Surely no one could survive what he had and be left normal.

Day by day, sometimes even hour by hour, he had suffered through and emerged so strong that no one could touch him now.

He was granite. And he fully intended to stay that way.

Sin cocked his head as he heard a sound. It was the soft whispering of leather against stone. So slight, most men would not have heard it at all, but for a man whose lack of vigilance had cost him dearly in his youth, it was mammoth.

From the shadows he saw a man emerge with a dagger. In an instant, he knew the man who attacked him. Though why it surprised him, he had no idea. Roger's enmity toward him was nothing new.

Sin rolled his eyes as the fool rushed him with the dagger raised. "Roger, this is a mistake."

Before the knight could comment, two more attacked.

Sin sighed disgustedly. They knew he was unarmed. No one was allowed through the main entrance of the throne room bearing arms. Not that it mattered.

He caught Roger with his foot and kicked him back. The knight went sprawling.

The next man he knew not at all. It didn't matter. Sin hit the ground in a roll and knocked him off balance, then twisted the sword from his grasp.

Sin heard the rasping swoosh of Roger tossing a dagger toward his back and the door opening. Instinctively, he dropped to the floor. The dagger whizzed past and embedded itself into the chest of the man he had been about to fight. The man gasped as he sank to his knees.

The man he'd disarmed ran out the open door while Sin turned to see Callie standing there in shock.

Roger started for him, but Callie jerked at the rug beneath Roger's feet and sent the man sprawling.

Hiding his amusement at her aid, Sin angled his stolen sword at Roger as the knight slowly regained his feet while Callie stepped back to observe them.

The knight's eyes glared his hatred and Sin was amazed Roger didn't run and hide. It was what the knight did best.

Sin lowered his confiscated sword. "Care to explain?"

"Explain what? That someone needs to kill you? Everyone knows you need to die. How many sleeping throats have you cut in the name of Henry?"

Sin heard a soft gasp at the words. He glanced behind Roger to see Caledonia covering her mouth with one hand, her eyes wide. Now she knew the truth of him.

So be it. He'd never hidden from what he was.

Perhaps it was for the best. Now she would hate him as everyone else did. It would make avoiding her all the easier.

And yet something inside him shriveled at the thought of her hating him. It made no sense to him at all. But then, few things in life did.

Roger looked to the woman and his eyes narrowed. "Does she know you were a *hashishin*?"

Sin took a deep breath as he recalled the way his masters had *thoroughly* trained him in ways to take a man's life. He saw the confusion on Caledonia's face as she regarded the two of them.

"She doesn't know the Saracen term *assassin*, Roger."

"She knows the term *murderer*. That's what you are. You are a filthy murdering dog with no conscience or morals."

Sin lifted the tip of the sword to Roger's throat. "You've said enough. Any more words, and I will show you firsthand what my Saracen trainers taught me."

Roger paled.

The gilded oak doors opened to admit Henry and his guard. The king drew up sharply as he caught sight of Sin in the middle of the room with his sword at Roger's throat. "What is this?"

Henry's guards came around to protect their king.

Sin stepped back and handed the sword hilt first to one of the guards. "Nothing of any great import, Sire. 'Tis only another attempt on my life."

Callie stood in shock at Sin's bored tone. It was as if he thought little of the fact that the man had just sought his death.

Rage suffused Henry's face as he confronted the handsome knight who was almost a head shorter than him. "Any good reason why you felt the need to kill our advisor?"

Roger glared his hatred at Sin. "He killed my father in cold blood and yet you reward him like some treasured hound. 'Tis obscene the way no one dares make him pay for what he's done."

Henry's eyes narrowed dangerously. "We understand you are upset, but we stringently advise you to counsel that tongue, lest you find our wrath falling full force onto your head."

Roger stepped back and turned his chastised gaze to the floor.

Henry glanced to Sin. "Is it true? Did you kill his father?"

Callie saw pain flare in Sin's eyes a moment before he shielded it.

Sin shrugged. "How would I know? I never knew my victims' names."

By Sin's expression, she could tell he did remember their faces. There was such a haunted look to him that she had no doubt it troubled him still.

"See?" Roger snarled. "He doesn't deny it. I want justice for my family."

"Justice, sir, or were you after a more selfish end?" The words left her mouth before she realized she'd spoken.

Suddenly all the men turned to look at her.

Callie shifted nervously. "I was told you came to kill him so that one of you could marry me and put down my people."

"You lie!"

Henry cocked a brow at her words. "How do you know this?"

"Their plot was overheard by someone I trust."

Sin was stunned by her words. In the whole of his

life, no one had ever defended him. He was so used to being cast out and left to his own ends that her actions baffled him.

Now her sudden appearance in the throne room made sense. "Is this why you came here?"

She nodded. "I wanted to forewarn you."

He stood in complete disbelief.

Henry narrowed his eyes on Roger. "A witness to your plot, Roger. What say you now?"

"There was another conspirator as well," Callie said.

Henry looked to Sin.

"Aye," Sin concurred reluctantly, "Thomas of Wallingford. He ran off."

Henry sent his guard in search of the man. His eyes cold, he looked to Roger and instructed his other guard. "Send him to the tower. We shall deal with him later."

Once the three of them were alone, the king approached Callie with one arched brow. "By your actions, may we assume you will abide by your marriage?"

"Might I speak alone with Lord Sin on the matter, Majesty?"

Henry focused a suspicious stare on her, but ultimately allowed them to leave his presence.

Sin led her from the throne room and down the hall to a set of stairs. They walked along in silence until Sin took her to a courtyard behind the keep.

The small area was surrounded by gray stone walls that were covered in ivy and honeysuckle. It was a peaceful afternoon, with nary a sound to intrude on them.

Callie watched him stand proudly before her, his dark hair falling becomingly over his face. Lord Sin was a dangerously handsome man. One who could devastate a woman with nothing more than a simple smile. She couldn't help wondering what it would be like to be held by him. To taste those lips on hers.

She shouldn't be having such thoughts of him, and yet she couldn't quite stop herself.

He clasped his hands behind his back and eyed her a bit impatiently. "Well?"

Callie sorted through her jumbled emotions as best she could. "May I be honest with you?"

"I certainly prefer it to dishonesty."

She smiled at that. He was such an odd man.

"I . . ." She paused as she searched her mind for the best way to broach her concerns.

"You . . . ?"

She fidgeted with the sleeve of her gown. She knew so little of this man that she wasn't sure what to say.

Finally she lifted her chin and did what she did best. She blurted it out. "You and your king have asked me to bind myself eternally to you. To entrust my life and my people into your hands. I wanted you to know that I take my oaths very seriously. And if we are to do this, then I wish to spend a little time getting to know you."

Sin opened his mouth to tell her of his plan to find the Raider and leave her in peace, then paused.

She would never agree to his going home with her to hand one of her people over to Henry, or worse, kill him. If she had any intention of doing that, the rebel leader would already be on his way to London.

Nay, he would have to let her think he was agreeable to this match. "Very well," he said. "How do you suggest we get to know one another before the morrow?"

"Will you dine with me this evening? Here. Just the two of us?"

He arched a brow at that. "Us alone?"

"And Aelfa, of course. But no one else."

It was a strange request she made. Yet he could see no harm in humoring her. "What time?"

"Vespers?"

He nodded. "I shall see you then."

Callie watched him leave her. For the first time, she noticed the way he walked. Like a stalking lion waiting for a predator to jump out at him.

He was a fierce man, this knight. Fierce and lonely.

And soon to be her husband.

Swallowing at the thought, she went to make preparations for the night.

Sin was alone in his room, sitting at his desk, when he heard a knock at the door. "Enter."

He half expected it to be Caledonia, so when Simon entered, it surprised him.

"What brings you here?" Sin asked as Simon closed the door and leaned against it.

"I was wondering when we'd be leaving for Scotland. I wanted to send word to Draven. I thought we could stop in for a short visit, since Ravenswood is on the way."

Sin let out a slow breath. "I truly appreciate your offer, Simon, but I have no intention of taking you with me."

"You need someone to go with you."

"I need no one. I assure you, I will be fine."

Simon crossed his arms over his chest as he eyed Sin speculatively. "Do you remember what you said to me the first night you came to Ravenswood?"

"Nay. I barely recall that night."

"I asked you if you were afraid of being so far from your family. You said that you had no family. That you belonged nowhere and to no one. Do you remember it now?"

Sin shrugged. "Vaguely."

"Well, it seems to me the man before me is still that nine-year-old boy who stood defiantly before Harold. You still have one shoulder braced to take a blow while your hand is curled into a fist to strike back."

Pain assailed Sin as unwanted memories rushed through him. He'd spent the better part of his life trying to forget the very things Simon wanted him to remember, and the last thing he wanted was to dredge up such horrors.

"Simon, is there a point to this?"

"Aye, there is. When Draven and I tried to befriend you, you would say nothing to us. You drew into yourself even worse than Draven did. He at least kept himself open to me. But you . . . you refused all comfort."

Sin held his silence. He had never refused comfort. It was simply forbidden to him. Every time Harold had caught him speaking to Draven or Simon, he had been punished for it. Harold had despised him with a passionate zeal. Older than both Draven and Simon, Sin had never had a protector.

Sin had always been alone. There had never been a choice in the matter.

"I want to go with you, Sin. Haven't you spent enough of your life with nothing but enemies at your back?"

Sin sighed. "You know you don't owe me for what I did."

"I know that. It's not why I want to go."

Sin frowned at that. He would never understand Simon's mind. "Then why? Why would you want to spend a week's time journeying to a land where they will despise you?"

"Because they tell me a friend of mine is going there alone."

Sin shook his head. Simon was a strange man. Inside, he knew Simon had no business going along. The man had no idea what they were in for. But Sin did.

He was used to it. But Simon . . . Simon was a fool to want to do this.

"Well?" Simon prompted.

"We leave day after tomorrow."

Simon nodded. "Good. I shall send my squire home to his parents until I return." Simon pushed himself away from the door. He had a devilish gleam in his eyes. "I *will* return, won't I?"

"Only if you learn not to annoy me. Otherwise I might just feed you to the Scots myself."

Laughing, Simon opened the door. "By the way, I learned from the lady's maid that her favorite color is green."

"Why are you telling me this?"

"Just thought you might want to know. I'll be around if you need me."

Sin leaned back in his chair as he thought about everything Simon had said.

It was a cold place, his world. He spent his days tending whatever matters Henry needed and his nights alone in his room listening for the next attack.

He wondered why today that bothered him when it never had before. He'd merely accepted it as fact.

It must have been the time he'd spent journeying with Maggie and Braden, he decided. He'd grown soft in their company. Grown used to people who saw him as something other than a monster.

He swallowed as his thoughts turned to Caledonia and her angelic, unassuming face.

Tonight he wouldn't be alone. Tonight he would be with a beguiling woman who possessed brave, friendly eyes and a sharp wit.

For the first time in his life, he looked forward to the sun setting.

Callie smoothed the front of her dress with her hands. Vespers had come and passed with no word of Lord Sin.

She was more nervous than she should be and a little irritated that perhaps he had forgotten.

"Should I go look for him, milady?" Aelfa offered.

Before she could respond, she saw Lord Sin approach in the gathering shadows.

Her breath caught in her throat. Still dressed all in black, he cut a striking figure. Freshly shaved, he wore his hair brushed back from his face and it warmed her that he had taken time to freshen his appearance for her.

She smiled at him.

"Forgive me for being late, milady," he said, giving her a courtly bow. "It took longer in town than I thought it would."

A chill went down her spine as he lifted her hand and placed a gallant kiss on the back of her knuckles.

"You're quite forgiven," she said, noting the breathlessness of her voice.

What was it about this man that made her so hot, and yet cold as well? So shivery, yet warm?

His answering smile made her weak in the knees. He was so close to her now, she could smell the fresh, clean scent of him. Feel the heat of his body warm hers. His strength and power overwhelmed her senses.

With a mental shake, she redirected her thoughts away from how much she would love to kiss this man and feel his arms around her. "I hope you enjoy what I brought." She indicated the platters on the blanket she had spread on the ground. "We tried to find someone who knew what you preferred to eat, but no one seemed to be able to suggest anything that wasn't frightening."

"Mmm," he said. "Let me guess. I like to drink the blood of innocents, feast on the entrails of knights and eat the hearts of small children everywhere."

"Aye, that was much the consensus."

A strange light came into his midnight-black eyes as he looked away from her. "Well, I hope you didn't go to such trouble to feed me. I fear 'tis off season for good blood, and knights can be rather testy when you disembowel them."

It amazed her that he could joke about it. What she had learned this afternoon made her heart ache. Out of all the hundreds in this castle, no one knew anything about the man before her. Not even the king.

Henry couldn't tell her what Sin enjoyed doing, what songs he preferred, what activities he liked, not even his favorite color.

Not even Simon knew.

"I'm afraid to disappoint you," she said with a wistful sigh as she continued to tease him, "but all we have is roasted pheasant, stewed apples and leeks with onion sauce and wine. But if you prefer the other . . ."

He smiled at her. "How is it you understand my humor when no one else does?"

"I have no idea except to say that my brother is a bit morbid as well. He rather revels in it at times."

"You think I'm morbid?"

"Aren't you? You dress in black and like to frighten people. Isn't that the very definition of the word?"

"I suppose."

Callie set him down upon the blanket and poured them wine. She glanced over his left shoulder to see Aelfa motioning to her that she would be on the other side of the wall should she need her. Nodding at the maid, Callie handed Lord Sin a cup. "So tell me, other than being morbid, what else do you prefer to do?"

Sin shrugged. "I ride a great deal."

"And?"

"That's it."

Callie wrinkled her nose as she regarded him. "It's a very short list."

"Unlike yours. I'll wager your list is long. Infinite, probably."

He was teasing her and she enjoyed it a great deal. For the first time, she realized he was a different man around her. He never teased anyone else and he seemed a bit more relaxed in her presence. The thought thrilled her. "As a matter of fact, my list is quite infinite."

"You probably enjoy dancing and singing."

"Aye. Do you?"

"I've never attempted either."

"Not once?"

He shook his head.

"Why?"

He took a deep drink of wine and set the cup aside. "Never had time as a youth, and as a man I never had any inclination."

"Oh. I don't suppose you read?"

"Nay."

"So, what is it you do when you're home and not serving your king?"

"I train."

"And when you're not training?"

"I think about training."

"And when you're not doing that?"

"I'm resting so that I can train when I rise."

She grimaced at his earnestness. "Are you being honest, or are you just being irritating?"

"I'm always honest, milady, and am told most often irritating."

Her heart lurched at the casual way he said that. He was so accepting of the way others treated him.

"Always honest, eh? I don't think I've ever met a man who could claim that."

His black eyes burned into hers. "I've done many things in my life, things that I wish I'd never done, but I have never lied."

Somehow that comforted her.

"Tell me, Lord Sin—"

"Sin," he said, interrupting her.

"What?"

"Just call me Sin. I'm not one for titles."

"But you are an earl, are you not?" She'd heard one of the courtiers refer to him as such. The man had told her Sin had lands all over England, Normandy and Outremer.

"I am a man, Caledonia. I'm not a title, and the only thing I wish to be master of is myself."

It was the first time she'd heard her name from his lips. A tingle swept over her. There was something very intimate about the way he had spoken her name. "Is that why you don't show a coat of arms?"

Sin didn't answer. "Why don't you tell me about you, milady?"

He was a sly one, trying deftly to distract her, but she wasn't about to let him get away with such tactics. "I know all about me; 'tis you I don't know."

"Aye, but I know nothing of you. Nothing except you are fearless."

She rubbed her neck nervously. "Far from fearless. I have been terrified since the moment my father died." She couldn't believe those words came out of her mouth. She'd told no one of that.

"Why?"

"He was everything to my clan. He held them to-gether when one half wanted to attack the English and the other half just wanted peace."

Sin nodded as if he understood, and she felt a sud-den connection with him, though why she would feel such, she couldn't imagine. "Your uncle is laird now?"

"Aye. They wanted to elect me, but I refused. I knew such a thing would hurt my brother Dermot. He already feels very competitive with me because of our mothers. I had no wish to make it worse for him."

Sin took a bite of pheasant. "What about your mothers would make him feel competitive?"

"My mother was cousin to King David." Callie paused as she saw hatred flare in his eyes at the men-tion of the former Scottish king. "You don't like him?"

"Let's just say the one time I met him, we did not get along."

"But he was such a good man."

Sin looked away.

Callie swallowed her nervousness. Would his ha-tred of her cousin spill over onto her? There was no doubt that Sin had no use whatsoever for David, but she couldn't imagine why. Davey had been nothing but kind to her when she had lived at his court.

"And Dermot and Jamie's mother?" he asked.

"She was a very young shepherdess. I was Jamie's age when my father met her. He fell in love and mar-ried her within a month's time."

Sin's gaze dropped to his trencher. "Do you remem-ber your mother?"

Callie smiled as happiness welled up inside her. It always did that when she remembered her mother.

"Aye. She was beautiful and kind. An angel. I was only five when she died, but I remember so much of her."

She saw the sadness in his eyes.

"What of you? Tell me of your mother."

"What about your stepmother?" he asked, instead of answering her question. "Was she kind to you?"

What a peculiar question; but then, given the way most people looked upon stepparents, maybe it wasn't so strange after all. "Morna is wonderful. You'll like her much, I think. She's been trying to find me a husband."

He frowned at that. "Why haven't you married before now?"

Callie drew in a deep breath as she thought about it. In truth, she'd always wanted to be a wife and mother. She could think of nothing better than having a home filled with children.

"My betrothed died before we married," she whispered, "then my father died before I had a chance to look for another. Since his death, I haven't even wanted to consider it, for fear someone would use me to try and take control of the clan from my uncle."

"Peace is important to you?"

"Very much so. I've lost enough of my family. I've no wish to lose more."

His black gaze searched hers and she saw the respect he felt for her. It warmed her greatly. "You're very wise, Caledonia."

"Callie." She smiled gently. "My family and friends all call me Callie."

Sin stared at her, unable to believe she would offer him her nickname. In that moment, he could almost let himself dream of a life with her. Of sharing endless nights like this.

But in his heart he knew better. He wasn't the kind of man a woman like her needed.

"Do you want children?" The question slipped out before he could stop it.

She blushed. "Aye. I would love to have dozens of them."

His groin tightened at the thought. At the moment, he would love to offer his services, but that was another thing he could never do.

"And you?" she asked. "How many children do you want?"

"None."

"Not even a son?"

He shook his head. "I don't want any children. Ever."

"Why?"

Sin clenched his teeth. He didn't want children because he refused to bring anyone so defenseless into the world. Look at her little brother. Her father was dead, and she and Jamie were left to the hands of his enemies.

He would never take such a chance. Never allow a child of his to suffer.

"Men like me don't father children."

"Men like . . ." Her eyes grew wide and more color flooded her cheeks. She pulled away. "Forgive me, milord, I didn't realize you preferred the company of other men."

Sin choked. "I most assuredly do not, milady. My desires are definitely toward women."

The humor returned to her eyes. "Oh. Well, you said—"

"But I didn't mean it the way you took it."

"Then why don't you want children?"

"This subject is closed."

Callie realized he wasn't going to give her anything more than that. Very well; she would work on that later. For now, she would focus on other things.

"What did you do today?" she asked. "You said you went into town."

"I was making plans to leave for Scotland."

Her heart soared. "You're taking me home?"

"Aye."

"When?"

"Day after tomorrow."

Joy ripped through her. Thoughtless in her excitement, she launched herself into his arms and squeezed him tight as her heart pounded.

Sin sat in shock as she wrapped herself around him. No one had ever hugged him before. Not once. He swallowed at the sensation of her bosom flattened against his chest, of her breath on his neck and the tenderness of her arms around his neck.

She felt wonderful.

Awkwardly, he placed his own arms around her. His blood pounded through his veins as his body roared to life with a heated demand so fierce it left him breathless.

All he could think of was the warmth of her body on his, the way her cheek felt pressed against his.

Before he realized what he was doing, he tilted her chin up with his hand and lowered his mouth to her parted lips.

Sin moaned at the taste of her mouth. The feel of her breath mingling with his as her tongue hesitantly swept against his. She smelled of woman and lilacs, of pure, blissful heaven. He cupped her face in his hands, and just inhaled the scents and feelings of the only tender moment he'd ever known.

His blood rushed in his ears as his body burned for her, and it took every ounce of his strength not to unlace her gown and sample more of her.

Sample all of her.

Callie's head swam at the taste of the man, of the power of his arms around her. His tongue teased hers relentlessly. A deep-seated ache threatened to overwhelm her as he stirred feelings and sensations in her body she'd never before known.

His arms tightened around her body and she could feel the muscles of his back flexing beneath her hands. Goodness, but he was all solid muscle. All manly power.

And she wanted him in a way she'd never wanted anything. The female in her awoke with such a ferocious demand that she was stunned it didn't incinerate her. What was this fire inside her? This ache she had, to strip off his clothes and touch every part of him with her hands? Her lips?

For the first time in her life, she understood what her friends meant when they spoke in hushed whispers about their husbands. No wonder they blushed and giggled.

Kissing was wonderful!

He ran his hands down her back to her ribs. Callie throbbed even more as she arched against him. Instinctively, she rubbed herself against him. He answered her with an animalistic growl as he deepened his kiss and moved his hand to cup her breast through the fabric of her gown. She moaned at the feel of him.

Sin hissed at the way her breast overfilled his hand. At the way she tasted of such sweet innocence and fire. Her hands sought out his body, stroking him, inflaming him. And all he could think of was laying her back and . . .

He pulled back and stared at her half-open eyes. Her lips were swollen as she breathed raggedly. He could just imagine how she would look in his bed. Imagine how it would feel to claim her.

Tomorrow, she would be his. He could take her then, over and over, until they were both spent.

But in his heart, he knew that would never happen. He would never allow that to happen.

"Why do you look at me that way?" she asked.

"What way is that?"

"Forlornly. You remind me of a wishful dreamer staring after something he thinks he can never have."

Sin blinked and forced all the feelings from his body as he released her. He gently extricated himself from her and the temptation she offered. "I didn't realize I was doing that."

"You do it quite a bit, actually."

"Well then, I shall have to be more careful, shan't I?"

She leaned forward as if to impart a great secret. "I think you've spent way too much time trying to keep anyone from seeing your emotions."

He snorted at her. "Except for you. You seem to be able to see into my thoughts with uncanny accuracy."

"My father claimed it was my mother's blood. Legend has it her family came from the fey folk."

Sin looked away. "I don't believe in such tales."

"I figured as much. You strike me as a man who will only believe in what he can see or touch."

"Exactly."

"But you know, sometimes it's what you don't see that has the most power."

"Meaning?"

"Love for one thing. It's the most powerful thing on earth, and yet you can't see it or touch it. You can only feel it."

He shook his head at her whimsical words. "Spoken like a true romantic spirit."

"You don't believe it?"

"Remember what you said. I don't believe in anything I can't see or touch."

"So, you've never been in love?"

"Nay. You?"

"Never."

"Then how do you know it's so powerful?"

"Morna told me all about it. She has it for my father even though he's been dead nigh on three years."

Sin didn't like the direction of their conversation, so he sought to distract her to more familiar and comfortable things. "I'm sorry about your father. How did he die?"

"It was an accident in battle. His horse threw him while they were under attack."

Sin picked at his food. He had seen many men perish in such a manner. "I'm glad you weren't there when it happened."

"I wasn't, but poor Dermot was. He hasn't been the same since."

"That must have been terrible for him."

She nodded. "What of you? Were you there when your brother died?"

"Nay. I was in the Holy Land when it happened."

"Was it an accident for him as well?"

Sin swallowed. "Nay, he killed himself."

She gasped at the news and quickly crossed herself. "The poor lad. Why?"

"He felt this love you speak of, and sadly the woman he loved didn't return his devotion, but rather she ran away with another of our brothers."

"I can't imagine anything worse."

Sin could. In fact, he had lived through things much worse. But then, life was nothing if not pain.

They ate in silence for a time, while Callie studied her would-be husband. There was such an air of reserved sadness about him. One of hurt vulnerability, which made no sense to her. How could a man so strong be vulnerable?

A mighty oak can be felled by even the tiniest of insects when one allows them to continually gnaw at it. She hadn't thought about her mother's saying in a very long time. And yet it was true.

She had a feeling there was much that gnawed at the man before her. Though he carried an air of aloofness, surely it bothered him that everyone he met either bore him fear or hatred.

When they finished eating, Sin escorted her to her room. Callie hesitated at the door. Come the morning, the two of them would be united, and she didn't know much more about him now than she had before.

"Thank you, Sin, for humoring me this evening."

Sin gave a subtle nod. He'd enjoyed this night

much more than he cared to admit. Normally he took his meals in the silence of his own room. The sound of her voice had been a pleasant change.

Before he knew what she was doing, she placed a tender hand to his face, rose up on her tiptoes and kissed his left cheek. His breath caught at the sensation of her feathery-light lips against his flesh. The warmth of her hand on him.

His body reacted instantly, hardening with desire for her, and he wanted nothing more than to pull her into his arms and make love to her for the rest of the night.

But he couldn't seem to move. He was held immobile by her gentleness.

"Good night, Sin," she breathed, leaving him.

He didn't move until she'd stepped into her room and closed the door.

Sin stared at the door, his heart pounding as banished desires flooded him.

In the space of a few seconds, he remembered every time in his life he had ached for someone to hold him. Someone to just pretend they cared for him. Reality had forced him long ago to stop thinking of such things. To stop yearning for desires that would never come true.

And yet . . .

That hope was back. It was back and it was crippling in its ferocity.

Don't . . .

He knew better than to let himself be fooled. Foolish desires amounted to nothing but more pain. And he'd been dealt more than his fair share of that emotion.

Sooner or later, she would reject him. He held no

doubts. And it would hurt a lot less if he kept himself away from her.

He would take her home to the wild hills that had birthed her and then he would set her free to find a man she could love. A man with whom she had something in common. Someone who knew how to dance and how to sing.

Someone who knew how to love.

And yet even as the thought crossed his mind, a part of his heart ached at the thought of her with another man.

But it was meant to be. Sooner or later, he would have to let her go.

Chapter 6

Callie trembled with nervousness as Aelfa helped her dress for her wedding ceremony. This was the day she had waited for the whole of her life, and yet she dreaded it as well. Once she made her vow before God, there would be no going back.

From this day onward, she would be wife to a man she knew very little about. Wife to a man who wanted no children and nothing to do with her beloved Scotland. She shivered, hoping that this was what she was meant to do.

Henry had sent a beautiful gown of gold cloth that was trimmed in diamonds, pearls and rubies. His note had said he hoped his gift met with her approval. It was a gown fit for royalty. Even so, she had decided not to wear it. Not that she meant any slight to Henry or his thoughtfulness. But if she was to marry so far from home, she wanted her heritage with her.

Dressed in the nicest saffron kirtle she'd packed for her journey to her aunt's hall, Callie had her father's dark blue, green and yellow plaid wrapped around her. Aelfa had plaited two small braids and draped them gently to rest atop her auburn curls, which were held into a semblance of order by pearl-tipped pins. Callie felt like some fairy creature standing there in her Highland finery.

"You are beautiful, milady."

Callie smiled at the maid as Aelfa handed her the arrow-shaped pin for her plaid. "Thank you."

A knock sounded on the door.

She turned to see Simon pushing it open. He paused as soon as he saw her and grinned wolfishly. "They await you below, my lady."

Jamie opened the door wider and fell into the room from between Simon's legs. The lad had taken up with Simon as of yesterday and she hadn't seen much of him since.

Jamie's eyes were wider than moons as he regarded her. "Gor, Caledonia, you look like Queen Maeve. I hope you're not planning on eating your husband, too."

She laughed. "Nay, but I might be tempted to stew up a bit of a scamp if he doesn't behave."

Jamie stuck his tongue out and ran back into the hallway.

Laughing at the incorrigible imp, she took a deep breath and faced Simon.

"Are you all right, milady?" he asked as he offered her his arm.

She placed her hand in the crook of his elbow, grateful for his presence to see her down to the chapel. "I'm not sure. In spite of his reputation, I don't think Lord Sin is an evil man."

"Nay, but he is a lost one."

"Lost men can be found and brought home."

"Aye, but only if they are willing. Either way, at least you will be in your own home in a matter days."

Callie smiled at the thought. Home. She had missed it so terribly much. She'd been gone almost three months. Seana would have had her baby by now. Her brother Dermot had probably found another love, and Aster would no doubt be twice as gray from worrying over her and Jamie.

It would be good to see all of them again. Even if she had to marry an Englishman to get there.

He's a good man.

She believed that. It was the only thing that made this whole event tolerable. Well, that and the teasing man she'd glimpsed beneath the emotionless facade Sin showed to the world. For whatever reason they had been brought together, she trusted the Lord meant for her to do this. It was her faith that kept her going.

She allowed Simon to lead her to the king's private chapel in the back of the castle, far away from the bustle of the great hall. Aelfa followed them, with Jamie in tow.

The chapel was bright and cheery as they entered. The stained-glass depictions of the Stations of the Cross twinkled over the cobblestone floor. Henry sat to one side of the nave on a small throne, while Sin and the priest waited by the altar.

Her husband still wore his black armor. In truth, she had yet to see him wear anything else. She wondered if he owned any other clothes.

There were no other people in the chapel. Callie swallowed as another wave of trepidation ran through her. This was not how she'd dreamed her wedding would be. She'd always thought to be married in the large courtyard behind her home with her family and friends surrounding her. Aye, there would have been cheers and smiles aplenty, with good wishes and warm hugs.

A severe pang of homesickness washed over her. How she wished at least her uncle could be here with her. He had been like a second father to her and it pained her that he would miss this day. Closing her eyes, she imagined Aster's kind face, his eyes shining with pride as he handed her over to her husband.

She faltered as she realized he would never smile at Sin. Indeed, it would take much doing for her to get him not to snarl and snap. The day would surely never come that her uncle would welcome an Englishman into his family.

Saints above, please let this be the way to peace, she prayed.

Sin stiffened as he saw the pallor of Callie's face and the way she closed her eyes as if unable to bear seeing him at the altar. He couldn't blame her for it. Who wanted to wed the devil's own?

Since the moment the priest had walked in, the man had done nothing but eye Sin warily. Every time he thought Sin was looking the other way, the priest would cross himself and whisper a prayer to St. Jude to forgive him for what he was doing to the *poor innocent lamb* who was to be sacrificed to Lucifer.

Sin glanced down at his damp surcoat, where the priest had "accidentally" spilled holy water on him. No doubt the man had expected him to shriek in pain and explode into a puff of smoke.

His lips twisted cynically as a sudden movement of his hand made the priest start.

As Callie drew near, Sin reached his hand out to her. She offered him a tenuous smile. She left Simon's side and placed her tiny hand into his.

Sin paused at the softness of her touch. Her soft skin was a soothing balm to his warrior's calluses. A wave of tenderness tore through him, that she would come to him like this. Trust him not to hurt her or her brother.

He was humbled by it.

She looked up, and he saw the promise in her eyes, and it shook him all the way to his frozen heart. Perhaps there could be hope for them after all.

He listened to the priest begin Mass, but the words meant nothing compared to the foreign emotions welling up inside him. He wanted this woman who held a warrior's courage. This woman who could be so trusting of a man who knew nothing of trust.

She deserved so much more than this paltry ceremony. Sin knew very little of women, but the one thing he did know was how important such an event was to them. They spent endless hours of their lives with one another fantasizing over every detail.

His sister-in-law Maggie had been a basketful of nerves on her wedding day. He and his brother Lochlan had had their hands full trying to get her to the chapel on time. She'd babbled the entire way there telling them how much young women dreamed of their weddings. How she'd planned her day out carefully and if either one of them let anyone or anything botch it, she would bring down the wrath of plagues on both their heads.

He wished he could give Callie a day like that one had been. Maggie had been surrounded by her brothers and friends. Gifts and well wishes had been piled all around for them. There had been music and dancing, and all manner of happiness.

At least Henry had a reception supper planned for them, but they would be surrounded by strangers. Strangers who cared nothing for either one of them. His heart ached for what Callie was missing and he wished he could make it up to her.

He wanted—

"Sin!" Henry's voice intruded on his wandering thoughts. "Have you a ring or not?"

Blinking, Sin glanced to the priest, who was staring at him expectantly. Callie's brow was arched and he realized they must have been waiting several minutes for him to respond.

He reached into his purse and pulled out the small silver box. He'd spent hours at the jeweler's yesterday trying to find something Caledonia would like.

The task had seemed simple enough at the onset, but the many different choices had confused him. Rings came in any variety of colors and sizes, and it had struck him just how little he knew of his wife.

Still, he had listened carefully to the short, pudgy man about what ladies chose and what most men purchased for wedding rings. Indeed, his ears had rung for hours afterward.

He'd never bought a gift for anyone before and he'd had no idea what Callie would prefer.

After an eternity of careful debate, he had found one he hoped was perfect. . . .

Callie bit her lip as Sin placed the ring on her finger.

As she looked at it, tears filled her eyes. The dainty gold band was elegantly carved with roses and this-tles, and the deep, dark green emerald shone even in the dim light of the chapel. The roses and thistles were the perfect blend of his English heritage and her Scots blood.

Better still, she remembered Simon asking after her favorite color. How kind of Sin to base his choice on that. And her mother had always said that emeralds were the stones of love. That they signified the unifi-cation of the heart and soul, and would bring eternal love to the one who wore it.

Her husband's kindness truly knew no bounds.

Sin jerked as a tear fell onto his hand. Instinctively, he took the ring off her finger as remorse filled him.

He was no good at this sort of thing. A warrior through and through, he knew nothing of women and their trinkets. Leave it to him to bungle such an im-portant moment.

"Forgive me, milady," he said hoarsely. "I thought you would like it. I'll get another—"

She stopped his words by laying her fingers to his lips. "It is the most beautiful ring I have ever seen. I only cry because I am touched by the thought you must have put into it. Thank you."

Warmth flooded him. She smiled a smile that made his legs weak and his groin tight. She brushed her gen-tle fingers against his jaw and dropped her hand to his, then slid the ring back onto her finger.

Perhaps there was a chance for them after all . . .

Nay, Sin. Don't even think that. Don't think it at all. 'Tis an illusion. A fleeting moment. Sooner or later the truth will out and she will hate you.

His heart heavy, he listened as the priest joined them together.

Once it was over, Henry led them from the room to the great hall, where a feast had been laid out. The hall was crowded with somber nobles who eyed Callie with pity and Sin with open hatred.

Sin paused as he regarded the cold room. Granted, no one had ever cared much for his presence, but this went beyond the normal reserve and disdain the courtiers showed him.

One of Henry's marshals came forward. An older man in his late years, he wore an impeccable gray surcoat and had the look of a harbinger.

He bowed low before Henry and his guard. "Forgive me, Majesty, it seems Roger, the Earl of Warrington, was found murdered in his cell this morning." The man's suspicious gaze went to Sin. "His throat was cut."

A mortified condemnation rippled through the crowd.

Sin went numb at the news. He heard Simon's sharp intake of breath behind him and he felt Caledonia's hand drop in temperature.

Convicted without a trial. How very typical.

He stared blankly at the crowd, tempted to hunch over and run about like a crazed animal, dragging his knuckles. It was, after all, what they expected of him.

"Were there any witnesses?" Henry asked.

Again the marshal's gaze went to Sin. "None, Majesty. 'Tis as if a *phantom* had come and gone," he said, using the epitaph most often applied to Sin's crimes.

Against his common sense, Sin glanced to Callie. A

stern frown marred her face while she listened to Henry and the marshal speak.

When she locked gazes with Sin, he waited for her to condemn him as the others had. "He is the man who tried to kill you last night?"

"Indeed, madame."

He felt her hand grow even colder. Worse, he felt it tremble.

His stomach drew tight. He would expect the others to think the worst of him, but for some reason it bothered him greatly that she would.

"We shall have to investigate this matter," Henry said. "For now, we have a wedding—"

"Murderer!"

The word rang out across the hall.

Callie scanned the room's occupants until she saw a woman around two-score-and-five behind the massive crowd. The courtiers parted, giving the unknown woman a pathway from the door to Sin.

Her face flushed and her dark brown eyes bright with tears, the noblewoman approached Sin with the quiet dignity of a queen. Her long, red dress was a stark contrast to the lady's black hair and dark eyes. There was something oddly familiar about this stranger.

The woman stopped in front of Sin and gave him a glare of such loathing that Callie was amazed it didn't cause him to disintegrate right before her eyes.

He didn't move at all as he regarded the woman with the same contemptuous sneer.

"Damn you for killing my son. I wish you had died in the womb," the noblewoman said cruelly. "Better I should have killed myself than ever given birth to a monster such as you."

Callie gasped as she realized this was Sin's mother and it was his similarity to her that she had noted as the lady crossed the hall . . .

Which meant the man last night who had tried to kill him was his own brother. Callie's legs went weak with the knowledge.

"Thank you, Mother," Sin said stoically. "As always, I will cherish your well wishes."

Her black eyes lethal, his mother slapped Sin hard across the face, laying his cheek open.

Still Sin didn't move. He didn't flinch. Not even when his mother rotated the ring around on her finger in a hateful gesture to let all know she had cut his cheek on purpose.

"I demand justice," the woman cried, turning to Henry. "I want this bastard to pay for what he's done."

"You would condemn your own son, Countess?"

Tears ran down the lady's cheeks as she fought against her sobs. "I have no son. My only son died by the hands of a filthy killer." Raising her hands like claws, she rushed at Sin, who caught her by the forearms and held her back.

"I want you dead for it!" she shrieked in his face. "You're despicable and vile. I wish to God I had killed you the very hour of your birth."

His eyes blank, Sin said nothing as he kept her from clawing him.

Henry ordered his guard to take the distraught woman from the room and to escort her to her chambers.

Callie moved toward her husband and reached up to touch the bleeding cut on his cheek.

Sin flinched from her as if she were a viper. "It will heal," he said.

"Some wounds never heal, milord," Callie said as her heart ached for him. She couldn't imagine a mother being more cruel to her child than what she had just witnessed. She could only guess at what other atrocities the woman had visited upon him over the years.

No wonder he had refused to speak of his mother last night when she'd asked him about her.

Sin glanced to Henry, then he turned and stalked back down the hallway toward the chapel.

Callie followed him, with Henry one step behind her.

Once Sin reached the chapel, the priest took one look at Sin's angry visage, and hurried from the room.

Ignoring him, Sin grabbed their wedding papers from where they'd been left drying on the altar and started for the fire in the hearth.

Henry quickly stepped into his path. "What are you doing?"

The rage on Sin's face was terrifying. "I want this marriage dissolved. Now."

"Sin . . ." The king's voice was thick with warning.

"Step aside, Henry."

Callie held her breath. She'd never seen Sin like this. This was the man who really could kill someone in his sleep. He was cold. Icy. His eyes filled with turbulent agony.

"You burn those papers and I will see you in chains."

Sin gave him a hard, droll stare. "Think you that

matters to *me*? If you're trying to scare me, you will have to do better than that."

"Leave us," Henry said to everyone.

His guards hesitated.

"Now!" Henry roared.

They left, but Callie went no farther than the closed door. She glanced at the guard, who looked away sheepishly, then she pressed her ear to the door to hear them.

A heartbeat later, the guard did the same.

"Give me those papers, Sin."

Sin didn't move. He couldn't. Everyone in the great hall believed he had killed his own brother. Everyone, including Callie. He shouldn't care what Callie thought, and yet he did. He cared in a way that scared him. "Why did you do it?"

Henry shrugged. "It had to be done. Roger was a liability neither of us could afford."

How many times had he heard those words? How many times had he murdered for Henry? In truth, it was a miracle he hadn't been the one ordered to kill Roger.

"I won't marry a woman who believes I could cut the throat of my own brother."

"Whyever not? It's not as if you haven't done worse things in your life. Remember what the Saracens called you? *Melek in Ölüm.* The Angel of Death. It's what you've always been best at."

Sin winced at Henry's words. How stupid he had been to even hope he could start anew with Caledonia and live a quiet, normal life. He could never run from his past. From all the things he'd done to survive.

He stared at the papers in his hands and saw his signature below Callie's. Her dainty, graceful handwriting was a stark contrast to his clumsy attempt.

She was made of such goodness, such kindness. Everything about her was beautiful and he was nothing but evil. Ugly. A scarred soulless monster, incapable of anything save destruction.

Melek in Ölüm. The title rang in his ears. Even now he could hear his masters laughing as they trained him. He had gone by many names back then. Had committed crimes he wished he could bury in the farthest reaches of his mind. He didn't deserve a second chance at life. And he damned sure didn't deserve a woman as decent and kind as Callie.

Only a devil like Henry would seek to bind them together.

Through the pain of his memories, he saw an image of Callie's warm smile. Heard the beauty of her laughter.

She touched him on a level that made no sense whatsoever.

"Now," Henry said, reaching his arm out. "Hand me those papers."

Sin hesitated. But in the end, he found himself handing them over against his will.

Henry breathed a sigh of relief as he tucked the papers inside the leather pouch on the altar. "I am your friend, Sin. You know that. If not for me, you would have died alone in Outremer without ever being among your own kind again."

His own kind. Strange, Sin felt as alien here in England as he had ever felt with the Saracen tribes who had bought and sold him.

Henry tucked the pouch under his arm. "Why do you care what the wench thinks of you anyway?"

Sin cut a glare at Henry to let him know he had overstepped his bounds. "That lady happens to be my wife. I would caution you to show her due respect."

Henry rolled his eyes. "Not another one. I do you a favor and get a snapping lion at my heels. Please don't tell me you're going to be like Thomas à Becket and turn on me, too."

"You know me better than that."

"I thought I knew him better than that, too, and yet look how wrong I was." Henry stared at him speculatively for the span of several heartbeats. "By the way, if you're still thinking of thwarting this marriage by trickery, think again. Come morning, I want proof of consummation."

Sin arched a brow at that. "Don't tell me you wish to witness the event."

"Hardly. I've already verified her virginal state. Come morning if there is no blood, then I shall have my physicians examine her again. There had best be no maidenhead."

Sin gave him a dull stare. "You keep speaking as if I care whether or not I live or die. You have no real power over me, Henry, you know that. All that binds us together is my oath of loyalty to you."

Henry narrowed his eyes. "You and I have been at odds since I first brought up this matter. I've no wish to fight with you. I just want this settled. I need a strong yet passionless arm in Scotland. You are perfect to infiltrate her people and maintain peace. Between you and the MacAllisters, it will secure my northern borders and leave me free to scrape Philip off my weary heels. If this marriage is not consummated, then she will be able to break the pact as soon as she returns home."

"I know, Henry."

"Then why are you making this so much more difficult than it need be?"

Sin had no idea. It was just a feeling deep in his gut that if he consummated his marriage with Caledonia, then it would be eternal. And the last thing he wanted was to tie a woman like her to a man like him. It seemed foul and cruel.

"Very well," Sin conceded. "Come morning, you shall have your proof of the deed."

Henry smiled. "Then I shall leave you to your new bride."

As Henry left, Sin stared longingly at the papers he carried under his arm. How he wished he could undo this day.

In truth, he didn't care at all what the others thought of him. But it did matter to him what Callie thought. He didn't want to see her eyes dark with suspicion or, worse, hatred.

Taking a deep breath, he headed for the door and prepared himself to face her condemnation.

Callie's heart pounded as she pushed herself away from the door just moments before Henry threw it wide. She gave a quick curtsy to the king as he passed, then waited anxiously to see her husband.

So, Sin was innocent of the murder.

The news relieved her more than she ever would have thought possible. He was far from an innocent, but in this he'd had no part.

When he walked through the door, she bestowed her brightest smile on him.

Confusion darkened his midnight stare as he glanced about the crowd that watched him as if he were the lowest of life and unfit to share the earth with them. But she didn't care what they thought. Let them be fools if they must.

Her heart lurched at the sight of the drying blood on Sin's cheek. The wound was already purple and jagged, and it must pain him. It was an ugly blemish on a man so handsome.

She reached her hand up to touch him. "Let me—"

He shrugged off her touch and strode from the hall.

Callie swallowed the lump in her throat at his curtness. What would have made him behave that way?

Determined to find out, she went after him.

She caught up with her husband down the hallway, where servants bustled to get as far away from him as they could. "Where are you going?"

Sin paused at the melodic voice behind him. She had followed?

He turned about to find her directly behind him, with her skirts held in her hands so that she could match his much longer stride. Her trim ankles were bare to his view and the sight of them fired his blood. Not even the plaid she wore, which reminded him of a heritage he despised, could detract from the way he wanted to claim this lady.

His wife.

The truth tore through him.

"I want to be alone," he said more sternly than he intended.

"Well, how fine is that?" Her voice carried the full

weight of her sarcastic displeasure. "Here it is *our* wedding day and you wish to spend it alone. Fine, then, call me shoe leather and have done with it."

He frowned at her words. "I beg your pardon? Call you what?"

"Shoe leather." She gestured toward his feet. "You know, the inconsequential matter that you tread upon without thought. That is all I am to you, isn't it?"

He couldn't have been more stunned had she spat in his face. How could she ever think that, when to him she was the very essence of heaven itself? He couldn't imagine a woman more noble or precious, even if she did have an insufferable habit or two. "I have yet to treat you as if you were inconsequential."

"*Yet,* you say. Implying that the time will surely come when you will."

"I didn't say that, either."

"Didn't you?"

"Nay."

She looked up at him with a light smile at the corner of her lips and an impish gleam in her bright green eyes. "So then, I do have value to you."

More than she would ever know. "This was all a game?"

She shook her head. "Not a game. I merely wanted you to talk to me." She took a step forward and touched his arm.

Sin stared at the delicate hand on his biceps and it took all his strength not to crush her to him and claim her lips with his. Not to lift her in his arms and run with her to their room, where he could lose himself in the sweet softness of her body.

"I know you have been alone much of your life," she said gently. "But we are married now. No matter how this came about, I fully intend to abide by my vows. I would be a wife to you, Sin, if you will let me."

Therein lay the problem. He didn't know if he could. Every time he had ever reached out to someone, he had been hurt. Over the years, he'd learned to pull inward, to give no one that kind of power over him.

He had shut off his heart, his emotions, and learned to just be.

It was the only way to have peace in his life.

Now she wanted to change all that. He had hungered for love and acceptance for so long that he didn't dare reopen himself to any tenderness now. It would destroy him.

"I need to be alone for a while," he said, gentling his voice. "Please."

She withdrew her hand. "I will be waiting for you when you are ready."

That was the kindest thing anyone had ever said to him. Touched to a level so deep it defied explanation, he turned and made his way slowly toward the stables.

"I don't know if you'll ever reach him, milady."

Gasping in alarm, Callie turned in the hallway to see Simon drawing near from behind her. "You were eavesdropping?"

"Only a little."

She smiled at his honesty. "Where is Jamie?"

"Aelfa took him to your room. She and I will watch over him tonight for the two of you."

"Thank you."

He nodded.

As he started to leave, she stopped him. "Simon, is there anything you can tell me to help me with Sin?"

"He is a hard man, but a fair one. No one, including me, really knows your husband, milady. Sin just is. He asks for nothing and relies solely on himself. If there is a way of reaching him, I do not know it. All I know is that it won't be easy. But if you're willing to try, then I am willing to help."

"You're a good man, Simon."

He laughed aloud at that. "Beautiful women keep saying that to me, and yet they all end up married to another. Perhaps I should try being bad, and maybe then I could go home with the fair demoiselle."

Callie smiled at him. "I doubt you could ever be bad."

A young maid approached them timidly from up ahead. Callie greeted her.

"Beg pardon, milady," the girl said nervously as she curtsied before them. "My lady bade me give this to you. 'Tis a wedding gift."

Callie took the small box from the girl's shaking hands. "From whom?"

"The Countess of Rutherington."

"Sin's mother," Simon clarified.

Callie frowned. Why would she be sending a gift? It made no sense, given her actions toward Sin.

Curious, Callie opened the box and saw a small bottle.

"What the devil is that?" Simon asked.

Thinking it perfume, Callie opened the lid and

took a whiff of it. She knew the reeking smell in an instant. It came from the plant her mother had used to rid their hall of mice and other unsavory vermin.

It was a bottle of poison.

Chapter 7

Callie hesitated at the solar door where two guards stood on either side, making sure the countess didn't leave her rooms again. But a moment's hesitation was all she gave it. Her anger high, she strode between the men and threw the door open, then slammed it shut.

The countess looked up with a startled gasp from her perch on the bed as Callie charged unannounced into her room.

"What is the meaning of this?" Callie asked, moving to the bed to hand the countess the bottle of poison.

The lady wiped the tears from her eyes and drew a ragged breath as she ignored the bottle. She lifted her chin regally while toying with the edges of the pillow in her lap. "I thought you would have need of it tonight. Either for yourself or preferably for *him*. Either way it would spare you having to stomach such a repulsive monster in your bed."

Callie was aghast. What on earth was the woman

thinking? "How can you say that about your own son?"

The countess stiffened, her dark eyes snapping righteous fire. "He is no son of mine. That bastard destroys everything he touches. He always has. If you were wise, you'd drink that poison now and save yourself years of untold misery at his hands."

The countess's hatred of Sin mystified her. What could he have done to his mother to warrant such rampant hostility? "Why do you hate him so? What has he *ever* done to you?"

"What has he done?" she shrieked, rising from the bed and dropping her pillow to the floor. "He has ruined my life. That wretched demonic father of his seduced me when I was just a child. I spent one night with him that no one ever should have known about. Instead, I conceived. When my father found out, he was so enraged, he beat me so severely it would have swept any normal infant from my womb. But not *him*. He is the devil's own. He even survived when I drank potions that should have killed him."

Callie's stomach knotted at what the woman was describing. Her hatred of Sin was unimaginable.

"When he was born," the countess continued, "he almost killed me. I bled so that 'tis a wonder I ever survived. When they tried to hand him to me, I couldn't bear to even look at him. So I bade my maid procure a wet nurse and sent him immediately to his father."

"You sent a newborn bairn out into the world within hours of his birth?"

"Hours? I sent him out as soon as I had finally flushed him from my body."

Callie couldn't breathe as pain assailed her. She

saw the image of a newborn being handed off so clearly in her mind. How could anyone be so cruel?

Worse, there was no remorse in his mother's face. She felt fully justified in what she'd done to him.

It defied Callie's understanding.

Rage and hatred burned in the countess's eyes. "The man I wanted to marry refused to have me after I had been stretched by another man's child, so my father viciously married me off to a man older than he was."

"None of that is Sin's fault."

"Nay? Had he not been born, none of it would have happened." By the light in her eyes, 'twas obvious the past was replaying itself to her. "I sent him to his father and thought I was through with him forever. Then, years later, he showed up here at court and all the gossips started in again. I had to live with the disgrace daily. People whispering behind my back. Comments and aspersions being made about my dear baby Roger. My husband was a pious man and made me wear hair shirts beneath my gowns from that day until he died. I was humiliated and forced to beg penance constantly for it. And now that monster has taken the only thing good in my life. Roger was all that was important to me. The only thing that gave my putrid life any happiness."

Callie sympathized with the woman's grief and she wished she could ease the pain she knew the countess bore over the death of her son. But none of that changed what she'd done to her eldest, who had been nothing more than an innocent babe in dire need of a mother's love.

"Sin didn't kill him."

"You're a fool if you believe his lies."

Callie patted the countess's arm in sympathy, wishing she knew what to say to ease the woman's suffering.

But there was nothing she could do that would make his mother accept him or feel better. Shaking her head at the tragedy of it all, she handed the poison back to her. "I am very sorry for your loss, milady."

She turned and quietly left the countess to her conscience.

Sin spent the entire day riding. He'd left London behind and headed south. Part of him just wanted to keep going. He had lands all over England, Normandy and Outremer. Castles so strong not even Henry's entire army could breach them. No one had ever defeated him in battle. He could destroy nations if the mood took him.

There was no reason why he had to go back to London or to his wife.

None whatsoever.

No reason other than the fact that he liked the feel of her hand on his arm. The look of laughter that hung in her bright green eyes. The look of that peekaboo dimple that flashed when she spoke.

He closed his eyes as indecision ripped him apart.

Tonight she would be his. He could take her over and over until he was sweaty and spent, until they both were unable to move from exhaustion. She wouldn't deny him the right of her body. Wouldn't turn away from him in disgust or fear.

For once, he could have comfort and a welcoming touch. There was no doubt in his mind.

Sin closed his eyes and tried to imagine a world

where someone truly wanted him. A world filled with a woman who would smile at his approach. Whose face would light up in happiness at his presence.

Would it be so awful?

Callie wanted to be wife to him. Could he not be husband?

He could try.

Aye. He could at that. His heart suddenly lighter, he wheeled his horse about and headed back to London.

Sitting at the window with her dinner laid out on the small table, Callie watched the sun set with no sign of her husband anywhere. He'd left hours ago and no one knew where he was headed or when he would be back.

If he would be back.

She heard her door open. Hoping for Sin, she turned to see Aelfa entering the room with sad eyes. "He has yet to return, milady."

So this was it, then. Alone even on her wedding night. It didn't bode well for her future if he showed her so little regard today of all days.

Callie glanced to the ring on her finger. When she'd first seen it, she'd hoped that maybe there could be happiness between them. That maybe he might be willing to accept her into his life.

She was such a fool.

"He could still return," Aelfa offered charitably.

Callie picked at the dinner she had hoped to share with her husband. As she sat there staring at his empty trencher across from her, she became angry. This was her wedding night! How dare he treat her this way.

How could he have so little regard for her? The more she thought about it, the angrier she became. She had been nothing but kind and cordial to him. Had shown him only respect, and then he couldn't even be bothered to show himself for supper?

Well, she wasn't some nothing. It was one thing to need time alone, quite another to wallow in self-pity and leave her guessing about where he was and when, if ever, he might decide to return to her.

By all the saints above, she wasn't going to sit here another minute and feel this lowly and unwanted. If he didn't want her, fine. She wasn't going to spend the rest of her life trying to please him when it was obvious he didn't want to be pleased at all.

"Where is Simon?" she asked Aelfa.

"He is with Jamie in his room."

"Could you please watch Jamie for a short time and ask Simon to come to me?"

Aelfa looked a bit confused, but didn't hesitate with her answer. "Aye, milady. Gladly."

Callie got up as the maid left and quickly washed her face and straightened her appearance.

It didn't take long for Simon to join her, and yet she'd managed to down two goblets of wine while waiting for him.

"Can I be of service, milady?"

"Aye, Simon. I hear music below, and since my husband seems wont to ignore me, I would appreciate it if you would escort me to the hall where I can actually enjoy my wedding night."

She saw the hesitation on his face.

"Please, Simon. Otherwise I shall just sit here until I become so angry that I might do him harm."

He laughed at that. "I would like to see that, I think."

But he escorted her below.

Callie decided she would enjoy this night. Partaking of the wine and music, she danced with Simon until her head was light and dizzy from it.

Sin entered his wife's chambers and drew up short. There was no sign of her anywhere. A cold meal, barely touched, rested on the table by the window.

Where was she?

Frowning, he glanced around the room, trying to discern what mood she might have been in when she left.

Surely she wouldn't have escaped now after they were wed. She'd told him she would be waiting.

Pain pierced his chest at the thought of her fleeing from him. It was so severe that it momentarily took his breath. He hadn't realized until that instant just how much he'd looked forward to seeing her when he arrived, to finding her here with a welcoming smile on her face.

Stunned by the realization, he headed below to find Simon and see if he had word of her.

The crowd in the great hall was thick. Music, voices and laughter rang throughout the madness of it. Couples danced in the center while some groups stood off to the side and people lined the tables that were filled to overflowing with food and drink.

Every time Sin drew near a group, they would grow silent and stare at him with repugnance etched into their faces. And as soon as he passed, their heads would go together and they would whisper.

Sin didn't care. He had no use for them, either.

As he skimmed the courtiers, his gaze was drawn by a flash of Highland plaid in the center of the tables where people were dancing.

His breath caught at the sight of his wife in Simon's arms. Callie was leaning back against Simon's chest and smiling up at him with an open, happy expression.

Sin saw red as possessive anger tore through him. How dare she look at Simon like that! The pain of it ate at him. He'd wanted her to greet him with that expression, and now she directed it toward another man.

Wanting blood, he stalked toward them.

"Callie," Simon said with a laugh as he reached for the goblet in her hand, "give me that cup. You've had enough wine for one night."

She pulled it from Simon's reach, then stepped away from him, spilling half the cup's contents across the floor. "Pop and dandies, Simon," she laughed back. "I want more of it, not less."

"What goes here?" Sin demanded as he drew near.

Silence settled across the room. Sin felt the looks of all the courtiers on them as they watched curiously.

"I was dancing," Callie said, her gentle brogue a bit slurred and hard to understand. "And I was drinking." She frowned at the cup in her hand as if unable to understand where her wine had gone. Pouting, she looked up at Sin. "But now Simon won't let me do either."

"I'm trying to get her into bed," Simon confessed.

Sin arched a brow.

"Don't give me that look. She's drunk."

He arched his brow even higher.

"Oh, great Peter's hairy toes, Sin, you know me

better than that. I wasn't going to do anything other than summon her maid to care for her."

Callie snorted at that. "It's a very evil thing when a woman is this far into her cups and still no man wants to tup her."

The men exchanged shocked looks.

Seeking to get her away from the others before she destroyed herself entirely, Sin scooped her up in his arms and carried her from the hall.

She sighed, then wrapped her arms around his neck and laid her head on his shoulder. Sin trembled at the feel of her hand in his hair as she ran her fingers through it, lightly brushing them against his scalp.

"You are a strong one, aren't you?" Her wine-scented breath against his neck sent chills all over him. "I like the way your arms feel when you hold me."

Then she gave a sharp yank on his hair.

"Ow!" he said sharply. "What was that for?"

"I thought you left me." She kicked her legs and squirmed in his arms. "Put me down. I'm mad at you."

Sin tightened his hold on her. He wasn't about to put her down. Not until he had her safely in her room.

"Mad at me?" he asked incredulously. "For what?"

"You're a large, aggravating beastie. That's what you are. Turning my head and making me want you, then leaving the first minute you can."

In spite of himself, he grinned. There was something about this drunken lass's outspokenness he liked. "Making you want me, eh?"

"Aye. I want a kiss from you, husband."

He set her down only long enough to open the door to her room.

She swayed slightly, then threw her arms back around his neck and tried to kiss him. She missed his lips and planted a hot kiss on his jawbone.

Hot chills erupted like liquid fire all over his body.

He hissed as she licked his flesh with her tongue. "Mmmm," she moaned. "You're all prickly and hard."

She had no idea just how hard he was.

Sin kicked the door closed as she pulled back.

"Where were you?" she asked, trying to put her hands on her hips, but they fell limply to her sides.

"I was riding."

"Oh. Your favorite thing to do. How could I forget? It's the only thing you enjoy doing. That and training."

"Aye, and you like to dance. Tell me, were you drunk before or after you went downstairs?"

"Definitely after. There was this one tall man who said he'd be happy to take your place tonight if you didn't feel up for it."

"Oh, I'm *up* for it, all right."

Before he could think better of it, Sin stepped into her arms and pulled her close, then gave her a proper kiss.

She moaned against his lips, then pulled back. "Are you going to hurt me?" she asked.

"I don't plan on it." He frowned at her. "Why would you think that?"

"Aelfa said it would hurt when you stick your . . . um . . . male piece into me."

Sin arched a brow at her choice of words. He always had the oddest conversations with this woman. "I'll try and take care, then, not to hurt you."

She laughed at that. "So, you *are* going to stick your—"

"Please, Callie, have mercy on me."

Biting her lip so that he saw her little dimple, she slid her hands down his chest in innocent exploration of his body. Sin struggled to breathe as he fought the urge to take her wildly. He would have to be gentle with her. Careful. The last thing he ever wanted was to hurt this gentle lady.

"Such strength," she whispered, running her hands over his chest. She fumbled with the laces of his tunic until she bared part of his chest to her eager eyes. She peeled the edges of the collar back to see as much of his body as the tunic would allow. Sin stood perfectly still, afraid to move lest it frighten her. He would let her get used to him first, then . . . then she would be his.

"I like the way your skin looks. Can I touch it?"

"Madame, you may touch anything on me you like."

She smiled at that. "Really?"

He nodded.

Callie untucked his undertunic and ran her hand over the hard planes of his muscles. Oh, the man felt good beneath her hands. She pulled his tunic off, wanting to see more of him. She touched the scars along his ribs, then traced the one that lashed across his right nipple.

She frowned at all she saw. They were everywhere. So much pain. So much strength.

Suddenly she wanted to see all of him. She dropped his tunic to the floor, then reached for the laces of his chausses.

Oh, she liked this man even when he made her mad. She ran her hands through his hair, delighting in the feel of it as she tasted the heavenly heat of his mouth. Moaning, she surrendered all her weight to him and clung to his broad shoulders.

She felt his hands roaming her back, pulling at the laces of her gown. A shiver ran over her as she thought of what he was going to do to her tonight. He was going to see her in ways no man had ever seen her before. Touch her in places no one had before and do things with her she had only vaguely dreamed of.

The very thought made her blush.

Sin held his breath as her fingers flicked against his lower abdomen while she undid his chausses. As soon as she untied the tabs, the heavy chain-mail breeches sank to the floor, exposing him to her.

Callie swallowed at the sight of his swollen shaft nestled among the dark hairs. He was huge! Surely such a thing would cleave her in two. No wonder Aelfa had warned her of pain.

She'd never seen anything like it before.

Quite curious, she moved her hand slowly to touch him. As soon as her fingers brushed his velvety tip, he hissed and his shaft jerked, arching toward her hand.

She pulled back. "Did I hurt you?"

"Nay, love," he said raggedly. He took her hand into his and led it back to his shaft.

She shivered at the velvety, hard feel of him in her hand as she curled her fingers around him. She stared, in awe of the pleasure on his face. Aye, she liked giving him pleasure. Liked the way he stared at her as if he wanted to devour her.

With his hand on hers, he showed her how to caress him. How to run her hand up and down his shaft, then down to the soft sac below. Callie bit her lip at the power it gave her over him. She loved the way he felt in her hand.

Emboldened by his pleased look, she ran her hand down to gently cup his sac. He growled and hissed, then took her face into his hands and kissed her deeply.

Callie moaned at the taste of him as she gently kneaded him in her hand. He ran his hands through her hair, then down her back to the laces of her gown. Her heart pounded in sweet expectation.

In a matter of heartbeats, her gown sank to the floor and they stood bare skin to bare skin. She trembled at the sensation of his hot body against hers.

On fire, she clung to him.

Sin pulled back only long enough to look at her. His eyes blazed at her. Picking her up, he carried her to the bed.

Callie sighed as soon as she sank into the feather mattress. A sudden wave of dizziness assailed her and the room spun about crazily. Suddenly everything went black.

Sin dipped his head down to kiss her, then froze. "Caledonia?"

She didn't move.

He shook her gently. "Callie?"

Again, no response. She was out cold.

Cursing, Sin pulled back, his groin burning like the fires of hell.

Aggravated, he watched her skin gleaming and taunting him. If not for his raging body that demanded hers so rawly, he would laugh at this. But there was nothing funny about the pain of his unspent lust.

"It's just as well," he said, pulling the blanket over her. He took this night as a sign. He had no right to her. Not really.

She deserved an honorable champion. A man like Simon. Someone who could love her and give her the children she wanted so much. His heart ached at the knowledge that he could never be that carefree man who could laugh with her and share her peaceful life.

So be it. He would heed this omen and content himself with just seeing her home to her family and bringing the Scottish rebels out into the light to be punished.

Still, as he watched her sleeping, a bitter ache settled deep in his heart, making him wish he were a different man. A better man.

Sin lay down beside her and pulled her into his arms. He would just hold her for a little while. Pretend that they had a future together. Pretend he had something to offer her that was worth having.

Callie came awake to a ferocious pounding in her head. Moaning, she blinked her eyes open and flinched at the bright daylight streaming through the room.

The door opened, sending spikes of pain through her skull. "Och, now, please walk softly," she breathed.

"Pardon me, milady," Aelfa whispered. "But his lordship is waiting below to start your journey to Scotland."

Callie sat up quickly, then gasped as more pain hit her. She was married.

And she was going home!

She looked around the room, but there was no sign her husband had ever been here. Fuzzy memories tangled in her mind as she tried to recall the night before.

She remembered Sin looking angry and vaguely recalled him carrying her to the room. The last clear memory she had was the feel of his chest under her hand.

Aelfa came forward with a towel. "I had them draw a bath for you in the antechamber, milady. I thought you'd like to bathe this morning before you head out on your long trip."

"Thank you, Aelfa," she whispered, pushing the covers back.

Her heart stopped as she saw the bloody sheets.

Aelfa gasped at the sight and crossed herself. "Baby Jesus, Joseph and Mary, milady, are you all right? Gor, but I never saw such like that in all my life. Is it your time of the month?"

Callie shook her head. Nay, she was midcycle, and even so, she'd never bled like this. Her thighs were completely coated.

"You best be moving slowly, milady." Aelfa helped her stand. "Are you feeling all right? Sore?"

"I feel fine except for this ache in my head." Callie wrapped her plaid about herself and headed toward the tub in the next room. The blood in the bed concerned her. What had caused it?

Nothing seemed to be hurting her. She wasn't so naive as to think women bled like that every time they were with their husbands.

Whatever could have happened?

How very, very strange.

* * *

Sin frowned as he made his way through the great hall. Everyone was staring at him rather oddly. Even more oddly than normal.

He couldn't fathom their stares until Simon joined him.

"What did you do to Caledonia last night?" Simon asked.

Sin grabbed a raw apple from a platter on one of the tables, then led Simon toward the stairs. "Nothing."

"You didn't murder her in her bed?"

He paused midstep and glared at his friend. "What sort of question is that?"

"Don't be angry at me. That's the story everyone is bantering about this morning. It seems Henry ordered Aelfa to bring him your bedsheets. Now everyone believes you must have cut her head off for there to have been so much blood on them."

Sin set his jaw and said nothing in response. He'd never taken a virgin before, so in an effort to make it appear he had slept with his wife, he'd cut his own arm and used his blood for the sheets. Apparently he'd used too much.

"So what happened?" Simon prompted.

He ignored Simon as he gazed up the stairs to see Callie and Jamie coming down them. She wore her plaid around her saffron kirtle again. Her hair was plaited down both sides of her face, and her cheeks and eyes were bright this morning.

The woman took his breath away and made him ache to finish what the two of them had started the night before.

When she saw him, she smiled a smile that made

him instantly hot. Hard. One that reminded him all too well she'd fallen asleep before he had found any comfort whatsoever.

"Good morning, my husband."

His stomach clenched at the word. "My lady. How do you feel?"

"Still a bit of an ache in my head, but fine otherwise. You?"

He looked around at the courtiers, who gawked at her as if she were a ghost. "Never better, my lady."

Her smile widened.

Jamie ran past him to show Simon a handful of string.

"Are we leaving now?" Callie asked.

"I thought you would want to."

"Aye. The sooner, the better."

"Then come. We're all packed and ready."

Callie reached to take his arm, but he pulled away. Disheartened but far from daunted, she took a deep breath and followed him through the hall toward the door.

Henry met them outside the hall, his face grim. "You be careful," he said to Sin. "I don't want your head to come back to me in a sennight."

Sin nodded, then helped her to mount her horse.

As he reached for Jamie, the king stopped him. "The boy stays here as guarantee that no harm will befall you."

Jamie screeched out a denial.

Callie opened her mouth to respond, but before she could, Sin spoke. "The boy goes with us."

"Are you mad?" Henry demanded. "Without the child, there's no guarantee of your safety."

"The boy goes with us." The sharpness of Sin's voice surprised her. She doubted if Henry would allow any man save her husband to use that tone without putting irons on him.

"I assure you," Sin said more calmly, "I can handle myself even against the devil himself, but I will not leave an innocent boy here with no protector."

Henry stiffened. "You insult us if you think we would allow a ward of ours to—"

"I was once one of your wards, Sire." Sin gazed at Henry, his face expressionless.

Guilt flashed in Henry's eyes before he recovered himself. "Fine, then. Take him if you must."

Without another word, Sin picked Jamie up. The lad threw his arms around his neck and held him tight. She saw the confusion in Sin's eyes.

"I like you even if you are an English dog," Jamie announced, pulling back to pat Sin's head. "You're my favorite one. Well, you and Simon."

Sin gave a crooked smile. "Then I thank you, I think."

Jamie grinned as Sin put him on his horse. Without another comment, Sin pulled himself up into his saddle.

Henry took the bridle of Sin's mount and looked up at him. "We want word the minute you arrive at the MacNeely's castle and a note for every week thereafter. Should we not receive it, we will send an army to determine your well-being."

Sin looked much less than amused. "I will be fine."

Henry nodded a farewell and then they were off.

Sin led the group while Simon and Jamie rode abreast of Callie. Luckily, they traveled light. She and

Jamie had packed very little for their trip to their aunt's, and Simon and Sin seemed to need nothing more than the clothes on their backs.

But then, she had already learned her husband wasn't the typical Englishman who needed an entire entourage with him at all times.

They rode well into the afternoon before stopping for a small repast.

As soon as they dismounted, Jamie ran off into the woods to heed nature's call, while Callie set about unpacking some of the foodstuffs Aelfa had gathered for them.

They had left London behind hours ago, and all she could do was look forward to when she would be home again.

Closing her eyes, she swore she could almost feel her crisp, heather-scented Highlands seeping into her weary bones. She'd been gone far too long; but then, even a week away from home seemed an eternity.

Jamie came bounding back out of the woods at the speed of a dodging hare and accidentally ran into Sin as he fed the horses. The grain spilled all over Sin's boots and made a huge mess.

Callie held her breath, half expecting Sin to strike out or at the very least shout at the lad's clumsiness. He didn't. Instead, he picked the lad up and made sure he was unhurt, then brushed Jamie off and sent him on his way with a hushed warning to be more careful lest he hurt himself. Once Jamie was hurtling toward Simon, Sin dropped to his knees and silently cleaned up the mess Jamie had made.

His gentleness amazed her. The other Englishmen

had never once hesitated to cuff the lad for such carelessness. Even her Uncle Aster and Dermot were quite intolerant of Jamie's clumsy ways. Sin said nothing more about it. Not even when he had to remove his right boot and dump grain out of it.

As Simon and Jamie ran past him, Sin caught the lad up in his arms and tossed him up over his shoulder to dangle down his back as he walked. Jamie squealed with laughter as Sin toted him to where she sat with the food.

"Put me down!" Jamie said, his voice broken by laughter.

"You need to eat if you're to grow to any size." Sin flipped him over his shoulder and laid him gently on the ground by Callie's side.

Jamie scrambled up, but before he could run again, Sin caught him. "Must I tie you down?"

Jamie laughed, then dropped to the ground and sat with his legs crossed while Simon joined them.

"Will we camp outside the entire way?" she asked Sin as she handed Jamie some bread and chicken.

Sin shook his head. "There should be inns most of the way and Simon's brother lives farther north as well. Two days hence, we'll stop on his lands. So, you'll have a bed every night until we reach Scotland."

Heat descended over her face as a memory of last night flared. She remembered standing naked with her husband and holding him in her hand.

It pained her that she couldn't remember exactly what they'd done. She'd overheard many women through the years talking about what went on with men and women in the night. And once her friends had started marrying, she'd heard even more details about it. She'd never dared tell anyone how many nights she'd lain awake in her bed wondering if she'd ever experience it herself, and now that she had . . .

Well, it was quite unfair to have no memory of it.

Biting her lip, she wondered if he would claim her again tonight. Heat rushed over her face as she considered him lying beside her. Of his hardness deep inside her.

She glanced to her husband, then quickly looked away.

Sin saw the blush in her cheeks and wondered what caused it. His gaze dropped to her lap and in his mind he saw the ripe curves of her inner thighs. Felt the softness of her skin as he had rubbed his own blood over her to disguise what he had yet to do.

Touching her last night without easing the desire of his body had been the hardest thing he had ever done.

Even now he could remember the feel of her supple skin under his palm. The lavender smell of her hair. The taste of her lips.

How he wanted her. Ached for her. He shifted slightly, trying to alleviate the tightness of his chausses against the part of him that demanded her most.

Callie saw the look of hunger on Sin's face from the corner of her eye. He stared at her in such a way that it made her tremble with nervousness.

Simon cleared his throat. "Should I take Jamie for a walk to the next county?"

Sin dropped his gaze to his food. "Nay. We need to get back on the road. I don't want night to fall on us while we're in the woods."

"Very well, but remember, I did offer."

That was the last anyone spoke until after they resumed their long trek.

They traveled for the rest of the day. At dusk, they stopped at a small inn in a town she'd never heard of before. Jamie was so tired, he complained he couldn't make it inside. Ever patient with the lad, Sin pulled him from the horse and carried him.

Once she and Simon dismounted and their horses were turned over to the inn's servants, Sin led them into the inn, where a rotund man greeted them.

"I'll be needing three rooms for the night."

She widened her eyes at Sin's request. "Jamie can't sleep alone," she said. "He'll be frightened."

His little red head of tousled curls shot off Sin's shoulder. "I will not! Think you I'm a little lass, to be scared—"

"Nay, love," she said gently, smoothing down one of his wayward curls. "But you don't need to sleep alone in a strange place."

The innkeeper cleared his throat. "I'm afraid I only have two rooms left."

Sin nodded. "Very well, then, I'll take those." He shifted Jamie to his other side, then spoke to her. "You and Jamie will share a room."

"And you?" she asked.

"I'll sleep in the barn."

Simon stepped forward. "I'll—"

"Nay, Simon," Sin said, cutting him off. "I am more used to it than you are." His tone made it clear there would be no argument.

The innkeeper brought them food and they ate in silence. Exhausted from the trip, they retired as soon as they finished.

Callie tucked her brother into bed, and once he fell asleep, she left her room in search of her husband.

She found him outside her door, leaning against the wall with his sword beside him.

"Sin? What are you doing?"

" 'Twould appear I am sitting."

"And why are you sitting there?"

"Because it's rather difficult to sleep while standing."

Callie faltered as his meaning became clear. "You are sleeping outside my door? Why?"

"Because if I slept outside of Simon's door, the innkeeper might think I'm strange."

His sarcasm was beginning to wear on her. Still, a smile hovered on the edges of her lips. "You could come inside and sleep."

Sin stared at her body wrapped in plaid. Her curves evident from the light behind her, she wore her coppery hair loose around her shoulders. She looked like a goddess standing there. A breathtaking angel come to save his rotten soul.

And he wanted to devour her like some ravenous wolf. To take her into his arms and sate the aching burn in his blood. It was an urge so strong, he was quite amazed to find himself still on the floor and not inside her.

Nay, he couldn't sleep in her room. Not with her. Not when he felt so out of control with himself. "I am quite fine where I am."

"Sitting on the floor?"

"Exactly."

To his astonishment, she knelt beside him and kissed him lightly on the cheek. His skin burned from the softness of her lips. "Thank you, my fierce protector. I shall sleep much better knowing you are out here growing stiff and cold."

Sin arched a brow at her sarcasm. He was stiff, all right, but far from cold.

She rose and moved back into her room. "By the way, should you see Old Red Cap out to harm us, please give him my best."

Sin snorted as she closed the door. Little did his wife know, he *was* Old Red Cap.

Callie tried her best to sleep, but after an hour, she couldn't stand it anymore. The thought of Sin outside on the cold floor was more than she could stand.

Getting up, she grabbed her blanket and pillow and opened the door, then paused. Sin slept with his back to her, stretched out across the doorframe.

Her heart lurched at the sight of him lying there on the cold, hard floor, where his black armor no doubt bit into him. He didn't even have a blanket to cover him. There was no way he could possibly be comfortable lying that way.

Wanting to give him whatever comfort she could, she took a step forward.

Faster than she could blink, Sin rolled over, drawing his sword and angling it at her. The tip of it was barely an inch from her throat.

She gasped in panic.

Blinking and frowning, Sin lowered his sword. "Forgive me, milady. I should have warned you that I sleep lightly and that I come awake ready to fight."

"I shall remember that."

Awkwardly, she handed him the pillow and blanket in her hands. "I thought you might have need of these."

Sin stared at the items. In all his life, no one had ever seen to his comfort. Indeed, he remembered a time once when his stepmother had purchased apple drinks at a local fair for his brothers.

Barely seven, he had watched them gulp down the cider while his own parched throat had burned.

Might I have some, too, please? he'd asked.

His stepmother had curled her lip at him and scowled as if he had asked her to give over one of her limbs. *Find water if you're able. It's free and good enough for the worthless likes of you.*

It had been the last time he had ever asked for anything. "Thank you," he said, taking the pillow and blanket from Callie's hand.

She smiled and returned to her room.

Sin placed the pillow on the floor and lay down again. As soon as his head touched it, he caught a whiff of lavender. Callie's scent. Closing his eyes, he savored the sweet smell of her and imagined the way her thighs had felt as he ran his hand over them.

The entire time he'd touched her, all he had thought about was burying himself deep inside her. Feeling her arms holding him tightly.

Pain assailed him. Why was she kind to him when she, even more than the others, should hate him? He was her enemy. Her father had hated all things English, and yet she showed compassion and kindness to him.

Morbidly, he tucked his sword back under his body where he had learned long ago to sleep with it. The cool steel pressed against the heat of his chest as the hilt and chain mail bit into his flesh. It reminded him of what he was. A warrior. There was no place in his life for comfort. No place in his beleaguered heart for a wife.

Alone was what he knew and alone was how he intended to stay.

Callie stayed up most of the night, trying to think of ways to reach her husband. There had to be some way to get underneath his thick hide and make him accept her.

Morna would know. As soon as they reached her home, she would corner Morna and find out everything she needed. Aye, with Morna's help, Sin would be a cooked goose.

She wasn't about to grow old without children. Whether he admitted it or not, Sin liked children. No man watched over Jamie the way Sin did unless he had paternal feelings. And from what she'd seen, Sin would make a wonderful father.

"Sleep well, husband," she whispered. Because on the morrow she intended to begin the war she hoped would win her husband's heart.

Chapter 8

Well, so much for her war to win Sin's heart. The entire next morning was spent just trying to get him to speak.

Callie was at a loss as to what to do. By the time she awoke, their horses were already saddled and he and Simon were waiting for her and Jamie to resume their trip.

When she smiled and greeted Sin, the best he gave was a noncommittal grunt. In fact, the only response he gave to any question or comment she posed that entire morning was a noncommittal grunt.

By the time they stopped for a rest at midday, she was quite ready to throttle him. Or at the very least set a pack of wild dogs onto his hide.

Miffed beyond measure, she laid out their food, then went to her husband, who was busy tending the horses. "I was thinking of setting myself on fire tonight. Would you mind?"

He grunted again, then looked up sharply. "What?"

She smiled. "Ha! I knew it. I knew I could get you to talk. Just think, a whole word, too. Who knows, if I keep this up, I might have you speaking an entire sentence by week's end."

Sin tried to glower at her audacity, but the woman's charm was infectious. Not to mention she looked just a bit too adorable standing before him with her hair braided down her back and her cheeks bright. What was it about this woman, that every time she came near him, he wanted to kiss those plump, full lips? To bury his head in her neck and just inhale her sweet scent?

Her very presence set him on fire and left his entire body throbbing with need.

"I thought you wished to get home as quickly as possible," he said, noting the deepness of his voice.

"Aye, but we can talk while we do that. Have you noticed Simon hasn't had a bit of trouble asking me how I feel or if I am eager to see my family?"

He glanced to where Simon stood with Jamie while he added a feed sack to his horse. "I'm afraid I don't speak quite as much as Simon." Then again, he doubted if a herd of women spoke as much as Simon.

"I noticed. It's not exactly something you try to hide."

Sin picked up his brush and started rubbing down his horse. He couldn't fathom why Callie chose to be here with him when she could be with her brother and Simon. Especially given the way he had treated her this morning. "Why are you being so kind to me?"

Callie paused at the words. "You say that as if someone being kind is highly unusual."

"It is. In case you didn't notice in London, most people won't even meet my gaze."

She thought about that for a minute. "I think it's your glower that frightens them."

"I have no glower."

"I beg to differ on that point. You are quite ferocious with it."

"Then why aren't you intimidated?"

"I have absolutely no idea. My father always said I had more courage than ten men."

"I think your father was right."

She smiled at him and it did the strangest thing to his breathing, made his groin tighten instantly.

She waved her hand back and forth between them. "I want you to notice that right now, this instant, we are having a conversation. It's really not hard, now, is it? Think you we can carry this on for the rest of the day?"

He actually smiled at that. "I didn't mean to be curt with you this morning. I just don't like to talk while I travel."

"Very well, then, I shall forgive you. But only so long as you make it a point not to ignore me in the future."

"I shall try."

Sin watched her walk off, his heart heavy. She was a great beauty, and he didn't mean her looks. Her beauty was soul deep and possessed a brilliance he'd never known existed.

In that moment, he ached for her. Ached to be a man like Simon.

If he were honorable and decent . . .

He clenched his teeth. There was nothing to be done about it. He was what he was, and there was no way to change it.

Sighing in regret, he returned to tending his horse.

By the time they reached Ravenswood the next day, Callie was more than ready for a night of good, solid rest. The inn they'd stayed in the day before had been cramped and cold, the innkeeper sour and dour.

It had been a miserable night spent with Jamie's elbows and feet digging into her while she wondered where her husband was sleeping.

But tonight there would be plenty of room for Jamie to have his own bed and her husband would not be able to escape her. Aye, she would keep him by her side even if she had to tie him to her.

Simon had become more and more anxious the closer to Ravenswood they got, and as soon as the massive castle came into view, he spurred his horse forward, racing down the hill to the drawbridge.

"I think he's excited," she said to Sin.

"Aye, he and his brother have always been close. Much like you and Jamie."

She glanced to where Jamie slept, nestled in Sin's arms. Jamie had grown so weary an hour back that Sin had feared he would fall from his horse. Sin had stopped and pulled the lad to ride with him so that Jamie could nap in peace.

Jamie held the face of an angel while he slumbered and she didn't miss the gentleness of Sin. For a man who wanted no children, he showed a kind concern that many men lacked.

By the time they entered the well-kept, stylish bailey, Simon was standing with a very handsome, tall, dark-haired man and a blond lady who looked to be expecting a child any day. The man held a toddler in his arms and looked upon them with brotherly affection.

He must be Draven of Ravenswood.

"Sin," Draven greeted with a hint of reserve in his demeanor. "It's been a long time."

Sin reined his horse just before the three of them. Something insidious and painful crossed Sin's brow as he glanced around the lovely yard, which bustled with servants attending their duties.

A haunted look came into his dark eyes and was shared by the man before her.

"Aye, Draven," Sin said quietly, "it has. You look well and happy. Congratulations."

Draven smiled. "The same to you."

Simon came forward to take Jamie so that Sin could dismount. Sin, in turn, helped Callie from the saddle and led her to the others while the horses were led away by stable hands.

"My wife, Caledonia," he said to Draven.

Draven's eyes widened a bit in surprise, but he quickly concealed it. He turned to the pregnant lady and his face instantly softened. "My wife, Emily."

Simon laughed. "Could we be anymore stilted, gentlemen? These ladies would never know the trouble the two of you once brewed."

Draven laughed at that. "Us? I recall it was you doing most of it while we pulled you from harm's way."

"Lies!" Simon cried. "I was an innocent led astray by you demons of Lucifer."

"Innocent?" Sin asked Draven. "Remember that time he shot the bear with an arrow?"

Draven snorted. "Remember it? I am still scarred from it. And what of the wolf?"

Sin snorted, then lowered his voice to a child's falsetto. "Look, Draven, Sin, I found a puppy."

"A puppy with an angry mother."

"Oh, wonderful," Simon said sarcastically. "Now, why on earth did I want to put the two of you together again? I recant my words. Go back to your sullenness. Both of you."

Emily hugged Simon and squeezed his arm. "Poor Simon, ever the brunt of it."

Shifting Jamie's weight in his arms, Simon glanced at Callie, and by the look on his face, she knew he was remembering her trick of tying him to the bed. "You've no idea, Em."

Callie smiled serenely at him.

Emily reached out and took Callie's hand. "Come inside and let us see to a bed for your brother and a hot meal and rest for you and your husband."

There was an open and kind air about Emily of Ravenswood. One that made Callie feel instantly at home. Though she didn't know the woman at all, she felt a kinship with her.

As soon as they were inside, the toddler kicked Draven and demanded to be put down. "Hen, stay close."

The boy ran to the hearth and gathered an armful of toys, then ran to Callie to show her each one of them. He garbled and cooed at her in rapid succession, but she only caught a word or two of his speech.

"He's telling you that his grandfather bought the horse at Ransock's fair, where he got to play with a monkey."

Callie laughed. "Ah, that makes much more sense. How old is he?"

"A year and a half."

"When is the next due?"

"Within a month, I think."

Callie stared at Emily's plump belly with a touch of envy, and she wondered if she might have already conceived from her wedding night. It would be wonderful to have a child growing inside her. To feel the small fluttering of the baby and know it was hers to love . . .

She couldn't wait for the day.

Hen pulled at Callie's sleeve, wanting into her lap. Without hesitation, she sat him there and let him continue to show her his toys.

Sin watched the natural way Callie coddled the babe and his heart ached. Breathing deeply, he looked around the great hall. It was so strange to be back after all these years.

He couldn't remember the times he had been pinned before that same hearth while Harold maliciously beat him for any number of imagined reasons. In those days, the hall had been bleak and dark.

Now it was painted and welcoming. He barely recognized it. Even the dais with the lord's table had been moved to a different location.

Still, he knew this place. Felt the haunted memories of the past stirring. Painful, bitter memories he had spent his entire life trying to bury.

Draven placed a hand on his shoulder.

Instinctively, Sin started to knock it away, but forced himself to endure it. There was much about Draven that reminded him of Harold. The same dark hair, the same features and height. The only difference were the eyes. Harold's had been cruel and brown, while Draven possessed the light blue, kind eyes of his mother.

"The ghosts of the past are hard to exorcise, aren't they?"

Sin nodded. "I'm amazed you can live here."

"In truth, I only existed here until my wife forced herself upon me."

"Forced herself?"

Draven laughed. "You've no idea what a tigress resides in that angelic body."

Sin looked to Callie, who appeared as calm and serene as the Madonna herself. Aye, looks could be quite deceiving.

Draven offered him a cup of wine, but still couldn't meet his gaze for any length of time. Sin knew why. He'd never forgotten the day they had last seen each other.

The heat of Outremer had been searing. Barely fourteen, Sin had been Harold's squire for more than four years. The old earl had wanted to make peace with God and kill a few Saracens and so he had packed up his knights, son and squire and made for Jerusalem.

The journey had been arduous. Two of the knights had died en route and three more had been slain in battle. The last of Harold's knights had died of disease just the day before a bandit had robbed Harold of all his money.

Penniless, Harold had made for a slaver. The man had wanted Draven even though he was two years younger. Draven had been better fed and far less scarred.

"You'll not take my son," Harold had growled. "You can only have this one."

He had shoved a stunned Sin into the man's hands, where he had been inspected in the crudest and coldest of fashions. They had haggled over his worth and in the end he had been sold for less than the price of a good night's lodging.

When the slaver's men had come at him with irons, Sin had fought them with all his strength. But it hadn't been enough. And as they had dragged him away and the old man paid Harold, Sin had seen a flash of relief on Draven's boyish face that his father hadn't sold him instead.

Sin cleared his throat as he banished the memory. "I don't blame you, you know."

Guilt was etched into Draven's face. "I should have done something."

"Done what?"

"Fought him. Protested. I don't know." He took a deep breath. "Something."

"You were twelve years old, Draven. You were starving and scared. Had you moved, he would have either beaten you or sold you, too. Honestly, it's all right."

They both knew he was lying. As bad as Harold had been, he had been a saint compared to the Saracen who had bought Sin.

For a time, they watched the women and spoke of nothing in particular. And after a little while, they relaxed and remembered the boys they had once been. Coconspirators who had made mischief and mayhem.

And with Simon's help, they joined the ladies and retold some of their juicier stories.

"They tell me no one can defeat you in arms," Draven taunted Sin while Sin leaned against the hearth.

"I've heard the same of you."

Simon groaned. "Sweet Jesu, not this again."

"What, Simon?" Emily asked.

Simon shook his head. "Ladies, be prepared. You are about to witness the most horrendous thing on earth."

Callie frowned. "What?"

"Two champions at odds."

Callie laughed, until Sin spoke again.

"I could take you."

Draven snorted. "Nay. Only in your most fanciful dreams. But I, on the other hand, could make *you* cry like a girl."

"Ha! Never."

"You think not?"

"I know not."

"Then suit up and meet me outside."

"Draven!" Emily gasped. "They haven't been here hardly any length of time and you wish to spar with Lord Sin?"

"I'm not going to spar with him, Em, I'm going to sweep the list with him."

Sin scoffed. "You wish."

"Sin," Callie said as he pushed himself away from the hearth. "Are you not too tired?"

"Even half dead, I could beat him with one arm tied behind my back."

Draven smiled evilly. "Then do it."

"I will."

Simon groaned even louder.

Callie looked up at Simon. "They're not serious, are they?"

Emily answered for him. "I have an awful feeling they are."

Her awful feeling turned out to be correct when ten minutes later both men came back downstairs dressed for battle.

"Will you not at least eat first?" Simon called.

They shook their heads in unison and headed for the door. Their voices echoed through the room as they clattered down the foyer.

"Lay on, Sin, and taste your first defeat."

" 'Tis your own feet you'll be tasting, Draven-boy. There shall never come a day when you can best me."

Draven paused at the door and looked back to the hearth. "Come, Simon, and watch your foster brother eat crow."

The men slammed their helmets on, clanged their swords together, then headed outside.

"Simon?" Callie asked. "Should I be worried?"

They heard a scream from outside the door.

"I think we should be worried," Emily said as she scrambled to her feet and rushed for the door.

Simon grabbed Hen and they followed Emily to see the men outside in the yard.

"Alys?" Emily asked an attractive, dark-haired maid who appeared to be around Emily's age. The woman stood with her hand over her heart as if she'd suffered a horrendous fright. "Are you all right?"

"Aye," Alys said, "but your husband is dangerous with that sword, milady."

"You have no idea," Simon muttered as he approached the men. He flashed a bright smile at the maid, who blushed prettily, then hastened off.

As soon as the men locked swords, a small crowd of servants and knights formed to watch them. Emily and Callie exchanged a frustrated, weary look, then went to try and break them up.

It didn't work.

Hours went by as Sin and Draven attempted to pummel each other into the ground.

After a time, Jamie got up from his nap, played with Hen, then both were tucked into bed. Supper was served, eaten and then grew cold all the while they waited for the two combatants to grow up and join them.

Even the crowd outside dispersed as the watchers made their way to their own beds.

Finally, Emily had a brilliant idea. She and Callie made platters, then took them outside where their husbands were still fighting.

Someone, most likely Draven, had ordered rushlights lit around the list so that they could see each other even in the darkness of night. In spite of the lunacy of their actions, Callie did have to admire them. They were both extraordinary fighters, especially given the fact they had been at this for many hours.

"Mmmm," Emily said, taking a whiff of the roasted venison in cherry sauce. "Callie, you must take a bite of this. 'Tis the best venison our cook has ever prepared."

The men slowed a bit as they craned their necks to see.

Callie took a bite and moaned in exaggerated bliss. "You are right. 'Tis marvelous. Delicious." She cast a sideways glance to see the men stopping. "The best I have *ever* eaten."

Sin's stomach rumbled at the thought of the banquet the ladies held. He hadn't eaten much of anything that day. But Satan's throne would freeze before he ceded this battle to Draven.

"You're looking a bit weak," Draven taunted. "Methinks you need a bite to replenish your feeble strength."

"My strength is nowhere near as feeble as your brain."

They began hammering blows again.

Callie and Emily exchanged annoyed glares. Men!

They looked to Simon, whose platter was almost cleared of food. "What?" he asked innocently.

"What are we to do now?" Callie asked.

Simon shrugged and finished his food.

Emily set the platters aside and thought the matter through for several minutes. "My maid Alys once told me that if you flash a little ankle, a man will follow you anywhere."

Simon snorted. "Trust me, 'twould take more than an ankle to dislodge those two."

Emily loosened the top laces of her gown. Simon discreetly turned his back while she went closer to the men. "You know, Callie, 'tis rather warm out tonight. Perhaps I should dampen my kirtle until it's sodden and hangs transparent against my skin."

Draven stumbled at her words.

"Is that what you English do when you're warm?" Callie asked as she joined her. "At home we merely remove our plaids and walk about . . . bare."

Sin snapped his head toward her.

Callie fingered the pin on her shoulder. "It only takes unfastening one brooch to remove the entire thing."

Draven growled and rushed Sin, catching him about the middle and knocking him back.

Sin roared and attacked full force.

Emily sighed as they continued their battle. "I think we only made it worse."

They turned to look at Simon, who was now poking around the other two platters and eating the food from them.

"What?" he asked again as he realized he held their full attention.

Emily put her hands on her hips. "Is there truly nothing you can do?"

Simon dropped the food in his hand and straightened. "Should I do this, then I want both of you to promise me you will grab your husbands before I am gelded."

"We will," they promised in unison.

"You had better."

Straightening his tunic with a tug, Simon moved closer until he stood just a little way from the other two men. "Draven," he said, his voice falsetto. "What a big, strong warrior you are. Why, it makes my heart pound the way you move. You're such a great hero."

Sin laughed out loud.

Draven merely growled again.

Simon turned his attention away from his brother. "And Sin, such a great big, tough knight you are. Why, I just don't know if I can stand here and watch you. It makes me all jittery."

Sin laughed no longer.

Simon turned to look at Callie and Emily. "Ladies, while the men play with each other's swords, what say you we adjourn inside and Emily can show me all about damp kirtles and Cal—"

Before he could finish the sentence, Draven and Sin charged him.

Sin caught him about the neck at the same time Draven caught his waist. Together they lifted him from his feet and tossed him into a water trough.

No doubt they would have done more damage had Callie and Emily not run forward to grab them.

Callie pulled Sin's helm from his head and kissed him quickly before he could get away.

Sin froze at the taste of his wife's cool lips against his hot mouth.

He was weary beyond simple endurance, and sweating, yet she didn't seem to notice the stench of him.

She pulled back and gave him a smile. "Tell me honestly, are you not famished, my lord?"

Aye, he was. He starved for her in a way that was truly terrifying.

Draven made a disgusted noise, distracting him. "I'll go in when Sin cedes defeat."

"You'll go inside right now," his wife said, "or you'll be sleeping in the stable this night."

Sin opened his mouth to taunt Draven but was

stopped by Callie's hand on his lips. "One word from you and you shall join him."

Simon's laughter rang out as he dripped his way toward them. "Who would have ever thought the two greatest knights in England could be laid low by simple maids?"

Both men growled and would have seized Simon had their wives not taken their arms.

"Boys," Emily said, her voice stern. "Would you please behave and go inside to eat? You've done quite enough damage to poor Simon and to each other for one night."

"Yea," Simon said, wringing his shirt. "Besides, I know not why you're angry at me. You two get to go to bed with these two beautiful ladies, while I get to cuddle my pillow."

Emily patted his wet arm. "Poor Simon, ever abused. We shall have to find a wife for you, isn't that right, Callie?"

"Aye, we shall."

Callie could swear she saw a look of panic cross Simon's face.

They went inside to eat while Simon headed up to his room to dry off.

After the men had finished eating, Callie took Sin to their room, where she could help him remove his armor.

"You must be terribly sore," she said, noting the bruises and red marks on his flesh. Luckily, there were no wounds.

Sin scoffed. " 'Twas friendly exercise. I am fine."

"Friendly? Well then, I pray I never see you fight in earnest." She meant that, too. Though it had irritated her, his skill had been beyond measure. She'd never seen two men fight better than they had.

"Here," she said, urging him to sit on a stool so that she could rub his shoulders and arms.

Sin sat down. He couldn't fathom what she wanted until her soft, gentle hands began kneading his shoulders and neck. He moaned at the pleasure of it. No one had ever done such a thing for him before.

Chills exploded across his flesh as she ran her hands over his biceps, squeezing them as she went. His groin tightened and burned, stretching against his chausses, aching for possession of her.

Her touch was heaven, and more chills spread over his skin as he felt her breath against his flesh. Saints above, how he wanted her. Just one taste of her succulent flesh. One precious moment in her arms.

Callie swallowed at the hard feel of Sin's muscles under her hands. She'd done this countless times for her father, uncle and brother, and yet, with Sin, touching his skin made her mouth dry. Made her legs weak and her breasts tingle. A hot stab of desire sliced her middle as she throbbed for him.

The feel of his strength, of his hardness, was more than she could stand.

A knock sounded on the door.

"Enter."

A maid came in leading a brigade of servants with a tub and buckets of steaming water. "Lady Emily said his lordship would be needing a bath."

Callie smiled at the thoughtfulness.

Once the tub was filled, she stepped back for her husband to rise.

Sin didn't move. He stared at the tub as images

whirled through his mind. Callie wet and dripping, straddling his hips as he eased his aching loins.

Aye, he could just imagine her breasts shining in the light, her lips smiling at him as he pleasured her.

"Are you not going to bathe?" she asked.

It wasn't until he removed his chausses that Callie realized she hadn't really seen him naked on her wedding night. Or if she had, she had no memory of it.

She swallowed at the bare beauty of him. Of his body, so lithe and powerful. He was magnificent.

Sin made himself sit in the tub, but what he really wanted to do was take his wife into his arms and make love to her for the rest of the night.

And it was the one thing he couldn't do.

He had no intention of staying in Scotland. Ever. And he refused to take a chance on getting her with child. He would never be his father. Never take his pleasure, then leave a woman to tend a child of his.

To hate and despise his child.

To his dismay, she took the cloth from his hands and lathered it. Sin ground his teeth as he hardened even more. "I can do that myself."

"I know you *can*. But I wish to do this for you."

He would never understand her kindness, but then she thought them to be married. Only he knew the truth of their wedding night.

"Why are you so accepting of me as your husband?"

She set her soap aside. "My grandmother was Irish and she had a saying: *Lord grant me the serenity to accept the things I canna change.*"

She placed one hand against his shoulder as she started washing his back. "For whatever reason, you and I have been joined. I could fight you and hate you, but in the end it would change nothing. It would only make both our lives miserable. From what I have seen, you are a good man. So, I prefer to make peace for both our sakes, and to hope that maybe you can make my clan understand that the English settlers are inevitable. And that we can live harmoniously with one another."

Her words brought an unexpected pain to his heart. "So, you have no real care for me." The words were out before he could stop them.

She stilled her hand and moved forward so that she could meet his gaze. "I barely know you, Sin." Her earnest gaze bored into him until a light of humor lightened it. "Still, I like what I have seen." She returned to washing his back. "Except for tonight. I think you let your pride get the better of your common sense."

He smiled at that. Indeed he had.

"And I do care for you."

Her words startled him, and yet he understood her meaning. "As you would any stranger."

"Yea and nay. I daresay, I wouldn't scrub the back of a man I didn't know."

He grinned at that. "I should hope not."

She picked up a bucket to rinse his back. He sighed as the warm water slid over his flesh.

Callie set the bucket aside and returned to sit beside him. "I want to get to know you, Sin. I think knowing you would be a most wondrous thing."

He looked away as he took the cloth and started bathing his leg. "Truly, there is nothing about me worth knowing."

She caught his face in her hand and turned him until her gaze held his. "What did they do to you, to make you withdraw so far into yourself?"

Sin didn't answer. He couldn't. He'd spent the whole of his life trying to bury those memories. Trying never to look to the past for anything. He just existed. It was all he knew.

She heaved a weary breath. "You've left me again, haven't you? I can always tell. Your eyes turn dull, cold."

She rose to her feet. "Very well, I shall leave you in peace. But know this: One day I am going to find the heart you have buried away from the world."

"And what would you do with it if you found it?"

"I would hold it safe and keep it from the hurt that has shriveled it."

Said heart pounded at her words. "My lady, that organ knows nothing of love. It knows nothing of kindness. Even if you did find it, I assure you, it would be quite worthless to you."

"Perhaps or perhaps not. Either way, I intend to find out."

Her strength never ceased to amaze him.

She moved toward the bed and pulled her gown over her head. Sin's entire body burned at the sight of her naked form. Worse, she gifted him with a lush view of her backside as she climbed into bed.

In that moment, 'twas all he could do not to join her. All he could do not to run to the bed, roll her to her back and partake of the feast that was her body.

His tongue burned from want of her lips, her breasts. It would be pure bliss to have her wrap her body around his. Pure bliss to be her husband this night.

But he couldn't do it. She was accepting of him now, but things would change when he got her home. Her Highland brethren would never tolerate an English knight in their midst.

Not even his brother's clan had been able to do that. He'd stayed with the MacAllisters for a brief time after Braden and Maggie's wedding while his burns had healed. And though all had been coolly cordial, he had still seen the way the servants and villagers had shied away from him. The way no one wanted to spend more than a fleeting moment in his presence.

Even his stepmother, Aisleen, had been very coldly polite to him during his stay. Not once had she been able to meet his gaze. Of course, her cold aloofness was a vast improvement over the contempt and repulsion she'd shown him in his youth. Still, he had refused to stay where he was unwelcome.

He had to do that enough at Henry's court.

Sin looked back at the bed where his wife waited, his stomach hurting. No one had ever welcomed him before Caledonia.

She would give herself to him if he asked it.

And he wanted to ask. So much so that he burned with the yearning.

Don't do this to her or to you. Leave, Sin.

No good could come of tasting heaven when he couldn't stay in it. He'd learned that early in life. Memories of happiness only stuck the barb in deeper.

And he had been barbed enough.

* * *

Callie held her breath in nervous anticipation as she heard her husband leave the tub. He would come to her now, she was sure of it.

While the men had been fighting outside, Emily had told her much about how hard Draven had fought against the love Emily had offered him.

She took courage in hoping that if Emily had bent her stubborn husband to accept her, perhaps there was a chance for her and Sin as well.

Perhaps.

At least she thought that until she heard Sin walk across the floor and out the door.

Stung, she rolled over to make sure she had heard correctly.

Aye, she had. Her husband was nowhere to be found.

Grinding her teeth in frustration, she lay there and let the pain of rejection wash over her.

Very well, then, if he didn't want her, so be it. She wasn't going to lie around and ache like this. She had made her offer. He had rejected it.

He had no use for her. Fine. She would be home in a few days and then she could do as he did and just pretend he didn't exist. Fine. Wonderful.

If that was what he wanted, she would give it to him.

And yet, even as her anger spoke loudly in her head, there was a tiny part of her that wanted the kind of marriage her parents had shared. The kind of marriage Morna had had with Callie's father. The kind Emily shared with Draven. One of love and respect.

"I know not what to do," she breathed. But inside

she did. She would have to continue the fight for his heart.

She only hoped he didn't fight her with the same determination he'd shown with Draven. If he did, then she would have no hope whatsoever of winning.

Chapter 9

They left early the next morning. Callie barely had time to say good-bye to Emily and Draven before Sin whisked the four of them back on the road to Scotland.

The next few days were eventless and marked only by her husband's reluctance to acknowledge her presence in any way.

By the time they reached the border of the Mac-Neely lands, she was ready to strangle him. But the sight of her home eclipsed every bit of her irritation at her husband.

She was home! Spurring her horse, she raced ahead of the others.

Sin caught up to her and pulled her to a stop.

"What is it you do?" she asked.

"We're being watched."

She frowned at his words. "By whom?"

He didn't answer. "Simon, put the boy on your horse and stand ready to get him and Callie to safety."

Simon obeyed without question.

No sooner had Simon placed Jamie before him than a cry went up through the forest. Callie's heart hammered as two score men surged out of the trees to surround them. But it wasn't fear that made her heart race. It was joy. She knew these Highlanders. Knew and loved each and every one of their blessed faces.

Faster than she could blink, Sin dismounted to stand before her horse and unsheathed his sword, ready to take them all on. Her heart swelled at the sight. He might have been cold toward her the last few days, but he was still willing to fight and protect her. It was a good sign.

"Release the lass and lad or die!"

Sin took a step forward.

"Aster, please," Callie said, trying to diffuse the passionate nature of her kinsmen. "They have returned me."

Aster's gray hair was a bit shaggy and his face had new wrinkles to it. He looked at Sin and Simon skeptically. "Are you sure, turtledove?"

"Aye." She wanted desperately to tell them who Sin was, but thought better of it. Let them meet as friends and then she would deliver what was sure to be a cutting blow to her uncle.

Aster signaled the men to sheath their weapons. "Then it appears I owe you an apology, English."

Without speaking, Sin sheathed his sword and returned to his horse. Callie noticed the rigid way he sat. This was the Sin she had met on the turret stairs. A man of suspicion and danger.

Her own family held the same guarded nature. No one, not even Dermot, greeted her openly. All of them eyed Simon and Sin, ready to grab swords at any provocation.

"Uncle Aster, Uncle Aster," Jamie shouted excitedly, "Lord Sin married Callie and he disarmed her, too."

She cringed at Jamie's words. Especially when Aster cut a killing glare at the two knights. "And just which one of ye be this Lord Sin."

"I am."

The air between the two men was rife with antagonism.

"We were married a week past, in accordance with the Church," she said, hoping to allay some of the tension.

Aster became even colder than before. "Were you forced to it, lass?"

She saw the look in Sin's eyes, but he said nothing. He expected her to betray him, to leave him at the mercy of her kinsmen. "Nay, Uncle. I married him willingly."

"Are you mad?" Dermot snarled. His green eyes snapped with fury as the wind tugged at his long, dark brown hair. "To be bringing a Sassenach here? Where's your head, woman?"

"My head is fine, Dermot MacNeely, and I don't be needing to hear it from the likes of you. Sin is my husband and you're honor-bound to show him respect."

Dermot spat on the ground. "I'll die before I show respect to any S—" His sentence stopped as a dagger whizzed past his face, narrowly missing him.

Sin eyed him harshly. "Call me that one more time, boy, and you will die for it."

Dermot unsheathed his sword, but before he could ride forward, Tam grabbed his horse. "Calm down, lad. Your sister's home. Let's let Aster and Callie sort this through."

The look on Dermot's face should have splintered her husband into oblivion. Sin appeared immune to the hostility and yet something told her he wasn't.

Everyone's mood was subdued as Aster led them back to her family's castle. If not for Jamie's rapid chatter, the ride would have been in complete silence.

As soon as they entered the hall, Jamie's mother came running toward them. Morna was a beautiful, slender woman with long, dark brown hair the same shade as Dermot's. Her kind blue eyes were filled with joy at the sight of them.

"Och, my wee bairn!" Morna screamed, scooping Jamie up in her arms and holding him tight to her ample bosom. He kicked his legs in protest as she squeezed and kissed his face over and over again.

Sin watched the woman, who probably wasn't any more than a year or two older than him, greet her son. There had been a time once, long ago when he'd dreamed of coming home to such a welcome. But when the other boys who had been taken from Scotland had been sent home by Henry, all that had greeted him had been a curt, cold note sent by his father:

I have no use for a Sassenach in my home. Do with him as you please. He is not now, nor will he ever be, welcomed here.

The old wounds inside tore open, spilling aching pain throughout his entire body.

"My lord?"

He turned away from Callie and removed his gauntlets from his hands.

Callie frowned at Sin's back. The raw anguish in his eyes haunted her. When she stepped around him, she saw his face held its usual stoic expression.

Morna took Jamie upstairs, while Aster led her, Sin, Simon and Dermot into his counsel room.

"I dinna want him here," Dermot said in Gaelic.

Callie saw red. " 'Tis not your decision."

"The hell it's not. He's English."

"Dermot, Callie, settle down," Aster snapped. "This won't get any of us anywhere. Now then, tell me, Callie, what do you intend for us to do with him?"

"I intend for you to make him welcome."

Aster ran his hand through his graying hair. "Now, that's asking a wee much, don't you think, lass? I spent the best part of me youth fighting his kind. As did your dearly departed da. I want peace with them as much as you do, but not at this cost."

She glanced to her husband, who exchanged a peeved glare with Simon. "We are being rude by discussing this in front of him when he knows nothing of our language."

"He's a whoreson and if he can't understand us, then you'd best be sending him home."

"You're right about one thing." They all froze as Sin's flawless Gaelic rolled like thunder through the room. "I am a whoreson, but I have no intention of going home until there are no more raids against Englishmen." He stalked toward Dermot until they were toe to toe. "So if you want me to leave, then all you have to do is make peace."

"Wherever did you learn to speak our language, lad?" Aster asked. "I've never known a Sas . . . Englishman to speak it so well."

Sin cast a glance over his shoulder. "I'm just full of surprises."

Callie held her breath as the two men sized each other up. Like Sin, her uncle wasn't used to anyone questioning his supreme authority. He ruled their land with the power of a king, and all the clan owed their blood loyalty to him.

She cast a pleading look to Simon, hoping that if a battle ensued, he would help her break them apart.

Aster narrowed his gaze. "If you think for even one instant that I will let you capture any of my people and hand them over to your king, you are sadly mistaken."

Sin turned to face him. "Then I would caution you to make sure the rebels raid no more."

"How can I do that when I have no idea who they are?"

"You are laird of this clan. Don't tell me you don't know every man, woman and child who inhabits it. If you don't know the rebels by name, you most certainly know them by reputation and you know which of the men are most likely guilty."

Dermot raked a sneer over Sin and Simon. "There are only the two of them here, Uncle. I say we cut their throats and bury them."

Sin actually smiled at Dermot's threat as Simon cocked an amused brow.

When Sin spoke, his tone was low and lethal. "Better men than you, whelp, have tried, and they are all lying in their graves for it."

Dermot stiffened to his full youthful height, which was still a full head shorter than Sin. "You don't scare me."

"Then you are too foolish to live." Sin pulled a dagger from his boot. "Come here, boy, and I'll cut *your* throat and gladly put you out of both our miseries."

For the first time in her life, Callie saw her brother pale. "Sin," she said, in a teasing tone she hoped would lighten their moods and stave off their fighting. "Put that away before he thinks you mean it."

"I do mean it."

She rolled her eyes as her own temper ignited. "Och now, you men. Always bragging and bullying." She took the dagger from his hand and sheathed it back in his boot. "Next time, I'll confiscate it from you."

The incredulous look on Sin's face was laughable. In fact, Simon did laugh.

She turned on Dermot. "And you . . . you ought to be ashamed. Now go upstairs and say hello to your brother and let me speak with Aster without your hotheadedness interfering."

That only made Dermot madder. "I've as much right—"

"Dermot, obey!" she commanded.

Grumbling, he stalked from the room. "I'm not a child!" he snapped before slamming the door shut behind him.

Callie took a deep breath. Finally, a moment of peace to try and negotiate a miracle.

She turned back to the men. "All right, now, where were we?"

"Your uncle was telling you why he and the rest of your clan can't welcome me into their midst."

"It's nothing against you personally," Aster said. "I have finally succeeded in quieting down the rebels. Your presence here will no doubt set them off again."

Sin crossed his arms over his chest. "Was it your leadership that quelled them or the fact that Henry held Callie?"

Aster turned a peculiar shade of red. "Now, see here, I dinna have time for this. I have an envoy of allies coming in from a northern clan. The last thing—"

Sin stiffened. "To what purpose do they come?"

Aster blustered even more that Sin would dare question him about clan concerns. "It's none of your bloody damned English business."

Sin took a step forward, his face dark with warning. "As an advisor to Henry—"

"Great Peter's knucklebone, Callie!" Aster cried, turning on her with a fierce glower. "It's not bad enough you bring back an Englishman? Did you have to find one who is an advisor to the king?"

She disregarded his question. Much like Sin, she wanted to know who was coming and why. "Who is coming, Aster? I don't see the harm in his knowing."

A tic formed at Aster's jaw. For several minutes, he said nothing at all as he looked back and forth between them.

Finally he spoke. "The MacAllisters are coming."

Sin frowned. "Lochlan MacAllister?"

"You know of him?" Aster asked.

Callie arched a brow in surprise. The MacAllisters were a strong clan who wielded a tremendous amount of power over their fellow Highlanders. Their leader, Lochlan, was said to be wiser than King Solomon and the most skilled fighter in all of Scotland.

Ewan MacAllister was more myth than real. Legend said he'd taken to the hills, where he practiced ancient and black arts that called forth the souls of dead warriors to inhabit his body. A giant among men, Ewan had never been defeated in battle.

And Braden MacAllister . . . there wasn't a lass in all of Scotland who didn't know of him. More handsome than sin itself, he was said to be able to seduce any woman he met. When it came to fighting, everyone agreed the only person to match his skill was one of his brothers.

No one ever wanted to cross a MacAllister.

Sin snorted. "Aye, you could say that."

"Why are they coming?" Callie asked.

Aster took a seat at his desk and shuffled through papers. "Since they are on friendly terms with King Henry, I sent for them hoping to work a peace that would bring you home. Now I fear they will have wasted their journey. But no matter, I shall make them welcome and then send them back."

It made sense to her and she was relieved Aster had sought a peaceful way to get her back as opposed to marching himself down to London and getting killed. "When will they arrive?"

"Tomorrow or the next day."

Callie gathered Simon and Sin to her. "Come, gentlemen, let me show you both where you may wash and rest. Aster, would you please have food sent to my room and to the one across the hall from it?"

Rage suffused his face at her words. Aster growled low in his throat. Then he fairly shouted, "You canna be putting one of them in your room, lass! 'Tis indecent!"

She gaped at him. "My husband?"

Aster's face turned another shade of red. He blustered. "Aye, I forgot that. All right, then, I shall send Aggie up with food for all of you."

"Thank you."

Sin didn't speak as she led him across the hall and to a set of stairs. He saw the hate-filled stares they collected as they moved through the castle.

"You know," Simon said from behind him, "I haven't felt this much animosity since the last time I went to Paris."

"I told you to stay home."

"No doubt I shall wish I had listened." Simon cleared his throat. When he spoke next, it was in a deep, mocking tone. "Oh, but Simon, I am so glad you came along. Imagine, here I would be with only Callie and Jamie to befriend me." He changed his voice back to its normal tone. "Think nothing of it, Sin. My pleasure, really. 'Tis what friends are for."

Sin paused on the stairs and turned to face him with a droll stare. "Are you quite through?"

"Not really, why?"

Sin shook his head and laughed. "You're right, Simon. Thank you for coming."

Simon threw himself against the stone wall, his face a mask of shock and dismay. "Callie, quick, take cover, love. The castle is doomed. Sin said thank you to me. The end of the earth is upon us." He crossed himself. "Hail Mary full of grace."

Callie laughed while Sin glared.

"You are such a buffoon," he said. "You should have been a jester instead of a knight."

"True, but jesters don't get to carry a sword. Personally, I like my sword. You know, the whole knight image really makes the ladies lust for me. Not that any have lusted for me recently, since I have only been in the company of married women, but one is ever hopeful."

Simon paused, then drew his brows together sternly. "Oh, wait, I'm in Scotland, where they hate us English. Damn, my chances with the women have just fallen to nil." He sighed dramatically. "Wasn't there a monastery a few leagues back? Mayhap I should go take my vows and just save myself the embarrassment of being sneered at."

Callie laughed even harder. "Oh, Simon. I, for one, am very happy that you came along. We shall just have to teach you to wear a plaid and speak a little Gaelic."

Simon cleared his throat and whispered to Sin loud enough so that Callie could hear him. "Is it true the men wear nothing beneath their plaids?"

"Aye."

He shuddered and met her gaze. "I'll be keeping my breeches on, if it's all the same to you."

"Your choice," she said, opening the door to Simon's room.

Simon entered and closed the door, while Sin followed her across the hall to her chambers.

Sin paused in the doorway as he looked around the cheery room. The large bed was draped with burgundy serge, and warm blankets and pelts covered the mattress. There was an elegant carved trunk beneath the window of rose-tinted glass and on top was an assortment of dolls. The walls around them had been painted in light blues and white in soothing geometrical patterns.

He felt strange entering here. As if he were intruding into something very private.

"Will you not come in?" she asked.

Sin forced himself over the threshold, yet he couldn't stop the feeling that he had no business here. With her.

He dropped his saddlebags by the trunk and unbelted his sword.

Callie watched the stiff way he moved. He was so guarded and cold. She ached for the playful Sin she had glimpsed in London and for a very brief time on the stairs with Simon.

She folded down the bedcovers so that he could rest should he need to. "Would you like for me to summon a bath for you?"

"Nay. I'll just rest for a bit."

She stepped closer to him. "Are you all right?"

"I'm fine."

She reached up to touch his face and half expected him to dodge her hand.

He didn't.

Sin knew he should move away, but the comfort of her hand on his skin held him immobile. He'd been in caustic environments, surrounded by people who hated him the whole of his life. There was nothing new about this situation. Nothing except for the friendship she and Simon offered him.

For the first time in his life, he didn't feel all alone. And before he realized what he was doing, he dipped his head down and captured her lips with his own.

He moaned at the taste of her mouth, the sweetness of her breath. She wrapped her arms around him, drawing him even closer to her warmth.

Sin felt himself slipping even more. He wanted her in a way he'd never wanted anything else in his life. He wanted to hold her inside his withered heart, to keep her safe and protected, and yet he knew the foolishness of the thought.

He could never subject a woman like this to the horror of being an outcast. Her people were part of her and they would never accept him.

If his own brothers' people couldn't tolerate him, what hope did he have for these strangers? At least the members of the MacAllister clan had seen him as a child. Knew he technically belonged to them.

But even then, they had never really accepted him.

They had seen the scorn their lady bore for him and they had followed suit. While his brothers had been welcomed, he had always been an afterthought. Provided they even remembered him afterward.

He pulled back from her. "You should go visit with your family."

"You are my family, Sin."

Sin choked as a tidal wave of emotions tore through him. The force of it actually made his eyes tear for an instant. Aching and lost, he moved away from her.

"Milord?"

"Leave me," he growled.

"Sin?" She touched his arm.

Sin tore himself away from her and the confusing emotions she stirred. He needed time alone. Time to think through all this. Time to quell his body and soothe his soul.

"Just go!" he roared. "Leave me in peace."

Callie didn't know what to do. She'd never seen a

man in so much pain and she couldn't fathom the cause. He was so angry and, in truth, frightening like this.

Part of her wanted to wrap her arms around him and hold him close, but she didn't dare. He reminded her of a viper coiled and ready to strike out. Unwilling to push him, she nodded. "Should you need me, I will be below with my uncle."

Sin heard the door close behind her. He was so volatile, he wanted to tear something into pieces.

Most of all, he just wanted the pain in his heart to stop. He wanted to go downstairs and claim his wife. To live in the bliss of her acceptance.

Was that so much to ask?

In his mind's eye, he saw the way Draven had been with his wife and child. He ached with envy. A warm hearth and loving arms were not something he could ever have.

If your own mother can't stomach you, why should I? His stepmother's angry words echoed through him.

Sin raked his hands through his hair and he did his best to squelch the memories. He didn't want to think of the past.

"I don't want anything," he snarled.

And he didn't. Not Callie, not his lands. Nothing. He just wanted . . .

Closing his eyes, he summoned the cocoon of empty numbness that he had lived in for so long. Here, there was no pain. No past.

There was nothing.

It was the only comfort a man like him could hope

for. Aye, here, if not the heaven of his wife's touch, there was a facsimile of peace. And it was enough.

But inside, he knew better. Callie had ripped him from his cocoon and he would never be the same.

Chapter 10

Callie spent the afternoon visiting with her family and friends, catching up on all the news and events she had missed over the last few months. Seana had had a little boy named Graham. Susannah had married her betrothed and now she thought she might be with child. Morna had kept the village brewer company while worried out of her mind about Callie and Jamie.

And Dermot had been in love three times in the last two months. At least that was what Morna had told her. Callie wanted to ask her brother about the matter, but had a hard time, since he refused to get near her due to his unreasonable anger toward Sin.

Still, it was so good to see all of them again. Even Dermot, who really was behaving like a doormat. One all prickly and ready to chafe her feet if she got close to him.

Luckily her Aunt Diera, whom they had been planning to visit when they had been taken by Henry, was all healed and better from her fall.

All of them were delighted by her news of marriage until they learned Sin was an English lord. Then, one by one, she watched their faces fall and their eyes turn sharp with warning and loathing.

Callie was depressed by it. This wasn't going to be easy. Morna was the only one who even attempted to be happy for her.

Now Callie sat alone with Morna, kneading bread in the kitchen while they caught up on all the weeks she had been in London.

Morna's face was gentle as they worked, her eyes full of understanding. "I know 'tis hard, lovey, but what the others think isn't important. It's what you and Sin think."

"Why are you the only one who can accept him?"

Morna smiled while she floured her hands. Her long, dark brown hair was coiled becomingly around her head and she wore a red and green plaid over her kirtle. "Because I was once in Sin's shoes. When your da met me, I knew in an instant I would never love another man the way I loved him. He was the only thing in my world and I wanted him so much that my heart wept constantly in fear that he would have nothing to do with me."

"My father loved you."

"Aye, he did. But he was a fierce laird almost twice my age, and I the simple daughter of a shepherd. There were those such as Aster who fought hard to keep him from me."

The news surprised her. She couldn't recall a single time when Aster hadn't been respectful and kind to Morna. Indeed, she remembered him welcoming her into the family with open arms. "Aster?"

"Aye, he thought I was only after your father's money and position and that your da was a blind fool for running after a lass who was barely more than a child. He did everything he could to keep us apart. And there were others who thought the widower of a royal noblewoman had no business wasting time with the likes of me."

Callie gasped indignantly at such snobbery. How dare anyone say such about someone as kind and loving as her precious Morna?

Morna handed her a pan for her loaf. "Even a little queen gem named Caledonia didn't want me around."

Callie blushed as she recalled the first year Morna had lived with them. In truth, she had been a rude little runt. But then, her heart had broken at the thought of her father forgetting her and her mother. She'd been terrified that he would love Morna more and send her off to live in the woods by herself.

They were all stupid fears, but as a young lass, they had seemed well founded. Luckily, Morna had possessed the strength and patience of a saint and had eventually won her over. "I am sorry for that."

Morna patted her hand. "Don't be. I'm just glad you eventually came around to liking me."

"I love you, Morna. I couldn't love you more if you were my mother."

Morna gave her a warm hug. "And I feel the very same for you."

Callie squeezed her stepmother's hand as Morna released her. "I'm glad you stayed, but I fear Sin won't. He has responsibilities in England that are bound to take him away."

"Do you want him to stay?"

"Aye, for some reason I do."

Morna gave her a probing stare. "For what reason?"

Callie turned her attention to the loaf she was shaping. Images of Sin whirled through her mind. His kindness with Jamie, his stubbornness with Draven. She remembered the way he felt in her arms, holding her. The way his hard muscles felt underneath her hands.

His lips on hers.

Most of all, she remembered the way he looked the first time she had been nice to him. The shocked disbelief in his eyes.

"He's a good man in need of someone to love him, I think."

Morna stepped away to put her loaves in the oven. "Well, I will do whatever I can to help. I'll even take a stick to Aster's backside if need be."

Callie laughed at that. She'd love to witness the event.

Excusing herself, Callie put her loaves in, wiped her hands off, then went out into the great hall where the pantry was located. She remembered Sin liking the honey bread he had purchased for Jamie in London and wanted to surprise him with some tonight.

She paused as she entered the room.

To her instant dismay, there was a group of men milling around Aster in the great hall. At least a score of them. They spoke in low tones and it was the talk of them that scared her most.

"We don't want no English devil in our midst. I say we send him back in pieces."

Callie saw red.

"David MacDaniel," she said, striding across the room to stand in front of the big, burly brunette who had spoken those words. He stood even in height to her and wore a red and black plaid. He was handsome enough, but too bullish for her tastes. Not that it mattered. She just pitied his poor wife for having to deal with his mulish ways.

Callie put her hands on her hips and gave him a chiding glare. "I can't believe you'd say such a thing about my husband."

He refused to back down. "Why? It's the truth. If there's one Sassenach here, then there will be more sent. How long do you think it'll be before Henry overruns us?"

"Let's make an example of him! Show the English what we do when they dare—"

"Why don't you do that?"

Silence descended instantly.

Callie turned to see Sin walking slowly down the stairs. He moved like a dangerous black lion. His shoulders were thrown back, his gait one of deadly precision. His black gaze swept the men with a steely glint that made several of them gulp audibly.

They stepped back, allowing Sin to approach the center of the group. An aura of power clung to him and sent a shiver over her.

Again she was struck by how little this lethal knight reminded her of the playful man who had teased her in the courtyard in London. When Sin wore his warrior's cloak, he was truly something to behold, and yet she missed the more playful side of him. The side of him that could make her laugh and was full of tenderness.

But both sides of him made her quiver with desire.

He swept the men surrounding him with a cool, measuring glance. "You want me out of here? Pick twelve of your best and meet me outside in three minutes. If I win, all of you will do as I say . . . and if you win, I'll go home."

David snorted. "What kind of fools do you take us for? We know better than to trust the word of an Englishman."

A taunting, evil smile hovered at the edges of Sin's lips as he moved to stand before David. "What, are you afraid you can't beat me?"

A roar went through the men.

"Those who are willing to try, meet me outside." Sin strode casually from the hall, out the door.

Callie ran after him, her heart pounding in fear.

Twelve men against him? It was ludicrous! They would pound him into gravel.

Outside the door, on the stoop, she took his arm and pulled him to a stop. "Are you insane? They will mangle you."

An amused gleam came into his dark eyes as he reached one hand up to cup her cheek. "Nay, *mon ange,* they won't do anything more than hurt themselves by trying."

Och, she could strangle him. "Must everything with you be a fight?"

A haunted look filled his eyes and he dropped his hand away from her cheek, leaving it cold without his warmth. "It's all I know, Callie. Now stand aside."

She saw the men coming outside. Her heart pounded even more furiously. She didn't want him to do this.

"Aster!" she shouted to her uncle. "Stop them."

"Nay, he issued the challenge and I will see it met."

Before she could protest further, twelve men charged Sin. Callie crossed herself and cringed as they plowed into her husband and knocked him off his feet.

He rolled and came up standing, and when the next man charged, Sin grabbed his arm and flipped him up and over, to land on his back.

Gaping, she watched as he single-handedly brought all twelve men to the ground. Over and over. Every time one came at him, the man ended up at Sin's feet. Her husband never drew a weapon and none of her clansmen ever got a single blow on him.

She'd never seen anything like it in her life.

Still her clansmen fought, and with every move they made, Sin made a countermove that had them flat in the dirt.

"He is a devil!" Aster snarled. "No man can fight like that."

After several minutes, all twelve men lay on the ground, panting.

"Do you yield?" Sin asked as he surveyed her fallen clansmen. He wasn't even breathing heavily. The only sign of their struggle was the dust on his clothes. "Or shall we continue this?"

Her clansmen pushed themselves up slowly. They looked at each other shamefaced. She could tell none wanted to admit defeat, but no one wanted to go at Sin another time, either.

The only one of the men to approach him again was Tavish MacTierney. Not too much shorter than Sin, he was twice as thick, with beefy, muscled arms. The man had never been defeated in a fight before. He walked up to Sin slowly, calmly, then held his hand out to him.

"Tavish be my name, lad. It was a fair fight and I'll be holding no grudges. One day, I'd really like you to show me how you did that."

Sin stared at the proffered hand. It was a gesture he hadn't expected.

"I'd be glad to." He shook arms with the tall man, who reminded him quite a bit of his brother Ewan.

Tavish nodded, dusted his clothes off, then headed away from them, toward the castle gates.

The other men curled their lips while their eyes spoke loudly of the hatred they bore him.

Sin walked straight toward Aster, who glared his open hostility at him while the rest of the men dispersed. Their Gaelic insults were mumbled, but Sin heard and understood them all.

Aster didn't even try to mask his feelings. So be it. He didn't need the old man's help to find the Raider.

Sin feigned a warm, taunting smile at Aster. "Looks like I'll be staying, then."

The old man looked as if Sin had just offered him a piece of excrement.

Callie breathed a sigh of relief even though she knew things were far from fine. In time they would see the man her husband was, and she hoped then they would learn tolerance.

She stepped forward, wanting to take Sin's hand.

Faster than she could move, Sin grabbed her roughly, shoved her in front of him and held her at arm's length. His grip was so tight on her upper arms that she protested audibly. He refused to let go.

Aster's glare turned murderous.

A strange popping sound rent the air and Sin took a step forward, his gaze turning dull as his grip tightened even more. The familiar tic returned to his jaw.

Then as quickly as he had grabbed her, he let go.

"What was that about?" she asked as she rubbed her upper arms where his grip had bitten into her flesh.

Without answering, Sin whirled about, and it was then she saw the arrow that was embedded into his left shoulder.

Horror assailed her, and as she stared at the macabre sight of the arrow, she realized what Sin had done. He had known the arrow was coming and had held her still to make sure the arrow struck him and not her.

Her husband had saved her life.

"Find whoever did this," Aster roared to the others before they could leave. "I want the head of whatever idiot took such a chance with Callie's life!"

As the men ran about the yard looking for the culprit, Aster moved toward them. "Are you all right?"

"Nay, I am shot," Sin said, his tone wry. Other than grimacing, he seemed completely oblivious to the wound. "And in truth I am quite vexed. When I find the coward who did this, I shall gladly give you his ballocks."

Callie ached for the pain he must be in. "We need to get you inside. . . ." Her voice trailed off as Sin stepped away from her and headed toward the wall.

She exchanged a puzzled frown with Aster. Whatever was Sin doing?

Aster shrugged as if reading her thoughts.

To her horror, Sin went to the wall and threw his

back against it, driving the arrow completely through his body.

Tears welled in her eyes as she fought down a scream and watched Sin snap the head of the arrow off with his good hand. His face pale, he walked stiffly toward them, then gave Aster his back. "Pull it out."

By his expression, she could tell her uncle had never seen anything like it. "Good God, man, how can you stand to move?"

"If this was the worst wound of my life, I would be very fortunate indeed. Now pull it out so the wound can be stitched."

Aster shook his head in disbelief as he took the arrow in his hand and Callie bit her lip in sympathetic pain.

Sin's jaw flexed.

Instinctively, she took Sin's right hand in hers and braced her left hand against his uninjured shoulder. He leaned forward against her arm, tensing in expectation of Aster's actions.

Callie held his right hand between her breasts and stroked his fingers, seeking to give him whatever comfort she could.

With a frown, Sin looked at their hands joined, but said nothing. His gaze held hers and she saw the pain and anger that burned deep inside him.

"Thank you," she whispered. "But I wish you had just told me to duck."

Her words succeeded in lightening his face.

At least until Aster braced one hand against Sin's injured shoulder, then tugged the wooden spindle free. Sin cursed loudly as he staggered forward a step.

Callie pulled him into her arms, holding him tight,

wishing she could take the pain from his body and make the wound heal instantly.

Sin didn't know what to say as his shoulder throbbed. The fierce pain was overshadowed by the warm softness of her breasts against his chest, of the sweet feminine lavender scent of her hair. Closing his eyes, he inhaled the soothing smell and just let her comfort wash over him.

She had her arm wrapped about his neck, her small hand buried in his hair as she held him to her. It was the most wondrous thing he'd ever felt, and for a moment he could almost pretend to be her husband in truth.

His lips were so close to her delectable smell that all he had to do was turn his head ever so slightly and he could bury them in the curve of her neck. He hardened at the thought. Not even the pain of his wound could override the desire he held for her.

"I will find and punish whoever did this," she whispered, pulling back to stare up at him. The sincerity of those light green eyes amazed him. He stared in wonderment and ached to show her just how much those words meant to him. "I will not see you harmed."

He didn't know how to respond to that. "It's just a flesh wound," he said dismissively.

"It could have killed you."

"Pity it didn't." Aster's barely audible words cut through him, quelling his lust instantly.

Nay, there would never be anything between him and Callie except wishful dreams. The thought stung him much more deeply than it should have.

Ignoring her uncle's comment, Callie took his hand and led Sin into the castle.

They were going up the stairs as Simon was headed down them.

Simon nodded a greeting, walked past, then backed up the stairs to stop them. "Are you bleeding?" Simon indicated the tear in Sin's surcoat.

"It would appear so," Sin answered sarcastically.

"Good Lord, what happened?"

Sin shrugged. "Apparently someone doesn't want me here. No doubt you, either, so guard your back, little brother. The last thing I want to do is tell Draven you're dead."

"Have no fear. The last thing I want you to do is tell him I'm dead." Simon paused and looked back toward his room. "I'm thinking perhaps I should return to my room and don my armor before I go eat."

"Not a bad plan."

Callie interrupted them. "Gentlemen, please, I need to see to this wound lest he bleed to death from it."

Sin dismissed her worry. "It missed the artery. I assure you, I won't bleed to death from this."

Callie frowned at her husband and his calm acceptance of everything. It was as if he expected nothing more than to be insulted and wounded. "Then humor me, please."

Without further voiced complaints, he followed her to their room, though the look in his eyes told her that many an unspoken complaint circled in his mind.

Callie helped him pull his surcoat off. She frowned as she studied the hole where the arrow had pierced him. "Strange. You can barely see the blood on the cloth, and yet I feel it." There was a lot of blood on the cloth, actually.

Sin looked up from his inspection of his wound.

"The black is tinted with red dye to mask any injuries I might have. In battle, it confuses and scares my enemies who know they have injured me and yet can't see the blood."

"Hence the invincible devil epitaph they have applied to you?"

He nodded as he took a seat on the edge of her bed and held a clean cloth to his shoulder.

Callie prepared her needle and thread and did her best not to notice just how delectable her husband's body was when bared. The dim light in the room caught against the rich, tawny flesh, making it even more mouthwatering. Och, but the man was handsome.

" 'Tis an interesting trick. Where did you learn it?" she asked, trying to distract herself.

She didn't really expect an answer, so when she got one, it surprised her.

"While I lived with the Saracens. It was one of the lessons they taught me."

Now she understood the strange tactics he'd used to defeat her clansmen. "The fighting you used below— they taught you that as well?"

"Aye."

How strange, for him to be so revealing. Callie took the cloth from his hand and inspected the ravaged skin. Her stomach clenched at the new wound that lanced across skin already scarred from previous injuries. She ran her fingers over him, aching at the thought of what he had already lived through. His hard skin was so warm and his hair brushed against her hand as she prepared his shoulder by cleansing it with a wine-drenched cloth.

Her poor husband.

"How long did you live there?" she asked, trying to distract herself from his lush, muscled skin and the desire she had to kiss it and him.

"Almost five years."

Callie paused. Five years. It was a long time to live among one's enemies. She tried to imagine what it would have been like for her to live in London for that long while yearning to be home. No wonder he had told her he understood her need to return to her family.

Of all men, he knew it on a level she couldn't even begin to fathom.

"Why did you live with them for so long?" she asked as she drew the first stitch.

He tensed only the tiniest bit before he spoke. "I had no choice. I was their slave. Every time I tried to escape, they brought me back."

Her heart lurched at his words. By the ragged note in his voice she could tell they had made him suffer greatly for those attempts at freedom. Her gaze dropped to the long, jagged scars across his back and she wondered how many beatings he must have suffered at their hands.

And he had been just a lad. No older than Dermot. She swallowed as it dawned on her that he would have been even *younger* than Dermot.

She carefully made another stitch. "How did you finally get away?"

"Henry. They sent me to kill him, and as I was sneaking through his camp, I had a thought that if ever I was to have freedom again, Henry would be the only one who could help me. So instead of cutting his throat, I bargained with him."

She tied off her thread and cut it. "I'm still surprised he helped you."

"As was I. I honestly expected him to kill me once I let him up. But I figured either way I would be free."

The horror of it. She couldn't imagine trying to make such a decision. "How old were you?"

"Ten-and-eight."

"You were just a child."

"I was never a child."

Nay, he wasn't. And that was the worst part about all of this. He'd spent the whole of his life as an outsider. Here, in England and in Outremer. She couldn't imagine living like that.

Callie silently stitched the wound on his chest, then looked at his forearms where her sword had cut him. "I'm so sorry for hurting you."

Sin looked up at her words. The sincerity scorched him. "You didn't hurt me."

She alone had never hurt him. Not yet anyway.

He stared at the tendrils of her red curls falling over her shoulders, the gentleness in her green eyes. He felt her unwillingness to hurt him as she touched his skin. It made his entire body burn ferociously, demanding he take her in his arms and ease the ache in both his heart and his loins.

She was so incredible. And he wanted her with a passion so fierce, he wondered if it would destroy him.

She dipped her head down to his, and just as he opened his lips to taste her, a loud commotion filled the air.

People shouted as a group of horses came into the courtyard below.

Callie pulled away instantly, leaving him to curse the interruption while she went to the window to see what was going on. He joined her there and looked out over her shoulder.

In the courtyard below were three riders. Her clansmen and servants were rushing about to welcome them like long-lost family as Aster and Dermot left the castle and offered up a greeting to their guests.

"The MacAllisters are here," Callie said with a note of reverence in her voice.

Sin forced himself not to smile. She had no idea what was in store for her now.

His brother Braden rode his fierce stallion Deamhan, who pawed and stamped at the ground in aggravation at having to stop. The horse and man had much the same temperament.

Braden's long, black hair was tangled by the ride and his dark green and black plaid was worn as haphazardly as ever.

Ewan rode next to him on the back of a roan, while the fair-haired Lochlan swung his leg over his dapple-gray and slid masterfully to the ground.

It was good to see them again.

Callie turned to face him, her cheeks bright. He arched a brow at her exuberance, somewhat stung by it. She seemed happier to see them than she did to be with him.

"I'll go make sure they have food and drink. You dress and I will meet you below."

Sin frowned as she rushed from the room with a light step. He looked back out the window at the cheerful crowd below that warmly welcomed his brothers. Their shouts of greeting rang in his ears as Aster clapped Lochlan on the back like a father welcoming home his beloved son and Dermot laughed with Braden.

He supposed some things never changed.

Callie's heart pounded as she headed down the stairs. A powerful clan, the MacAllisters had once been an ally to her own. But over the last decade, their ties had dwindled. Still, it would be good for her clan to renew the alliance, and since the MacAllister was on such good terms with the English king, mayhap it would help quell the rebels as well.

She reached the hall at the same time Aster was showing the men inside.

Callie paused as she straightened her dress. They were giants all! Standing head and shoulders above her uncle and brother, the MacAllisters made her feel very petite. Only Sin could compete with their height.

"My niece, Caledonia," Aster said, directing their attention to her.

Callie swallowed nervously. The combined effect of the MacAllister brothers on a woman's senses was earth-shattering and quite disconcerting.

The blond man stepped forward. He was devastatingly handsome with stern blue eyes. "Lochlan MacAllister, my lady, 'tis a pleasure to meet you." His deep voice sent a shiver over her.

"My brother Ewan."

She looked to the giant on his left. He was like a large black bear, his hair long and in need of a trim.

"And Braden."

Callie nodded, hiding a smile. He was more handsome than a man had a right to be, and she knew the reputation of this particular MacAllister brother, who was said to be able to slay a man with a single blow and fell a woman with a single kiss.

She smiled at the three of them. " 'Tis a pleasure to meet all of you. Please, come and be seated."

As she led them toward the laird's table, Aster fell in by their sides.

"I'm sorry to have you waste your trip, lads. I had no idea the English intended to send my kin home to me."

"I'm surprised as well," Braden said. "It's not like Henry to give up hostages voluntarily."

"He didn't," Dermot sneered as he walked behind them. "He sent her home with a Sassenach husband."

"Is it anyone we know?" Braden asked.

"Doubtful," Aster answered. "I've never heard of him. Callie, isn't he an earl?"

"Aye, Uncle."

Lochlan raised a brow. "Earl of what?"

Callie paused as she realized she didn't know. No one had ever mentioned his properties to her. "I'm not really sure. But I was told he has vast holdings."

Callie stood to the side of the table, ready to see to the men's needs. The servants entered with ale and platters of meat and bread at the same time Simon joined them. He approached the table with his kind, open honesty that she found so very charming.

The MacAllister brothers watched him suspiciously as he neared her.

"The MacAllisters?" Simon asked.

Callie nodded.

Simon approached them. His smile widened and

his eyes gleamed in instant friendship. He looked like a man greeting old friends he hadn't seen in a long time. "I feel as if I already know the three of you."

Braden stared at him with a stern frown. "You are?"

"Simon of Ravenswood. And you would have to be Braden."

"I don't know any Ravenswood. How did you know me?"

"Youngest and full of mischief." He turned to Lochlan. "You would be Lochlan, who never met a rule he didn't love. Always steadfast and ready to lay your life down for any member of your family or clan." Then he looked at Ewan. "And you are the quiet one. Serious and short-tempered, ever ready to battle. Oh, the stories I've heard about the three of you."

The brothers exchanged nervous glances.

"Heard from whom?" Lochlan asked.

"From me, you worthless lickspittle. So tell me what miracle dragged the three of you from your holes and got your lazy hides all the way here. And a day early, no less."

Everyone in the hall froze at the harsh words.

No one with any sense would ever dare insult a single MacAllister, never mind the three of them at once.

Gasping, Callie turned her attention to the entranceway, where Sin stood, dressed in his armor, with this arms crossed over his chest. She could read nothing in his features. He merely stood there stoically as he regarded the men he'd just insulted.

Aster bellowed in rage. "How dare you insult my guests!" He turned to her with a glower. "You see the peace he brings?"

The three MacAllisters rose slowly to their feet. Like a giant wall, they moved in unison around the table toward her husband.

Callie swallowed while she saw Dermot's amused smile. Her brother was looking forward to this confrontation.

She crossed herself.

As soon as the brothers were in arm's reach of Sin, they laughed and swarmed him.

She stood in stunned shock as the MacAllister brothers grabbed Sin into hugs and he bristled, cursed, and slapped at their hands.

"Ow!" Sin snapped. "Let me go, you damned ogres."

"Have your burns not healed?" Lochlan asked with a worried frown.

"Aye, they have, but I've a new wound throbbing, and if you don't stop, you'll have it bleeding again."

"New one how?" Braden asked, his frown mirroring Lochlan's as he pulled at Sin's clothes as if looking for the wound. "What happened? Have you seen a physician for it?"

A loud whistle rent the air.

The men stopped talking and everyone turned to look at Callie.

"Would someone please tell me what is going on here?"

Ewan passed a disgruntled glare at her. "We happen to be saying hello to our wayward brother. If you don't mind, we don't get to see him much."

Callie's jaw went as slack as her uncle's and Dermot's. Nay . . .

Had she heard that correctly? If it were true, why had Sin never bothered mentioning it to her?

Why on earth would he hide something like that?

Crossing the room, she confronted her husband. "You're a MacAllister?"

There was a pain so profound in his eyes that it made her breath catch.

Lochlan stiffened. "Of course he is." Then he saw the look on Sin's face, too, and under his breath she heard him speak to him. "Regardless of the past, you have always been a MacAllister."

A tic started in Sin's jaw and when he spoke, his tone was equally as low. He cut a harsh glare to Lochlan. "If you recall, I was very publicly denounced. Twice."

She saw the shame on Lochlan's face as he dropped his troubled gaze to the floor.

Aster approached them. "Are you telling me this lad is a Highlander? Henry married my niece to a MacAllister?"

"*You* married her?" Braden gasped in disbelief. "*You?*"

Sin snorted. "Makes you want to run for cover before the Apocalypse strikes, doesn't it?"

Braden shoved him good-naturedly.

"Ow," Sin said again, shoving at Braden's hand. "I told you I was wounded. What are you going to do next, break out the saltcellar and rub it in?"

This was the first time since she'd met him that she truly saw her husband relaxed and unguarded. There was even an air of good humor about him.

Ewan grabbed her up and hugged her hard. "Welcome to the family," he said, planting a kiss on her cheek.

"Put her down before you hurt her," Sin snapped.

Ewan growled at him and refused to release her. "Now, lass, why would you be wanting to marry his surly hide when you had me and Lochlan to choose from?"

"Because you didn't ask her," Sin said wryly.

"Aye, well, I might have, had I seen her first."

"Well, you didn't. Now put my wife down."

Ewan set her back on her feet, then winked at her. "Possessive of her. Now, that's a good sign."

"Aye," Sin concurred, "but a bad omen for you if you don't be keeping your hands off her."

Lochlan laughed. "You talk like that, *braither,* and I can almost hear the burr in your voice."

Sin scoffed at him. "Wishful thinking on your part."

"You know," Braden said, indicating Simon with the tilt of his head, "we still don't know why he knows so much about us."

Sin stepped back and pulled Simon forward to meet his brothers. "He was one of my foster brothers."

"You must be the one who annoyed him on my behalf," Braden said, offering Simon his arm. "I hope you did a good job of it."

Simon shook arms with him. "I certainly tried to, anyway."

The men laughed as Aster herded them back toward the table. Callie watched and listened to the brothers and marveled in the changes their presence had on her husband.

With them here, she was hoping to corner one of his brothers and find out more about why her husband was so unwilling to accept her.

Most of all, she wanted to know why Sin hadn't bothered to tell her he was a Scot.

Chapter 11

The men sat for hours bantering and laughing. Callie listened, her heart warmed by their affection for one another. The MacAllisters even accepted Simon into their midst, and unlike her clansmen, they had no problem whatsoever with his English breeding.

She learned much of their past, including a lot of information about their brother Kieran who had killed himself. But she learned very little about Sin. It was almost as if they knew his past hurt him and so they sought only to mention tiny slices of it.

It was the wee hours of the night before they decided to find their beds. Callie yawned as she showed the men where they were to sleep.

At last she found herself headed to her room to be alone with her husband.

Sin was still smiling.

"You're very handsome when you do that."

"Do what?"

"Smile."

He frowned at her words.

"Here, now, I didn't mean to make you stop."

He cast a reluctant look to the bed, then moved away from her.

"Why didn't you tell me you were a MacAllister?" she asked quietly.

"Because I'm not."

Her frown matched his as she tried to sort it out. He definitely wasn't related through his mother. "I don't understand."

He sighed as he unbelted his sword and set it aside. "My father sired me the first year of his marriage. He was away from home, visiting a friend in London without his wife, and for whatever reason, my mother caught his fancy. She was scarce more than a girl back then, and they tell me his accent and wild ways enchanted her. I was conceived in the back of a barn in a manner my mother assured me was most humiliating and painful for her.

"As soon as she bore me, she sent me and my wet nurse to Scotland to live with my father. An old servant who was there that night told me that my stepmother took one look at me and was so distraught she almost miscarried Lochlan."

He spoke the words calmly and without emotion. Even so, it had to hurt him deep in his heart and soul. There was no way it couldn't.

She wanted to go to him and offer comfort, but was afraid if she tried he would stop talking. So she listened quietly, while her heart broke a little more with every word he uttered.

"From that moment on, my father wanted nothing to do with me. He ignored me every time I tried to speak to him. If I approached him, he turned his back and walked away.

"To my stepmother, I was nothing but a painful reminder of my father's infidelity. She despised everything about me. Because of his guilt and shame over what he'd done, my father went out of his way to prove to his wife that he bore no special favor toward me. My brothers had the best of everything and I had whatever was left over."

She swallowed against the tears that choked her, but she refused to let him see them. "He sent you back to England to be with your mother?"

"He tried, once, when I was seven. It was the middle of winter." He paused and leaned with one arm against the mantel to stare at the fire as if recalling the event. He looked so lost, standing there with his raw hurt etched plainly along the lines of his handsome face. Callie didn't know how she maintained the strength to keep herself from going to him. Perhaps it was the strength of him that held her together and allowed her to just listen as he told a story she was sure he had never told before.

When he spoke again, she heard the hidden agony inside his heart. "I remember being so cold the entire way. My father had sent next to no coin with us and the knight who was taking us to my mother would rent a room for himself and leave us to the stable or barn."

Callie cringed at the dispassionate way he spoke.

"My nurse kept telling me that my mother would be delighted to see me. She assured me that all mothers loved their children and that my mother would treat me just as Aisleen treated my brothers. She said my mother would grab me up in her arms and kiss me home."

Callie closed her eyes to stave off the sympathetic pain inside her. Knowing his mother as she did, she could well imagine his reception.

"We arrived on Christmas Eve. There were presents strewn about, and my nurse led me across the great hall to where my mother sat at the lord's table with a baby boy in her lap. She held him so lovingly as she laughed and teased him. I was joy-filled at the sight and thought that at last I would have the mother I had yearned for. That she would see me standing there in my worn-out shoes and tattered plaid, and hug me close and tell me how glad she was to have me there at last."

Callie felt a tear slide down her face and she was glad he wasn't looking at her to see it.

"When my nurse told her who I was and why we were there, she shrieked in outrage. Angrily, she threw her wine in my face and said that she only had one son and that I was never again to disgrace her with my presence. Then she had us thrown out into the cold night."

Sin took a deep, ragged breath as he continued to watch the fire. It was as if he refused to look at her for fear she, too, would reject him.

He lifted one foot to kick a piece of wood back into the grate. "I knew then that there was no such thing as a family for me. I was neither Scot nor English. I was nothing but a homeless bastard. Unwanted. Useless. My nurse returned me to my father, and his contempt for me grew until the day when King David's men came for a son. They wanted hostages to send to

King Stephen in England to ensure that no more Scots would raid his lands or attack his people."

"So he sent you."

He nodded. "Aisleen told him if he sent one of her sons, she would kill herself. Not that she needed to say it. All of us boys knew who was going to be sent." He laughed bitterly. "It was the only time in my entire life my father had ever looked at me or spoken to me."

Sin wiped a hand across his face as if thinking about the past made him weary. "My father and I passed angry words, and in the end he grabbed me by my shirt and shoved me into the hands of David's men. He said I was never to be welcomed into his home again, and as far as he was concerned I no longer existed."

Her tears fell freely as Callie tried to imagine the horror that had been his life. Never wanted, never loved. No wonder he was so distant with her.

Worse, she thought about how her clan had greeted his brothers after the way they had treated him and Simon. The way she herself had left his side to see to his brothers' needs while he had been left up here with a fresh wound. Alone.

He was always alone.

Dear Lord, how she wished she could go back and change this afternoon. He had been pushed aside more than anyone ever should. And she ached for him. She wept for the way he'd been treated, and in her heart she knew she would never be able to let him leave her and walk alone again.

"I will always want you with me, Sin."

He curled his lips at that and pushed himself away

from the hearth. "Don't mock me," he snarled angrily. "I don't need your pity."

Nay, what he needed was her love. But he had lived so long without anyone's love that she wondered if it was too late for him. Maybe there was such a thing as being too strong.

"It's not pity I feel for you." She moved to touch his arm. To her amazement, he didn't move away. She ran her hand gently over the biceps of his uninjured side and up to his face, until she forced him to look at her and see the sincerity of her eyes. "You are my husband, Sin, sworn before God. I will always be here for you."

Sin swallowed at her words, unable to fathom them, unable to believe she really meant them. It was a game she was playing with him, and he could only guess why she would want to do this to him.

He stared at the floor as he remembered the times in his life he had deceived himself. The times he had lain beaten by Harold, thinking that his father had only been angry at him when he had sent him away. That if he was a good enough lad and did as the English asked and spoke no angry words to Harold, that he would be allowed to go home as King Stephen had promised. That his father would welcome him back with open arms.

In the end, his father had continued to shun him. His father's letter to Henry hadn't even borne Sin's name upon it. It bore no reference to him as a son at all. It had been cold. Harsh. A final rejection that still resonated in his heart.

He remembered the sting of the Saracen whips, the

beatings he'd endured during his training. The only thing that kept him sane was the belief that if he could escape them and get back to England, all would be right. His mother's people would surely welcome him back into their fold.

And yet, after Henry returned him to London, he had been sneered at, hated and feared. They had treated him worse than a leper, worse than a heretic.

Not even God Himself could love something like you. The pope's condemnation rang in his ears.

Nay, he was still that little boy who had stood before his mother on Christmas Eve with his heart full of hopeful longing. What had he ever gotten for such foolish dreams?

Nothing but more ridicule. Nothing but more hurt.

His heart had withered and died years ago from lack of use. If he opened himself up to Callie now, he was sure she would betray him.

It was the only thing in life he counted on. The only thing that was a certainty.

Reluctantly, he removed her hand from his face. " 'Tis late. You need to go to bed."

"Where will you sleep?"

"On the floor before the hearth."

Callie's lip quivered as she fought against the tears inside her. Her frustration mounted. How she wished she knew a way to reach him. To make him believe in her. In them.

But he had shut himself off from her again.

She watched as he removed his surcoat and armor. His tawny shoulders gleaming in the firelight, he took a pelt from the bed and lay down to cuddle with his sword. She clenched her fists at her sides, wanting to choke him for his stubbornness.

What was it going to take to reach this man?

Whenever you fail to win them over, lass, then mayhap you should partake of their leisure. Her father's words rang in her head, giving her the inspiration she needed.

She undressed until she wore nothing but her thin underkirtle, then she grabbed a pillow from the bed.

Sin listened to his wife moving about as he stared into the fire in the grate. He wanted nothing more than to join her in her bed. To go over there and pull her into his arms and finally experience the only piece of heaven a man like him could ever hope for.

But then, he was used to disappointment.

Suddenly a pillow was placed against the back of his head. Frowning, he leaned back to see Callie making a pallet behind him.

"What are you doing?"

She shrugged as she sat on the floor and pulled his blanket over her. "I am being Ruth. I am making my bed where my husband is. If you won't join me in my bed, then I will join you in yours."

"You're being ridiculous."

"*I* am?" She leaned up on one elbow to stare at him. "It seems to me ridiculous is lying on a cold, cobbled floor when you have a comfortable bed waiting for you just a few feet away."

He closed his eyes, unable to deal with her and the raw emotions that were still churning inside him. He'd told her things tonight that he had never spoken of before. No one, not even his brothers, had ever known what his mother had said or done to him that night.

He was weak and he was tired and all he wanted was respite from his past.

"Go to bed, Callie."

She didn't. She merely snuggled down beside him and continued talking. "Why? Did I do something wrong on our wedding night? Did I displease you somehow?"

Sin choked as he remembered just how warm and welcoming she had been then, too. She'd never done anything to displease him. Not until this moment when she refused to do as he asked. "Nay. I was not displeased."

"Then why won't you make love to me?"

An image of her naked and hot in his arms scorched him. His body roared to life over her handful of words. She was the first woman to beg him for his favor. It was erotic and sensual, and it made him burn. "I can't believe I'm having this discussion with you."

"Fine, then, no discussion. You lie there with your wounded shoulder and just pretend I don't exist. Which you're very good at, by the way."

The hurt in her voice stung him. He didn't want to hurt her. All he wanted was for her to leave him alone. Just leave him to the little bit of tranquillity his beleaguered soul could find.

"Callie, it's not you. Why can't you just accept the fact that I am a faithless, worthless bastard and leave me in peace?"

"Like everyone else does?"

"Aye."

She sat up and leaned over him. Her breasts rubbed against his arm, making his shaft jerk in response to her innocent touch. Her unadorned beauty held him transfixed as her coppery curls tumbled around her face and the firelight gleamed in her green eyes. Her cheeks were pink from her anger and she narrowed a hard glare at him.

"Because I don't believe you're faithless and I know you're not worthless. As for being a bastard, that was hardly your fault." She rested her chin on his biceps and stared at him with a hunger in her eyes he found unbelievable. How could this woman want anything to do with him?

"I would love you, husband, if you would let me."

Those words . . .

They tore him apart and left him so vulnerable to her. He didn't dare trust in them. He knew better.

"And if I did? What of your family? Are you willing to leave them behind forever? Do you honestly believe for one minute they would accept an Englishman into their hearts?"

"You're not English, you're a Scot."

"Nay. I was born in England, and for the most part raised there. I was cast out of Scotland and told never to return. I hate being in this place more than you can ever understand, and the first chance I get to go back to London, I will take it. Will you be willing to stay with me then?"

Her eyes snapped angrily as she thought about that horrible place. "I despise London. The filth and stench. And they hate me there."

"Then you *do* understand how I feel here."

Callie's breath caught at his words. Dear saints,

she did know. That horrendous agony that had clenched her heart day after day as she feared she would never see her beloved Highlands again. It had been unbearable.

"Why did you marry me?" she asked quietly, half afraid of the answer he would give.

"Because I knew no other way to get you home. I saw what the others did to Jamie, how they treated and scorned him. He's a good lad with a good heart. I didn't want him to become like me. So, I brought you back here before it was too late for the two of you."

Callie froze at the wealth of emotion that overwhelmed her. In that moment, she knew she loved him. There was no doubt. The fierceness of the emotion ripped through her, filled her and made her want to take him into her arms and hold him for eternity.

This man, so strong, so full of pain, who could look beyond himself and still help others even though no one had ever helped him. It amazed her. It scared her, but most of all it touched her profoundly.

She ran her hand along the edge of his jaw. "I am going to make you want to stay here with me."

His eyes turned dull. "I assure you, you can't."

"Is that a challenge?"

"Nay, dove. Merely a statement of fact."

Maybe in his mind, but in her heart it was a challenge, and Callie loved a good challenge. Somehow, some way, she was going to break through his defenses and find the heart inside him. She would make him want to stay. She would be what he needed and how he needed it.

No matter what.

Sin rolled over and gave her his back. He expected her to get up. She didn't.

Instead, she settled down behind him and traced the scars along his back. It was such a strange sensation, to have her hand giving him pleasure over the things that had brought him such tremendous pain.

When she leaned forward and placed her lips over the arrow wound, he trembled. His body burned with desire for her. It would be so easy at this moment to roll over, take her into his arms and plant himself deep inside her. To ease the ache between his legs with her body.

He swore he could already feel her breasts in his hands again. Taste the sweetness of her skin.

But it was a fool's dream.

There was no safety in this world. No happiness for someone like him. Love was for other men. Men who were lucky and blessed. Men who knew how to love someone.

Tonight, though, he felt his loneliness on a level he'd never experienced before. He was cold. Empty and aching.

And all he wanted was respite from the pain inside him.

Before he realized what he was doing, he rolled over to look at her. Her eyes were so gentle that they warmed the cold place inside him. When she reached up to place her fingers against his lips, he felt his resistance to her shatter.

How could she be so open and giving?

He would never understand this woman.

She opened her lips in invitation to him. And without thought, he took it.

Callie moaned at the taste of him as he pulled her forcefully into his arms. His kiss was one of pure passion and of longing, and it stole her breath. She felt him fist his hand in the back of her kirtle as he pressed her closer to his body. He plundered her mouth as if it held all the treasure of the earth and he was desperate for it.

His arms clutched at her as his tongue danced with hers in a heated, intense rhythm that made her breathless and weak.

Heaven help her, but she wanted this man. It didn't matter to her what crimes he had committed. What he had done to survive the horrors of his past. All that mattered was the way he touched her heart.

He made her laugh, made her feel needed and desirable. Most of all, he made her feel like a woman. He awoke something deep inside her. A part of her she'd never known existed.

When she looked into his eyes, she could see the future. See the children she wanted to birth and the home she wanted to make for all of them.

Sin couldn't fathom why he didn't shove her away from him. He should. It would be the noble thing to do. But then, he and nobility were strangers. He was a beast who knew nothing save basic survival skills.

He only knew how to protect himself from harm.

And yet, when he looked at her, he could only think of being the man she needed. Of holding her close for the rest of eternity.

How he wished there were some way he could erase his past and be the kind of man a woman like this deserved.

"I want you, Sin," she breathed against his lips.

God help him, he couldn't resist that plea.

But he wouldn't take her here on the floor with no regard for her comfort. Animal he might be, but she was a gentle-born lady.

Against her protests, he picked her up in his arms and carried her to her bed.

"You're hurting your shoulder," she said, holding him tight so as to present as little weight in his arms as she could.

"You don't weigh enough to hurt me."

She looked doubtful as he laid her back against the feather mattress, her hands resting gently on his shoulders. The softness of her touch singed him, and Sin took a moment to savor the sight of her, warm and waiting for him. She lay there with her green eyes staring up at him as if he were all the things he'd ever wanted to be.

In her eyes, he was noble. Decent. Heroic. He was the man he'd always wanted to be.

He should leave. He knew it. He had no business doing this with her.

Yet he couldn't leave. He doubted if anything on this earth or beyond could get him out of this room tonight.

Callie saw the look in his tormented eyes and for a moment she thought he would pull away from her.

Instead, he untied his laces, removed his chausses and joined her in the bed. She shivered at the sight of his naked body lying beside hers.

His power and lithe grace was overwhelming. Her body ached and burned for his. She throbbed with a need she barely understood. All she knew was that she wanted him. She wanted to feel him inside her and share herself with him, to let him take whatever comfort or solace he could.

He lifted his hand to the laces of her kirtle and slowly opened the neck of it until she was bared to his hungry gaze. Callie shivered at the dark, intense look on his face as he stared at her naked breasts.

She moaned as he trailed his hand over her tight, swollen nipples as if savoring the sight and feel of them before he took one in to his palm and gently squeezed. She hissed at the pleasurable sensation and her body melted. She was so hot and wet for him, aching with her need and with her heart.

Callie wanted to claim his body, too, to touch him in ways she hoped no other woman had ever touched him. Tonight he would be hers and she intended to do whatever it took to make him understand just what a hero he was to her.

He buried his lips against her throat, his breath branding her with heat. She'd been so drunk the last time that she could barely recall him. But this . . . this was vivid. Vivid and hot, and she was filled with fear and curiosity.

She explored his body with her hands and delighted in the lean, masculine planes and dips. He was so hard and firm compared to her. His cheeks were scratchy from his whiskers. And the manly scent of him sent her reeling.

Sin shook from the force of his raw emotions. She touched him on levels he'd never known existed. As he looked into her eyes, he saw heaven itself. No woman had ever touched him like this. He'd never allowed himself such a comfort.

Never dared hope to possess it.

She was so giving to him. He drank the tenderness from her lips and tasted the goodness that was innate to her and so missing from him. She was an angel, and when he looked at her, he could almost believe in such things as heaven.

Rolling over, he pulled her on top of him so that he could cup her face in his hands and just stare into those precious green eyes and the promises they held.

Dare he believe them?

She moved her head and kissed his open palm. The gesture shook him. His heart pounding, he watched as she kissed her way up his arm to his lips.

Closing his eyes, he pulled her kirtle over her head, and relished the feel of her naked body against his. Tonight, he would do what he had never done before. He would open himself up to her and pray that on the morrow she wouldn't despise him for it.

Callie moaned at the heat of his body under hers. Desire swept through her. She hated that she had no memory of him from their wedding night. No memory of holding him in her arms.

He gently rolled her over and placed himself between her legs. She felt the hairs of his legs rubbing against her inner thighs as he kissed her, his hard shaft resting against her thigh.

It was such a strange feeling, to be so exposed to him. And yet it was so natural that they would share themselves. She reached up and ran her hands along his cheeks to bury them in his hair as she saw the needful hunger in his eyes.

"I am so glad you are my husband," she breathed.

Pain and ecstasy mixed in his dark eyes as he stared at her as if unable to believe he'd heard her.

He looked as if he were dreaming and terrified of waking.

His muscles rippling beneath her hands, he pressed the tip of his shaft against her core.

Callie held her breath. After tonight, there would be no forgetting the feel of her husband.

He brushed his hand against her cheek. His eyes held hers as mutual understanding and care passed between them. It was a priceless moment of sharing and it went a long way in giving her hope for them.

Then he dipped his head and claimed her lips in a passionate, fiery kiss. He drove himself deep inside her body.

She tensed as pain overrode her pleasure.

He froze.

"I'm sorry," Sin whispered. "Does it hurt much?"

Callie swallowed and shook her head. The pain was already subsiding into a dull ache as her body stretched to accommodate the large size of him. It had just startled her. Since she had already lost her maidenhead, she'd expected tonight to be free of pain. At least that was what she'd been told.

He braced himself on his arms to look down at her. Callie stared up at his face and the concern in his eyes as she felt him deep and hard inside her body. He was so incredibly handsome.

"I am fine, Sin," she said, offering him a timid smile. It was so very intimate, to look at him while they were joined this way.

With every breath he took, she could feel him throbbing inside her. Feel him rigid and hard all over and in her.

Instinctively, she moved her hips, drawing him in

deeper as her muscles tightened around his shaft. He growled in response, and a look of such pleasure crossed his face that it spurred her to bolder actions as she writhed beneath him.

Sin held his breath at the sight of her lying beneath him while she milked his body with hers. He held himself rigidly still, even though it was killing him. He wanted her to want him, not to fear the desires of her own body.

She should take as much pleasure from this night as he did. More so, in fact. And he loved watching her discover her sexual power and bliss as he did the same.

Growling at how good she felt, he thrust himself deeper into her. They hissed in unison.

Never once had he dreamed making love could be like this. Never had he dared to hope of a night where he could be with a woman so unreservedly and know that she was with him by her own free will.

Her red curls fanned out on either side of her face, reminding him of some beautiful fey creature who had stumbled upon him and claimed him with her magic. And she felt so good surrounding him. Surely there was no better pleasure than her warmth.

She ran her hands over his chest, up his arms and brushed them through his hair.

He lowered himself to her and gathered her into his arms. Then, slowly, very slowly, he began to gently rock himself between her thighs.

Callie sighed in pleasure at the feel of him so deep, hard and strong inside her. How could she have forgotten this? She wrapped her arms around him and listened to his rapid breathing as he moved.

Arching her back to draw him in even deeper, she

kissed his uninjured shoulder and inhaled the scent of him. He quickened his thrusts, sliding himself in and out of her, deeper and deeper. Her head spun from the sensations of his skin on hers, of his breath against her neck.

She breathed his name as she clung to him and met him stroke for stroke. Her body felt out of control. She was hot and tingly. And just as she was sure she would die from the pleasure of him, her body erupted into an ecstasy so intense that she screamed from it.

Sin ground his teeth at the sensation of her body gripping his while he kissed her deeply. Holding her tighter, he felt his own body release. With one last forceful thrust, he buried himself deep inside her and felt the waves of pleasure rippling through him as he gave her a part of him he'd never given another single soul.

He lay completely still, holding her for what seemed an eternity, and yet it seemed no time at all.

"Is it always like that?" she asked, her voice awed.

Sin drew a ragged breath as he drifted down from heaven, back into his body. "I don't know."

He tensed as soon as the words left his lips.

She looked at him curiously. "Don't know or you won't tell me?"

He started to cover the slip with a lie, and yet he couldn't bring himself to do it. Nay, he wouldn't lie to her. Not after she had given so much.

Embarrassed, he looked away. "I've never been with a woman before tonight."

Callie was shocked by his confession. How could that be? She'd heard numerous rumors of his sexual conquests from other women in London.

Of course, she'd also heard that he ate small children every morn, and had horns that sprouted from his forehead whenever he neared a church.

"What of our wedding night?" she asked.

"You passed out before we finished."

"But the blood that was on me and in my bed—where did it come from?"

"It was mine. I didn't think you'd want to suffer the humiliation of Henry's physicians examining you and finding you virgin, so I opened up one of the cuts on my arms and used the blood to shield you."

The full depth of his loneliness slammed into her. Dear saints, he had never been intimate even on the most basic level with another person.

It was unheard of for a man of his stature and prowess to remain untouched.

"I can't believe you haven't—"

"What kind of craven bastard do you think I am?" he asked, his eyes angry. "After all I have been through in my life, think you I would *ever* take a chance on leaving behind a baby to a woman who would hate it because of my actions? I would sooner have died celibate than learn a child of mine was in this world suffering because I was a selfish ass who couldn't control myself."

And yet he had taken a chance with her. After tonight, it was quite possible that she could have his child inside her. Which meant that he trusted her, at least on some level.

Touched by his words, she pulled him into her arms.

Sin held her close and hoped in his heart that he was sterile. He hoped there would be no issue from this night. He couldn't stand the thought of a child being born to the hardship and heartaches of this world.

He never should have touched her. It was wrong and he wished the arrow that afternoon had pierced his heart. He should have let her family defeat him and returned to England.

He should have done anything other than make love to her.

And yet even as these thoughts whirled through his mind, he looked into her angelic face and saw what he had waited a lifetime for.

All he had to do was find the courage to take it.

To his chagrin, he who had stood strong and alone all his life was now a coward who was terrified of a mere woman. Because she did scare him. She and these unknown feelings inside him. When he looked at her, all those long-buried dreams surfaced and made him wish for things he had no right to wish for. Home. Family . . . love.

Be grateful for what you have, boy. All bastards like you are fit for is wiping the asses of your betters. Harold's angry voice tore through him.

Unable to breathe, he reluctantly withdrew from her, got up and dressed.

"Sin?"

The sound of her voice sliced through him. He paused at the door, torn between the need inside him to return to bed and take her into his arms and hold her forever, and the fear of her eventual rejection that made him want to bolt like a frightened animal.

For the first time in his life, he chose retreat. "I'll be back in a minute."

With no direction, Sin headed down to the great hall, where he found his brother Ewan still sitting at the table, drinking ale alone.

"Why are you still awake?" Sin asked as he took the vacant seat next to his brother.

Ewan drained the cup and poured more. "I'm not dead with exhaustion yet. You?"

"Same."

Sin grabbed a cup and poured it full.

Ewan grunted at him as Sin downed the contents in one gulp. "What a pair we make, eh?"

Sin poured another goblet full. "How so?"

"Both of us tormented by our pasts."

Sin fell silent as more memories surged. He knew the guilt and pain of his brother. Knew how much the past wore on Ewan's battered conscience. "Thinking of Kieran tonight?"

Ewan nodded. "Every night. His face haunts me each time I try to sleep."

"Aye, I well understand. I see the men I've killed." He took another swig of ale. "I never knew most of their names."

"That would be easier than knowing you killed your own brother."

Sin pushed his chair back so that he could level a glare at Ewan. "Kieran killed himself."

"Aye, over what *I* did to him."

"It's still not your fault." Ewan had been nothing more than the pawn of a beautiful woman who had possessed no heart. Kieran had made his own decision and poor Ewan had been left behind to suffer for both their actions.

Sin felt for him and would give anything to alleviate Ewan's pain. But he doubted if there was enough time in infinity to ease his brother's heart.

Ewan started to pour more ale, then tossed the goblet over his shoulder and drank from the pitcher instead. "Damned cups are never large enough," he muttered. He tilted his head to look at Sin. "So, why are you here, when you have such a beautiful bride warming your bed?"

That was an easy question to answer. "Because I'm a hypocritical fool."

"Well, at least you know it."

Sin smiled wryly. "You know, I'm thinking tonight that I owe Braden an apology."

"For what?"

"Words I said to him while we were in MacDouglas territory with Maggie. I'm finding it much easier to give advice than to live it."

Ewan frowned. "Remember, brother, that I am drunk and none of that made a bit of sense to my fogged mind."

Sin took a deep breath. "I told Braden that he should take a chance with Maggie and find out if they were meant to be together. Now I find myself unable to live up to those words."

"You want to take a chance with Maggie?"

Sin tossed a small loaf of bread at his brother. "Why don't you go to bed and sleep it off?"

"I will eventually. Not drunk enough yet."

Sin arched a brow at that. The entire time he'd stayed in Scotland with his brothers while he healed his burn wounds, he'd noted how often Ewan stayed up well into the night, drinking alone. "Tell me, does Lochlan know how much you drink?"

"No one knows. Not even me."

Sin grabbed Ewan's arm before his brother could take another drink. "Maybe you should refrain some."

Ewan growled and shrugged his hold off. "Since you can't live by your own advice, then don't try to be giving it to me."

Sin shook his head as Ewan finished off the entire pitcher, then got up to find more.

Ewan had believed Isobail ingen Kaid had loved him. First he had fought Kieran to possess her, even to the point where they had almost killed each other over her, then Ewan had defied their father and brothers to run away and marry her.

Before Ewan could marry her, she'd run off with another man and left him all alone in northern England. Heartbroken, Ewan had returned home to find his family mourning the death of Kieran, who had committed suicide the day Ewan had left with Isobail.

The double blow had ruined Ewan.

Ewan had taken that chance for happiness and he had ended up embittered and alone, living in a cave in the hills with no one to care or notice how much ale he consumed.

Sometimes the chance for happiness wasn't worth taking.

Sin stared at his own cup. He could count his pleasant memories on the fingers of one hand. Happiness had always been beyond his reach.

He was a fool to think otherwise.

His heart heavy, he knew he couldn't keep Caledonia for his own. Come the morrow, he would concentrate on finding the rebels and then he would leave her.

Surely the pope would grant her an annulment. The man hated him with enough venom to gladly dissolve a marriage that should never have been.

Aye, he would set her free. It was the only decent thing for an indecent man to do.

Chapter 12

By midmorning of the next day, Sin was painfully aware of the fact that this might be the first time in his life he would actually fail his mission. None of Callie's people would speak to him. The instant he approached, they stubbornly set their jaws and hastened away.

Not that they were the first to treat him that way. But if he were to find the ones responsible for the attacks, he would need them to at least open their mouths in his presence.

He sat in the hall with his brothers and Simon, eating while he told them of his morning misadventure.

"Well," Braden said, "if you'd take to wearing Scot's clothes it would help. It's hard to warm up to a cold English knight."

Lochlan froze at his youngest brother's thoughtless words. Unlike Ewan and Braden, he knew the reason Sin disdained Scots attire. In his mind, he saw his father returning from the Kilgarigon fair with matching plaid cloth for him and his sons.

Braden had still been in swaddling. Their mother had wrapped the infant up in a portion of green and black plaid, while he, Kieran and Ewan had proudly donned plaids that matched their father's.

"There's my boys," his father had announced proudly as he looked them over and ruffled their hair.

Lochlan had been smiling until he caught sight of Sin in a corner. In their excitement, they had forgotten all about him, and as he typically did, Sin had withdrawn into the shadows, where he stood sullenly with his arms crossed over his chest.

Lochlan would never forget the look on his older brother's face as Sin watched them. Sin's young eyes had been filled with envy and pain.

Lochlan had turned to their father. "Da? Where is Sin's plaid?"

His father had ignored the question and continued to play with Ewan and Kieran.

His young mother had not been so kind. "Plaid cloth is for people of true Scots blood, Lochlan. They are not for half-blooded Sassenachs."

If he lived forever, Lochlan would never understand his mother's cruelty toward Sin. Nor his father's complete lack of regard.

He had found Sin later that day, alone in their room. Sin had been sitting in the middle of the floor with his arm cut open while he let blood trail from the wound into a bowl.

Horrified, Lochlan had run to him and covered the wound with a cloth to stop the bleeding. "What are you doing?" he'd asked.

"I'm trying to get rid of the English blood in me, but it doesn't look any different than yours." Sin's eyes had been hollow and empty. "How can I make it go away when I can't find the difference?"

Lochlan had bandaged Sin's arm, and they had never again spoken of that moment. But it had haunted Lochlan ever since.

Now Lochlan looked to Sin, who sat beside Simon. In truth, Sin's strength awed him.

"I'll not ever put another plaid on my body," Sin said to Braden.

"I'll do it," Simon volunteered cheerfully while he ate. "What the hell? I even have the red hair for it."

Lochlan smiled, even though he still ached with the pain of his memory. "I think we need to adopt Simon as an official MacAllister. What say you, brothers?"

Braden nodded. "I think he fits right in. Ewan?"

"I would nod, but my head hurts too much for it."

Sin snorted. "Given how much ale you consumed last night, I'm amazed you can even sit upright."

"How much did you drink last night?" Lochlan asked, suddenly concerned.

"Somewhere between too much and not enough."

Lochlan rolled his eyes, wishing he knew what to do to return Ewan to the man he'd been before Isobail had changed him.

"Back to the rebels," Lochlan said, trying to focus on an issue he could actually help with. "If they're no longer raiding Henry's people, why bother?"

Sin looked at him drolly. "Because they could start again at any time."

Suddenly a cry of alarm rang out.

The men ran for the door, with Ewan cursing every

step due to his head. Braden swung the door wide to show an English messenger entering the bailey on the back of a brown stallion.

Sin shook his head at the sight. By the faces of the Scots around the herald, it was obvious he was the only person they welcomed less than they had him.

As soon as the man spotted Sin and Simon, he relaxed a degree. If Sin hadn't been concerned about what brought the man into their midst, the gesture would have amused him, since it was the first time in his memory that anyone had actually been relieved by his presence.

The herald dismounted and brought a sealed parchment to him. "From my Lord Ranulf, who holds the lands of Oxley."

Sin popped the seal and read the message. His vision turned dark with every word he read. "Did he send word to Henry?"

"Aye, milord. And the king sent word that he will be headed this way to inspect the damage himself."

"What is it?" Lochlan asked.

Sin looked up to see his wife approaching them from the direction of the kitchens. He waited until she stood before him before he answered Lochlan's question. "It appears a group of MacNeelys raided Oxley's lands. He lost almost a score of cows and his village was burned to the ground. His people lost all their harvesting and now will be hard-pressed to make it through the winter." He gave Callie a hard stare to make her realize the exact gravity of the situation. "On a nearby tree they found a note saying: *English be gone from Scots soil*. And it was signed, *The MacNeely*."

Callie's face paled. "Aster didn't do that. He would never condone such."

"I know," Sin said sincerely, folding the message back up. "He knows better than to bring down the wrath of Henry on his head."

He looked to the messenger. "Tell your lord I shall personally see to the matter and find the man who did this."

The herald nodded.

"What do you intend to do?" Callie asked.

"I want you to round up every male in your clan over the age of ten-and-four and have them here by day's end. I want to have a word with them."

He wouldn't have thought it possible, but she actually paled even more. "I think that would be most unwise. They might attack you."

Lochlan stiffened. "They attack my brother and they attack us. You let them know that. I doubt there's a man born in your clan who wants to go to war with the MacAllisters."

She nodded. "I will do it."

Sin watched as his wife left to do his bidding. She wore her hair plaited today. Even so, tendrils of it had escaped the tight braids and were curling in a becoming fashion all around her face. As typical, she wore her father's plaid and made quite an appealing sight as she walked across the yard.

And with every step she took that swayed her hips, he felt himself growing harder and harder for her.

"She's beautiful, isn't she?" Lochlan asked.

"Like the first day of spring after a long, harsh winter." The words were out before Sin realized it.

Four pairs of eyes turned to him in astonishment.

"Poetry?" Ewan burst out laughing.

Sin shoved him.

Still, his brothers laughed. "Methinks Sin is smitten," Braden teased. "Lochlan, you'd best fetch a priest and exorcise him."

Sin growled at him. "He'd best fetch a priest to perform Last Rites for you before I kill you."

Braden laughed even harder.

"Oh, come now," Simon said to them. "Let's be kind to poor Sin."

"Thank you, Simon."

"After all, I think 'tis sweet."

Sin groaned as they continued to harass him.

"Sweet!" Lochlan howled. "Oh, aye, like a ferocious little lion cub."

Sin snorted. "I don't want to hear it from a man who parades himself around in a skirt."

His three brothers stiffened.

"Beg pardon?" Ewan asked.

"You heard me." Sin looked to Simon and smiled devilishly. "Now, I ask you, who is sweeter? The man in breeches or the geldings in skirts?"

They lunged for him.

Sin ducked and rolled out from under their feet.

"He's mine!" Ewan snarled.

Sin ran before they could catch him.

Callie looked up as her husband entered the stable behind her. He was running so fast, she barely recognized him. Two seconds after he entered the stable, she saw why.

His brothers and Simon were hot on his heels like a group of children playing chase.

"What is this?" she asked.

Sin ran behind her and put her between him and his brothers. " 'Tis nothing," he said, trying to be nonchalant and failing miserably.

The five men were panting from their exertion.

Lochlan caught his breath first. "Hiding behind a woman, are you? Since when did you turn craven?"

She looked over her shoulder to see the taunting look on Sin's face. "Not hiding. I just don't want to hurt you."

Ewan scoffed. "Aye, like we'd be the ones hurting."

The three MacAllisters lunged, but Callie brought them up short before they could reach her husband. "He is injured."

Braden narrowed his gaze on Sin. "Not half as injured as he's going to be."

Callie spread her arms wide to keep the brothers from her husband. "What is all this about, then?"

Lochlan drew himself up indignantly and appeared to be greatly offended by her question. "He insulted us."

"And so you're going to pummel him?" she asked incredulously.

"Aye," they answered in unison.

She ran her hand over her forehead. Already she could feel an ache there from trying to deal with the hotheaded group. She directed her stare to Lochlan. "And you are laird of what again?" She paused and clucked her tongue. "Oh, I forgot, a respected and feared clan."

Lochlan cleared his throat.

"That's right, my love," Sin said from behind her, "you tell him."

"And you . . ." She turned to face her husband. "King's advisor, was it?" She shook her head at them, even though inside she found their behavior charming and refreshing.

Sin cast them a sullen glare. "They started it."

"Oh, well, that makes it right, then." Tsking, she cast a chiding look to all of them. "Now, children, I have work to be about. What say the five of you make nice and return to your food?"

"My stomach votes for food," Simon said, stepping forward. Something in his demeanor reminded her of a lad trying to make amends for his wrongdoing. "For the record, I wasn't in on this. I was merely an innocent observer."

She fought down her smile. "I am quite sure, Simon, thank you."

He nodded and left.

Reluctantly the MacAllisters followed, but they kept glancing back over their shoulders as if to see if Sin would follow. No doubt, they intended to renew their bloodlust at first chance.

As Sin started to go, Callie caught his hand and pulled him back toward her. She reached up and brushed her hand through his tousled hair. "You know, I think I like this teasing side of you."

Immediately she saw a shadow descend over his eyes. He pulled away, but didn't go far.

"Where were you last night?" she asked. "I know you didn't return to bed."

"I couldn't sleep."

"Why?"

He shrugged.

Callie moved toward him, wanting him to open up

to her again like he'd done last night. "Sin, why must you withdraw from me? I thought we had settled some of this last night."

Sin swallowed as he saw the hurt in her eyes. He wanted desperately to reach out, pull her into his arms and kiss her until they were both blind from the pleasure of it. He wanted to feel himself inside her again. To hold her for the rest of eternity . . . and yet he dare not.

This morning had taught him well the depth of her clan's hatred for him. They would never accept him and he would never ask her to leave them. They were her family, and though she might call him that, too, he didn't believe it.

She barely knew him.

She'd spent her life caring for her clan, having them care for her. There was a bond between her and her people he refused to shatter.

What the two of them had . . .

It was unlike anything he'd ever experienced, but that didn't really mean much to a man who had seldom had anything at all.

It was lust he felt for her. Petty and sordid. There was nothing more to it. He was incapable of anything better than that and he knew it.

"I'd best be getting back to my brothers."

Callie sighed wistfully as her husband left. He hadn't bothered to answer her.

"How can you stand to let that Sassenach touch you?"

She gasped in startled alarm as she heard Dermot's voice from the loft above. She looked up, trying to see him through the breaks in the wooden planks, but couldn't find him. "What are you doing up there, Dermot MacNeely?"

She heard a soft, girlish giggle, followed by him shushing the lass. Callie's face flamed at the thought of what they had overheard and what the two of them had been doing up there.

Dermot jumped down from the loft. Belting his plaid, he approached her. "You need to send him back to England where he belongs."

She glanced to the ceiling, where the lass was still hidden but obviously would have little trouble overhearing them. "This is not a discussion I plan to have with you. Most especially not here."

Dermot grabbed her arm and hauled her outside. "There is talk in the clan. If you don't send that Sassenach home, there are those who will do it for you. And he'll be going back to Henry in pieces."

She pulled her arm from his grasp. "Who is saying that?"

"You know who."

"In that case, you'd best be telling your Raider to leave my husband alone. If he is harmed again, I won't rest until I have every one of your rebel hides in the stocks."

He gaped in disbelief. "You would choose a Sassenach over your own brother?"

"I would not want to, but I won't have him hurt. Now tell me who shot him yesterday."

He jutted his jaw out defiantly, and by the light in his eyes she could tell he knew the answer but would sooner die than tell it to her. "It was only a warning. Next time, they won't miss his heart."

Callie removed the anger from her tone and tried to

appeal to him more calmly. She loved her brother more than anything, and the last thing she wanted was to see him hurt for so foolish a cause.

"Dermot, please. Why must you be involved in this? If you will give me the names of the ones involved, I swear to you I won't turn them in, but I need to speak with them. We must have peace."

"Peace? Our father would be spinning in the earth to hear you say that. He hated the English, and if you were truly a daughter of his, you would never stand for that man to bed you. Let alone *beg* him for it."

For the first time in her life, Callie wanted to slap her brother. Her palm itched from the want of it. "Give me the name of the Raider."

"Or what?" he sneered. "Will you tell your precious Sassenach husband that I am one of the ones who raid?"

She was aghast at the very idea of it. "I have never betrayed you."

"And you better not." The cold fury in his eyes scared her. She'd never seen him like this before.

"Are you threatening me?"

The look softened ever so subtly. "I would never hurt you; however, I will not betray them. If your husband ever learns I am one of the rebels, he will have me tortured for the rest of the names. Are you willing to see me executed?"

"Of course not."

"Then get rid of him."

Oh, the lad could be insufferably stubborn. And selfish. How dare he stand there and make such demands? But it was time she let him know her stance on this issue. "I am his wife. If he leaves, I must leave, too."

"Then let us kill him."

She shook her head at him. Now he was being completely unreasonable. "Could you honestly do that?"

He shrugged nonchalantly. "Have you any idea the number of men he has killed? Jamie said he heard the English knights curse his name and relate the horrors that man has wreaked on others. He said your husband was known to cut the throats of sleeping men. It would only be justice to see him dead."

"I don't believe that to be justice," she breathed. "Desperate men do desperate things. You know Father's saying as well as I do. What my husband did, he did for survival. I won't hold that against him. He was a scared boy."

"A scared boy who cost many men their lives." He was so harsh and judgmental, and she wondered when he had changed. The Dermot she remembered was a dear lad who was quick to laugh and even quicker to let bygones be bygones. But this half-grown man before her was a stranger to her.

"Sin made mistakes," she insisted.

"He committed crimes and he should pay for them."

"You are not his judge."

Dermot glared at her. "Did you live with the English so long that they clouded your mind and won your heart?"

"You know better than that."

"Do I?"

Och, the lad was making her angrier and angrier. If she didn't leave soon, they were both going to say things they would regret even more.

"You are selfish, Dermot. You need to be growing up, lad, and learning that sometimes we have to compromise for the welfare of others."

"Compromise? You're talking of embracing an enemy my father gave his life trying to defeat."

"Dermot, please. Be reasonable. This is a different world we live in now. We need to—"

"You make your peace." He raked her with a disgusted glare. "But in my heart, I know I am right, and when I die and see Father again, I know I shall be able to look him in the eye with a clear conscience. Tell me, will you?"

Callie flinched at his words. "Of course I will."

He snorted in derision. "Then I wish you happiness with the lies you tell yourself." He stalked off.

Callie shouted after him, "Tell your rebel friends to be here tonight. My *husband* wishes a word with all the men of the clan."

He paused and turned to face her with a wry grin. "Oh, I'll tell them, all right. This is one meeting I wouldn't miss for anything."

A shiver ran down her spine. Whatever was she to do with Dermot? The lad had no sense, to be following the others. But then, he'd always been that way. Always let others lead him into mischief. She only hoped this time they didn't lead him to his grave.

*   *   *

Sin retired late in the afternoon to his chambers. He didn't tell his brothers of the ache in his shoulder or the fact he hadn't slept the night before. Much like Ewan, he'd spent the night in the hall.

He breathed a sigh of relief as he discovered the room empty of his wife's vivacious presence. He wished to be alone for a bit with nothing to cloud his mind.

After doffing his clothes, he slid himself into the bed. He should be able to take a brief nap before meeting with the men of her clan.

And for some morbid reason, he was actually looking forward to it. But he would need his head clear. His mind fully alert.

Closing his eyes, he let out a long, exhausted breath.

To his dismay, the door opened.

He froze, steeled for action should the intruder be an enemy.

It wasn't. He heard Callie's light footsteps as she crossed the room, oblivious to him. He slit his eyes open a hair to watch her set her laundry down on a small desk by the window. As she turned, she spied his clothes folded on the floor where he'd left them.

Her gaze traveled along the floor, then up the bed to where he lay. Sin didn't move. For some reason, he didn't want her to know he watched her.

A gentle smile curled her lips as her gaze fell on him. Very quietly, she pulled the shutters closed to darken the room for him, then she moved silently toward the bed.

She stopped by his side and placed one graceful, cool hand against his brow.

"You've a fever," she whispered. "Do you wish me to send for a physician?"

"How did you know I was awake?"

"You didn't flinch when I neared you. If you'd been asleep, you'd have me on the floor by now."

Her words cut him. "I would never harm you in such a way, Callie."

She smiled at that and brushed his hair back from his damp forehead. "I know, Sin. Do you wish a healer?"

He shook his head. "I just need to rest for a bit."

Callie traced her hand through the softness of his hair. He looked almost boyish, lying there with his cheeks pinkened by his fever. She glanced to the wound in his shoulder. There was no sign of infection. It appeared to be healing well, yet his fever concerned her.

"I sent a summons to all the men," she said quietly.

"Thank you."

She ran her hand from his hair, down his neck and arm to his hand. She held it in hers, staring at the scars that marked his flesh. His hand was so rough and masculine. Strong. Capable. And as she held it, she remembered the way his hands had felt on her body last night. The way his hands could both comfort and protect her.

She wrapped her other hand around his, holding it tight and hoping that she would have many afternoons like this when she could spend a quiet moment with him.

"Can I get you anything?" she asked.

Sin looked to where she toyed with his hand. The paleness of her soft, delicate skin was a sharp contrast to the dark roughness of his. Her hand was so tiny in comparison. So fine and dainty.

How could something so small shake him so profoundly? Those hands shouldn't have the power to do anything to him, and yet they made him hot and gave him a comfort that defied his best abilities to name.

He shook his head.

She lifted his hand to her lips and kissed his knuckles, making his body roar to life with a vicious demand for hers. "I'll make sure no one disturbs you."

She got up, leaned over and placed a kiss on his cheek. He savored the feel of her lips on his skin. And it took all his strength not to pull her into the bed with him and make love to her.

Instead, he let the kindness of her seep into him. The warmth of her lips touch the ragged edges of a heart that was just beginning to beat.

He heard her leave the room and close the door. Aching with regret, he balled his hand in the fur cover.

Why had she been given to him, when the very saints above knew there was no chance for them to have a life together?

But then, he knew.

Henry wanted peace and he was willing to sacrifice anything for it. Though Sin liked to pretend otherwise, he knew the truth of their relationship. When all was said and done, he was nothing more than a pawn to Henry. A servant, and should he ever fail to be useful to Henry, his life would be worthless.

Callie stood on the castle steps as the men of her clan gathered around. She'd had her servants prepare food and drink for the men in hopes of placating them.

To her complete and utter non-surprise, it didn't work. The air around them was rife with hostility. They all knew something wasn't right for them to be summoned here. They just didn't know what that something was.

"Caledonia, my sweet."

She turned at Fraser's voice. He stood just an inch taller than she and had bright blue eyes and dark blond hair. His smile always easy, he had a pleasant and open manner that she had often found soothing.

Before she had been captured by Henry, he had asked Aster for permission to court her. Though they had plenty in common and shared similar temperaments, she'd never felt romantically inclined toward him. He was like an older brother to her.

She offered him a genuine, if somewhat cool, smile. "Fraser, how are you?"

"Much better now that I know you are well. You've no idea how many times I urged your uncle to let us head to London to reclaim you. But he wouldn't hear of it."

A chill went up her spine at the underlying tone of his voice and the peculiar gleam in his eye. He was hiding something in that glib statement.

Could he be the rebel leader?

Like her father, he was a passionate hater of the English and he did have the demeanor of a man comfortable with ordering others about. It was possible. Not to mention he and Dermot were friends.

The crowd drew instantly silent.

Frowning, Callie looked around to find her husband standing in the doorway.

Sin's long, black hair spilled over his shoulders, vanishing into the blackness of his English surcoat and mail. He stood tall and proud with one gauntlet-covered hand on the hilt of his sword. Those piercing black eyes that could make her feel so deeply took in the entire scene at once, and he bore an aura of such power and lethal grace that it sent a shiver through her.

It was obvious to all, this was a man of authority. A man who saw more than just what was before him. And the men around her reacted to him like a group of restless predators who knew their leadership and territory was being threatened by this man's presence.

"Bloody hell, what's that Sassenach doing here?"

She didn't know the owner of that voice, but the sentiment was echoed all around her.

Her heart pounded in fear of what her clansmen would do. Most of them had yet to hear of her marriage and she wondered why Aster wasn't there to help.

The insults grew as Sin stood there in silence, sizing them up one by one. It was eerie to watch him, for she knew what he was doing. He was making a mental note of every man there, of his behavior and words. This was the Sin who held the king's ear. The knight no one had ever defeated in battle.

And the longer he stood there watching them while they insulted him, the angrier the clansmen became at his stoic silence.

"Where's the MacNeely?" one of the men shouted at Sin. "What have you done with him?"

Like a raging tide, the men were getting ready to attack Sin, who didn't seem the least bit concerned by their anger or animosity.

Terrified, she gathered her skirts and rushed to

stand by her husband's side. "Please!" she said loudly, holding her hands up to silence them.

When their voices quieted to a murmur, she spoke again. "Most of you are unaware that I am now married." She offered a smile to her husband and took his arm in hers. "Sin—"

A fierce curse sounded from Fraser. His eyes flaming, he strode up the stairs to sneer at her. "Tell me it's not true, Callie. Why would you be a whoring—"

Sin moved so fast she didn't even see his arm in motion. One minute Fraser was insulting her, and the next Sin had him by the throat.

Fraser tried to pry Sin's grip loose with both his hands, but it did no good.

The look on Sin's face was one of hell's wrath, and when he spoke his tone was low, lethal. "Insult my wife again or even look in her general direction, and I will rip your throat out. Do you understand?"

Fraser nodded.

Sin released him.

Fraser coughed and rubbed his throat. His fierce gaze bored into Sin, but he wisely held his tongue.

Sin looked out at her clansmen. "As for the rest of you, I have been sent here by King Henry to make sure no one else raids the English who live in the neighboring towns and areas." He centered his gaze on Fraser. "I know not who the rebels are, but I will find out and those responsible will be punished."

Snorts and insults rang out.

"Why should we fear you?"

Callie was unsure of who spoke.

Sin smiled slyly as he stepped slowly from the stairs

and walked among the men of her clan. She held her breath in fear of what they might do next.

"Let me tell you a little story," Sin said as he eyed them each in turn. "There was once a boy who wasn't even old enough to shave."

He paused at Dermot. "Beaten."

Then he looked to her Cousin Sean. "Naked." He continued to walk among them as he spoke. "He was sent out into the great desert with only a small dagger for protection."

Sin jumped back up on the stairs beside her and stood face-to-face with Fraser. His next words chilled her completely. "I have killed cobras with my bare hands and I have lived through conditions so horrendous, not even hell itself scares me."

His gaze panned through the crowd. "If any of you think for one minute that I have any soul left to prevent me from killing you, you're sadly mistaken. If you think for one minute," he continued, "any of you are capable of killing me, then I say try it. But make sure you've had a good confession beforehand, because I assure you it will be the very last mistake you make in this lifetime."

He focused his gaze on Dermot. "The raiding stops now."

Sin turned to walk back inside the castle. He'd barely taken a step before one of the men threw a cabbage at him.

Unsheathing his sword as he whirled around, he cleaved it in twain. The two halves fell harmlessly to the ground.

Utter silence descended. This time, he saw shock

and fear on the faces of the crowd as they finally realized the extent of his fighting skills.

Sin sheathed his sword. "*Never* attack me from
behind."

He swept one last menacing glare at them, then
walked inside.

Callie saw the reserve in the men who gathered
around to discuss what had just happened and how to
deal with Sin.

Fraser curled his lip at her and said nothing as he
went to join the men in the yard.

Callie ran after her husband.

She found him alone in the great hall, leaning on
both arms against the lord's table. His back was rigid
and he reminded her of an angry wolf. She approached him cautiously, but not in fear. She knew
him to be snappish in this mood. Still, she didn't think
he would turn his anger on her.

"That was amazing," she breathed. "How did you
know about the cabbage?"

"People act predictably." He pushed himself away
from the table and turned to face her with a frown.
"Except for you. You, I don't understand."

She smiled. "I think I might be flattered by that."

He rubbed his injured shoulder and looked away.
"They'll be outside right now trying to decide if they
should kill me or obey my mandate. Fraser and some
of the others will be arguing that I should be killed in
my sleep. He was to marry you, wasn't he?"

His quick turn of topic and acute perceptions surprised her. "He thought so. How did you know?"

"The way he looked at you."

"What else did you gather?"

"I know at least a score of the rebels by sight; by tomorrow I shall know their names."

Callie was dumbfounded. Her uncle, who had known these men for years, had yet to discern any of the rebels, including the fact that his own nephew was one of them. And yet Sin had managed to do it in a matter of minutes? It was inconceivable. "Are you serious?"

"Aye. Fraser is in with them, no doubt."

"Think you he leads them?"

He shook his head. "It's not in him."

"But he stood up to you. And I know the others respect him quite a bit."

"He stood up to me only because of you." Sin reached out to touch the stray piece of hair on her cheek. The softness of her skin was so soothing, and yet his heart ached at what he suspected.

He'd seen the way Fraser had looked to her brother when she had spoken. He had seen the look in her brother's eyes and the way Dermot had glanced at several others.

Dermot was in the thick of all this. Even worse, Sin had a suspicion that her brother might even be the rebel leader himself.

Aye, now that he thought about it, he held little doubt. It could only be fate that he would be sent here to kill the brother of the only woman he had ever cared for. It was just the type of twisted irony life would hand him.

It would destroy her to lose her brother because of him.

Callie would hate him forever.

Perhaps that would be for the best. If she hated him, then she would gladly seek out her annulment. She would refuse to stay married to the man who destroyed her brother.

You don't have to kill him. . . .

It was true. He could just as easily hand him over to Henry's custody.

Sin's gut knotted at the thought of it. If he sent Dermot to England . . .

Images of his childhood tore through him.

Worthless Scots cur. Not even fit to lick my boots. He could still feel the blows he'd taken, not just from Harold, but from all of the English who had hated his Scots blood.

Could he condemn another boy to such a life?

Nay. 'Twould be much kinder to kill Dermot outright than to leave him to such a fate.

He looked at Callie, trying to memorize her face. If he could have any wish, it would be to love her. To keep her safe from all harm.

But in this he was powerless. If he didn't hand Dermot over or kill him, Henry would destroy her entire clan, and her in the process of it.

Like so many other times in his life, his hands were tied. This he must do. There was no way around it.

Chapter 13

Sin didn't join them for supper that night, and as soon as it was over Callie went to find him. Simon suggested she try the castle parapets, and though it seemed an unlikely place, she went anyway.

True to Simon's prediction, she found Sin sitting alone, perched between the crenellation. He had his back braced against one stone wall, his foot against the one opposite it and his left leg dangled dangerously over the edge, out into the night.

"Thinking of jumping?" she asked.

"It would make you a rich widow if I did." He glanced at her over his shoulder. "Care to push me?"

There was something about his tone that made her wonder if it was a teasing comment or a sincere test to see if she would.

She moved to stand by his leg and gave him a chiding stare. "Nay, I rather like having you about. But you haven't been about this evening, have you?

You've been hiding again. Care to tell me why you are out here?"

"I wanted some fresh air."

"But up here?"

He shrugged. "I like it up here. People generally don't bother me."

She cocked a teasing brow. "Bothering you, am I?"

"Nay," he said, to her surprise. His gaze was warm and tender as he looked at her. It was a vast improvement over his normally empty stare.

He was gorgeous in the moonlight, leaning back against the wall. The moon was large and bright and allowed her to see his features plainly. There was something very masculine about the way he sat almost straddling the wall. He was at ease, and yet she knew he could spring into action like a hungry lion at the slightest provocation.

Shivery from the intensity of his presence, she reached out and touched his knee. "What are you thinking about?"

"Trying to guess where the rebels will strike next."

"You don't think you quelled them tonight?"

"Do you?"

"Nay," she answered honestly. The Raider had never ceased when Aster had publicly asked him to. And she supposed the Raider, being one of their clan, actually *liked* Aster. Therefore, it was rather hard to imagine he would stop for Sin, whom he no doubt hated.

Sin folded his hands over his taut stomach as he studied her face. "I'm sure all the rebels are together tonight, plotting. Did Dermot make an appearance at supper?"

Her heart stilled at his question. Could he possibly suspect . . .

"Aye. Why do you ask?"

"He didn't stay the whole meal, though."

Fear ran rampant through her. Where was he going with this line of questioning? In truth, she wasn't sure she wanted to find out. "How did you know?"

He gestured to the yard below and she saw a shadow moving toward the castle. "Dermot went to Fraser's a short time ago."

"They are old friends."

His gaze went back to her and sharpened on her, making her even more fearful than she'd been before. "Why are you suddenly so nervous?"

"Nervous?"

"Aye, you have the same look about you that you had the day I met you on the turret stairs and you were trying to escape."

The devil's hairy toes if he wasn't eerily perceptive at times. No wonder Henry valued him so. If she didn't know better, she'd swear the man had the gift of second sight. "How are you able to read people so easily?"

"It's what enabled me as a boy to be able to tell if my masters were going to allow me to approach them in peace or if I'd be searching the rushes for my teeth should I disturb them. Now answer my question."

Callie watched her brother walk toward the keep. In spite of their differences, she would never betray him. She'd never told anyone about the time she'd seen him riding back from a raid. Aster would kill him if he knew Dermot rode with the rebels.

"Shall I make it easier for you, then?" Sin asked.

"If you're afraid to tell me he is in with your rebels, that I already know."

She gaped. "How?"

"The way he acted earlier. I told you I knew them by their faces, and he is one I know by name."

She was flabbergasted by his abilities. "How can you be so certain?"

"You can't hide from the devil."

She put her hands on her hips as she glared at him. "I told you in London, you're not the devil."

"You're the only one who thinks not."

Och, the man was exasperating. "If you were the devil, you would be down there right now arresting Dermot. So why aren't you?"

"Because I'm waiting for him to reveal the Raider to me."

That took the anger right out of her. She had to save Dermot. There was no way she could watch her brother hang. Whatever it took to protect him, she would do. "If I can get him to tell me who the Raider is, will you let him go free?"

Sin blinked, then looked away. "He will never tell you that."

"I think he might. You have to understand him. Since my father died, he's been lost. He and my father were so close, and Dermot was there the day he died. Something inside him died as well; he's not the same lad he once was."

"You love him greatly."

She nodded, wanting him to know just how much Dermot meant to her. "I would do anything for my brother."

He fell silent.

Callie watched Sin for several minutes as she sorted through this entire ordeal. Like Aster, she knew the Raider must be stopped before he started a war between her clan and the English. Though her clan was a decent size, it was nowhere near large enough to wage war on an entire country, and with things being as they were in Scotland, she didn't know if her Cousin Malcolm would help them or not. As king of Scotland, Malcolm had his own concerns.

Dermot had told her the rebels believed they could convince other clans to join them against England, but she didn't hold to that delusion. If she didn't help Sin stop the rebels, all of them would be hanged as an example to the others who dared oppose the English king.

If the Raider had to be sacrificed for peace, then she was willing to pay the cost to protect the rest of them.

"Do you have any idea who the Raider could be?" she asked him.

"I'm rather certain I already know."

She gasped at his deadpan tone. "Then why haven't you acted?"

"I want proof."

She smiled wistfully at that. "You are a good man. Most men would already be jumping to their conclusions and acting on them."

His heated gaze bored into hers. "I am not a good man, Callie. Never delude yourself on that point. It's just, having suffered enough injustice in my life, I am in no hurry to deliver it up to anyone else." She saw his jaw clench. "But when I have proof of the identity of this Raider, Callie, I *will* see him punished for it."

"I wouldn't expect anything less than that."

He looked stunned by her words. "You're not angry?"

She shook her head. "I hurt in my heart at the thought of one of my clansmen being punished, but I am not angry. My father raised me with the belief that we are bound by honor to our people. My loyalty is with my clan and yours is with Henry. We can't let our emotions sway us. I understand that duty must always come first. This Raider has made his own decisions for what he believes in. I would rather the rebels lay aside their arms and join us in peace, but if they refuse to, then I will not fault you for doing that to which you're sworn."

Sin frowned at her. He was aghast and somewhat angry by her speech. His emotions made no sense to him and yet he felt them strongly. "How can you not hate me?"

This time, there was no mistaking the utter horror in her green eyes. "My God, Sin, are you so used to hatred that you can't accept the fact that someone, anyone, could care for you?"

He squelched the pain he felt at her words.

"Do you see these hands?" he asked, holding them up to her.

"Aye."

"Know you they have strangled men? They have shoved daggers into their hearts, swords into their bodies. These are the hands of a killer."

She took his right hand in hers and stared at him with a compassion that took his breath away. "They have also meted out justice. They have comforted me and Jamie. Protected Simon and Draven."

What would it take to make her see him as he really

was? He couldn't understand her steadfast refusal to see the truth. "I am a monster."

"You are a man, Sin. Plain and simple."

He wanted to believe her, but all he had to do was close his eyes and he could see the men he'd killed. Feel the guilt and pain of his past. He didn't deserve her kindness.

"What do you want from me?" he asked.

"I want you to be my husband. I want you to stay with me and be father to my children."

"Why? Because of some stupid oath made before a man Henry bribed?"

"Nay. Because of the way I feel when I look into those dark eyes of yours. Because of the way my heart pounds when I think of you."

Sin shook his head at her words. He didn't want the home she spoke of, and the thought of children . . .

"I will not ever be owned again by anyone, milady. My life is my own and I owe nothing to you, nor to Henry, nor to anyone else."

Callie released his hand as his words struck her like blows. It was then she understood why he bore no markings on his shield or surcoat. Nothing owned him and he owned nothing.

"I don't want to own you, Sin. I want to share your life."

"Share what? I have nothing to offer you."

A wave of irritation swept through her. Och, the stubborn oaf.

Suddenly she was tired of trying to make him see her way of thinking. "You know what? So long as you feel that way, you're right. You go ahead and keep to yourself. Stay up here brooding alone in the dark like some evil beastie who wants to walk the parapets at night, scaring people unto their wits' end. Wallow in your loneliness and the fact that you are beyond love. Go ahead and spurn me and my feelings. But know this: As long as you persist in this self-deprecation, then you are fulfilling the very doubts you have. No one will ever be able to love you unless you open yourself up to them."

Sin watched as she left the parapet, her words ringing in his ears.

Love.

He scoffed at the very word. It was a useless emotion. The quest for it had led many a man to his death. Look at his brother Kieran.

And even Ewan. Though Ewan's body might still be here, his heart and soul were gone. Torn asunder by love.

Sin was a knight of action. A man unto himself. He needed no one. Not now, not ever.

Callie fought against the wave of hopelessness that threatened to overwhelm her as she walked away from Sin, back to her room. Her brother was going to get himself killed and her husband rejected her as if she were poisonous.

Why? What was it with men, that they were ever seeking to destroy themselves?

Her father had been the same way. Fighting a hopeless war against an enemy who had never truly harmed him. He had merely wanted the English gone from Scottish soil and had given his life to that cause. And for what?

There was really no way to keep them out. All her father had done was pass on a legacy of suicide to his sons.

"Caledonia?"

She paused at the deep voice behind her and turned to see Lochlan drawing near.

"Are you all right?" he asked.

"Aye."

He cocked a blond brow. "You don't look all right."

She clenched her teeth and took a deep breath to calm the raging emotions inside her. "I am merely aggravated at your brother, but I am sure it will pass." Given a century or two, she might even be able to smile at the toad again.

He smiled knowingly. "He has a way of doing that to a person."

Callie studied the handsome, sculpted lines of Lochlan's face. He bore very little resemblance to Sin. The only thing the two men shared was height and the fact that both were incredibly pleasing to look at.

Nay, she corrected herself, they shared another trait. As she looked up into those clear blue eyes, she saw Lochlan was every bit as reserved and guarded. And his eyes were tinged by a soul-deep sadness.

"Tell me, was Sin always like this?"

"Like what? Moody, quiet?"

"Aye."

He nodded.

"Then it's hopeless, isn't it? There is no way to reach that man."

She saw the grimness of Lochlan's features as he considered her words. "Honestly, if there is a way, I do not know it. But I hope you will continue to try and reach him."

She frowned at his words and the odd look of him. Strange emotions swept across his face in the span of three heartbeats, and then his features returned to calm.

"You have guilt?" she asked, wondering at the source of it.

He sighed wearily and looked around them as if afraid someone might overhear. "More than you can fathom. I lead my clan and yet I know Sin is firstborn. I have no right to my father's legacy. Everything I have is his by right and by blood. Yet he refuses to take anything from me."

"Why did your father disown him?"

She amended her list to another thing the brothers shared. An angry tic started in Lochlan's jaw that reminded her much of Sin's.

When he spoke, his words wrung her heart. "In order to be disowned, you must first be recognized as a son. Sin never was. Ewan and Braden were too small to see what Kieran and I did. Our parents lavished the world on us, while Sin was delegated to a corner to watch. I hated any holiday where gifts were exchanged. We were given so much, while he received nothing at all. I remember one Christmas in particular when I felt so badly for him that I tried to split my gifts with him. He refused, saying that if they had meant for him to have gifts, they would have given him some. He told me I could keep all my gifts and most especially my pity."

"I don't understand why he was treated like that."

Lochlan shook his head. "In truth, neither do I. Believe it or not, my mother is a good woman who loves her sons completely. But she couldn't bear the sight of Sin. My father loved her beyond all reason, and so he refused to act as if he bore any favoritism to Sin at all. He went out of his way to prove to her that he didn't love Sin's mother and that Sin meant nothing to him as well. As a result, Sin was shunned. I can't recall a single time my father ever said his name or looked directly at him."

Her heart ached for her husband.

"Our birthdays were always marked by gifts and celebrations. And yet no one, not even Sin, knows what day he was born. All we know is he's a few months older than I am, but we don't know how many."

Callie struggled to breathe at what Lochlan was telling her. She couldn't imagine not knowing her own birthday.

Suddenly another thought occurred to her. "And his name? Where did it come from?"

"My mother gave it to him. When Braden was born and baptized, Sin wanted to know why no one had ever called him anything other than lad. He asked my father what his Christian name was and my father walked away in silence, shamedfaced at the fact no one had ever bothered to name Sin or have him baptized. So, my mother spoke up. She said if he wanted a name so much, then he should be named accordingly."

Callie saw the raw agony in his heart as he spoke his next words in a low tone. "My mother said he was conceived in sin, born in sin and that he would die that way. Therefore the only name to give him would be Sin."

Lochlan's eyes turned dull. "I shall never forget the stricken look on his face. Then he threw his shoulders back and told her, fine. Sin it would be. *The priest claims people love sin,* he said proudly. *Maybe if I am Sin, someone will love me, too.*"

Callie closed her eyes at the horror of it. How she regretted her harsh words to Sin. She should never have lost patience with him. He'd known enough heartache to last a million lifetimes.

"Lochlan, do you think a man can change?"

"I don't know, Callie. I just don't know."

Taking a deep breath, she said good-bye to him and made her way to her room. She had plans to make. Plans that included seducing her lost, wayward husband. And this time he would have no escape from her.

Chapter 14

It was long after midnight before Sin ventured toward his bed. Callie was sound asleep, curled on her side.

He stood there for quite some time, staring at her features, which were highlighted by the firelight. She was so breathtaking in her slumber. Nothing would give him greater pleasure than pulling the blankets back and joining her in bed. Gathering her in his arms and making love to her until the sun was high.

The taste and feel of her was branded into his soul, and he wondered if he would ever have the courage to leave her when the time came.

What would it be like to spend the rest of his life with her? To have laughter and love . . .

He closed his eyes. It wasn't for him. He'd learned long ago to hope for nothing except a comfortable bed of his own and a good meal. Those things he could possess.

Having Callie in his life would be like trying to contain the wind. She was beyond his reach. Far beyond it.

You could have her.

Nay, he could not. If he betrayed Henry for her, Henry would kill him and attack her clan. And if he betrayed Callie for Henry, she would hate him for killing her brother. Either way, he was damned.

Either way, he would lose her.

How could he choose between the two people to whom he owed the most? Henry, who had given him back his life, and Callie, who had given him back his soul.

God, how he wanted to hold her and just forget about his duties. Forget about the man he'd been. Have her soothe him in the way only she could.

The pain and fear inside him was so raw. So jagged.

Shaking his head to dispel the thought of her hating him, he made his way to the hearth. Weary and soul-sick, he lay down on the cold floor and forced himself to go to sleep.

Callie woke up a few hours after sunup to find her bed empty. Tears filled her eyes as she realized her husband had never come to her.

She wondered where he'd spent the night until she rolled over and saw him alone on the floor. A nasty burst of anger tore through her. She narrowed her gaze on him.

Why would he have done such a thing?

Suddenly aggravated beyond reason, she was seized by a childish impulse. Normally she would squelch it, but as she sat there, she realized one of the problems with her husband was that he'd been too stern and serious in his life.

A little taste of childish antics would do him good. Aye, she'd love to see the man who had been chased by his brothers into her barn. Sin needed many more such moments.

Before she could stop herself, she lobbed a pillow at his head.

Sin came awake instantly. His heart pounding, he rolled over with a dagger in his fist to confront his attacker. To his complete shock, he saw his wife approaching him with another pillow in her hand.

Sheathing his dagger, he relaxed, until she hit him with her pillow.

"What are you doing?"

She answered him with another smack. "I gave you a weapon; defend yourself, knave, or surrender."

Sin grabbed the pillow she'd tossed from the floor where it had landed and came to his feet. He fought her back as she beat him with the pillow and giggled.

In spite of himself, he laughed with her. She was so wonderfully beautiful in the morning light, with her coppery hair tousled, her cheeks rosy and her bare feet peeking out from beneath the hem of her white linen kirtle. Her smiles and laughter took his breath away.

He backed her toward the wall as feathers began to fly about the room. Just when he was sure he had her cornered, she dropped her pillow and ran at him.

Unprepared for her movement, he stumbled back three full steps. She ran her hands up and down his ribs, tickling him unmercifully. Sin laughed, dropping the pillow and wrapping his arms around her to stop her.

"Do you surrender to me?"

"Never," he taunted.

Fire glowed in her eyes. "Never? We shall have to see about that."

Sin picked her up and tossed her gently to the bed. He grinned triumphantly, then turned his back.

She launched herself from the bed and wrapped herself around his waist, piggyback-style.

Sin was laughing even harder as the door to their room opened.

They both froze to see her maid standing in the doorway, her eyes bulging at the sight of Sin wearing nothing but his breeches while Callie was draped over his back with her shapely legs bare and wrapped around his waist. Feathers were still hanging in the air, and unless he missed his guess, both of them had feathers in their hair.

Braden glanced into the room as he walked past in the hallway. Then he returned to stand behind the maid and eye them curiously. "Should I ask?"

Callie buried her head against Sin's neck and howled with laughter. Trying to look casual and normal, Sin shifted his weight and cleared his throat. "You see something unusual about a man waking with his wife?"

Braden exchanged a puzzled frown with the maid.

"I'll be back later," the maid whispered, backing out of the room and shutting the door.

Callie slid slowly down his back. But she didn't release him. Instead, she wrapped her arms around his waist and kissed his bare shoulder blade. "Good morning, Sin." The cheer in her voice astounded him.

Sin glanced at her over his shoulder. "Shall I ask now what brought on the pillow madness?"

"I was angry with you."

"For what?"

"Sleeping on the floor again. What is it with you and the floor? Most women have to fear their husbands are in the bed of another. Me, 'tis the hearth I envy."

Callie saw the wave of seriousness descend over his face. She narrowed her gaze at him. "Don't you dare."

"Dare what?"

"Turn those serious eyes on me, Sin . . . or else I'll bash you with my pillow again."

An astonished look replaced the sternness. "You've gone daft on me, haven't you?"

"Not daft. But definitely in the mood to do harm to you if need be. I am proclaiming this Fun Day. There will be no earnestness today. No moodiness or brooding."

Sin stared at her in disbelief. "You're serious, aren't you?"

"Quite. For every stern look I see, I shall punish you for it."

He arched his brow at that. "Punish me how?"

"In ways you've never been punished before. With pranks and tricks guaranteed to make you want to strangle me."

He smiled in spite of himself.

"See? It's easy to smile and make merry."

How he wished he could do as she asked. Spending the day with her would be wonderful indeed. But he had duties to attend. "I have a rebel to find."

"Then you can look until you go blind from it, but you'll enjoy this search or else I shall tickle you until you beg me for mercy."

The woman was insane. And yet he liked it. She reached up and brushed feathers out of his hair. "My first rule of business today is to make you wear something other than your armor."

"I won't wear a plaid."

"Fine, then, no plaid. But you've other clothes. I have seen them in the trunk."

True, he did own a pair of cloth breeches and a civilian tunic. But he couldn't recall a single time he'd worn them.

He had no idea why he was even considering her request, except for the strange realization that making her happy mattered to him. It shouldn't, but it did. And it was such a small request . . . how could he deny it?

"Very well, milady, no armor for today."

The pleased look on her face sent a raw stab of desire straight to his groin. The woman was truly beautiful. "There will be a quiet picnic for us at noon out in the meadow behind the castle."

He opened his mouth to protest, but she placed her hand over his lips. "No arguments. For this day, you will be mine and I will show you around the village. Look for your rebels if you must, but I intend to show you the other side of life."

"What other side of life?"

"The one worth living."

His eyes turned dull at the bitter reminder of his past. He had seen that side many times in his life and had no wish to see any more of it. "I have seen it, milady."

"Aye, but today you will live it."

This was complete and utter madness. And yet he couldn't find it within himself to turn her away.

She rose up on tiptoe until they were eye to eye. He saw her desire for him, and a tender emotion that made no sense to him whatsoever.

"Just give me this one day, Sin, and I will ask no more of you."

By her face, he saw how important this was to her. For whatever reason she wanted to do this, he would humor her. "Very well. You have this day when I shall try to be a nonbrooding, happy"—he cringed at the word—"man. Come the morrow, I return to being an ogre."

"I'll accept that so long as you agree to be mine completely today."

"Agreed."

Smiling, she kissed him lightly on the lips.

Sin growled at the satiny feel of her lips on his. Before he could stop himself, he crushed her to him and opened her mouth with his to taste the heaven of her tongue. She ran her hands over his naked back, her nails gently scraping his flesh.

Oh, but this woman felt incredible in his arms. So warm. So giving.

Closing his eyes, he lifted the hem of her kirtle until he could touch the bare skin of her hips, her back. Dear Lord, how he craved her.

"Make love to me, Sin," she whispered against his lips.

Her passion-laden words tore through him. But his reason still reigned supreme. "What if I leave you pregnant?"

She cupped his face in her hands and stared up at him with earnest eyes that scorched him. "Then I will love our child. Whether you stay or not, I shall keep our baby safe and make sure no one ever harms him. He will be as dear to me as his father is."

He felt his resistance slipping.

She returned to kissing him and trailed a hand down the front of his body, over the planes of his chest and stomach. Then she reached into the waistband of his breeches, her fingers brushing gently against his lower abdomen, until she could take him into her hand.

Sin hissed in pleasure as his thoughts scattered. His emotions raw, he reacted on primal impulse. Unable to wait another instant for her, he tore her kirtle from her and carried her to the bed, where he lay her down to devour her.

Callie stared up at him, knowing she had won this battle, and something inside told her it was an important victory.

She shivered as he left her only long enough to remove his breeches.

He returned hurriedly and gathered her into his arms, where he kissed her so furiously that it took her breath. This wasn't the same tender lover who had been so slow and easy with her before. He was like a beast possessed. One who couldn't get enough of her taste.

He trailed his hands over her body, making her shiver at how strong they were and yet so gentle. His hands had the power to destroy life, but with her they only gave pleasure.

Callie moaned as he dipped his head down and took her breast into his mouth. His tongue gently lapped at her hardened nipple, sending waves of ecstasy through her. She cupped his head to her, holding him close as her body burned for him.

"I love the way you taste," he breathed, running his tongue from her breast to her neck. "So warm and soft."

She trembled at his words, knowing he'd said them only to her. How she wished she knew of some magic to keep him with her, to make sure he never left her side again.

He kissed his way from her neck to her ear. She shuddered as he ran his tongue over the curve of it, then darted his tongue inside.

"I love the way you touch me," she whispered. "The way you feel on top of me. And I wish I could keep you here like this forever."

Sin pulled back as her words pierced his heart. How cruel, that they should want the same thing while fate conspired against them. He needed this woman in a way that made no sense.

He stared down at her face, which was framed by her curls. He'd never thought to see such heartfelt welcome on a woman's face. With her, he was home, and he trembled at the weight of his tangled emotions. At the need to hold her, protect her and the need to run away from the fear inside him.

How could he hurt her? Ever?

She reached up and laid her tender hand against his unshaven cheek. That touch scorched him and turned him inside out. There would never be another person in his life who would mean as much to him as she did in this moment.

Needing her in a way that shook him to his soul, he slid himself inside the warm heaven of her body.

Callie moaned at the feel of him deep inside her. The feel of his strength as he rocked himself between her thighs. He captured her lips with his and kissed her passionately, his tongue matching every stroke of his body.

She ran her hands over the hard planes of his back and felt his muscles rippling in time to his movements.

Suddenly he thrust himself deep inside, then stopped. He pulled back and braced himself on his arms so that he could look down at her. She laid her hands against his taut biceps and watched him watch her.

There was such a needful, hungry look in his eyes that it made her ache.

Slowly, he ran his gaze from her face, then down to her bare breasts and stomach, all the way to where they were joined. "You are beautiful," he said, his voice ragged.

She smiled as he dipped his head to kiss her again while he still held himself above her.

Sin closed his eyes and inhaled her sweet scent. Oh, the sexual things he wanted to do with and to this woman.

"Is something wrong?" she asked innocently.

"How could anything be wrong while I have you in my arms?"

Callie didn't know which of them was most surprised by that confession. Love for him flooded her heart. Smiling up at him, she wrapped her legs around his lean waist and brought him into her even deeper than before.

She kissed his lips as she used her body to give him pleasure. He shivered in her arms until he growled. His eyes hot, he lowered himself on top of her and took over the rhythm of their passion.

Callie kissed him furiously as she buried her hands in his hair and moaned at how delicious he felt on and inside her. She loved feeling him like this. Knowing he was all hers.

He made love to her fast, driving her up to a height she'd never felt before, and just when she was sure she could rise no higher, he pushed her up and beyond. To a level of pleasure so fierce it made her cry out.

She held him close as she felt him shuddering in her arms. He pulled back to stare down at her.

She smiled up at him. "See how much fun you've already had on Fun Day, my lord?" She wrinkled her nose at him impishly. "And to think we have yet to leave our room."

Sin laughed at her humor. "It does make me wonder how milady could ever improve this day."

"Oh, give me time and you will see."

Sin was fool enough to doubt that.

Once they were washed and dressed, she led him downstairs to break the fast. Lochlan, Braden and Simon were up and eating at the long table, but Ewan was still in his bed, no doubt sleeping off the keg of ale they had split the night before.

The great hall was empty and the early-morning light spilled in from the windows high above their heads. His brothers and Simon were trading good-natured insults and taunts as they joined them.

Callie sat him at the table, then hurried off to find food for them.

"She's in a most cheerful mood this morn, isn't she?" Lochlan asked.

Sin grunted as he grabbed the heel of Lochlan's bread and tore a piece from it. "She's terminally pleasant."

"She wasn't last night," Lochlan said as he reached for his cup.

Sin frowned at the odd note in his brother's voice. "What say you?"

Lochlan inclined his head toward where Callie had vanished. "When I left her last night, she looked as if she were about to cry."

"Over what?"

"You."

"Me?" he asked, baffled by Lochlan's words. "I did nothing to her." At least not yet. It was what was to come that made him want to throw himself from the top of her castle.

Until the inevitable day came that would divide them forever, the last thing he wanted was to cause her pain.

"Aye," Lochlan agreed, "it's the not doing anything to her that was the problem. It seems she was upset because you barely notice her at all."

That was wholly untrue. Sin noticed everything about her, and therein was the crux of his problem.

He didn't want to contemplate a future without her. "You know better than that."

"It matters not what I know. Only what she perceives."

Braden clucked his tongue as he joined their conversation. "And after all that advice you gave me about Maggie. For shame, Sin. I thought you were a man of action and not one of talk."

"Braden," Simon interrupted. "I think you might be forgetting one small detail. Sin is here to find one of Callie's kinsmen for Henry. How do you think your Maggie would have felt had you been an outsider and done that to her?"

Lochlan stiffened as he turned back to Sin. "You wouldn't really do that."

Sin sighed. "I am honor-bound to it."

"Sin," Lochlan said, his voice thick with warning, "you know the code of conduct that runs thick through everyone with a drop of Scots blood. You don't betray your kin, and most especially not into the hands of their enemy."

Sin arched a brow at Lochlan's words and watched as color darkened his cheeks. Interesting, that his brother would expect better behavior from him than their father had shown.

"That was different," Lochlan said, knowing Sin's thoughts. "It was wartime and that was the only way to cease hostilities."

"And if I don't stop the rebels, it will be wartime again. Henry is out of patience."

"Then, for your sake, I hope the rebel leader is someone in this clan your wife isn't overly fond of."

Sin stared at the table as his stomach knotted. In his gut, he already knew the culprit, even though his heart argued repeatedly that it must be someone else. Anyone else.

But it was Dermot MacNeely, as sure as he sat at the table listening to his brothers. His wife would curse and hate him forever when she found out. But there was nothing to be done about it.

"Well, I never . . ." Callie's voice broke off.

They looked up as Callie came into the room bearing a tray of fresh-baked bread and sliced cheese.

"When I left, the four of you looked fine, and here I come back and it's as if the Second Coming were upon us. Should I ask what tragedy has darkened the mood of this hall?"

" 'Twas only the absence of your beauty," Braden said, grinning. "We dwell in absolute darkness without it."

Sin snorted and tossed his piece of bread at his brother. "You'd best counsel your tongue, little brother, else I will counsel it for you."

Lochlan smiled. "Better still, let me tell Maggie and she'll have his ears boxed."

Braden feigned indignance. "I try and smooth over the matter with your lady and this is the payment I receive? Very well, you're on your own with the matter. See if I help you again."

Sin watched as his wife approached. More beautiful than the very angels in heaven, she eyed him with a determined stare. "Remember your promise to me, Sin. Only smiles are allowed today."

He gave her a fake smile that showed his teeth.

She rolled her eyes. " 'Tis better than a frown anyway."

Callie turned to face Simon and motioned for him to follow her. "My lord Simon, might I have a word with you in private?"

Sin arched a brow. "Why would you wish that?"

She reached across the table and touched the tip of his nose. "I merely wish to ask him a question away from your hearing."

"Why?"

"Because I don't wish you to hear it."

"Aye," Lochlan interjected, "what are you, Sin? Daft?"

Sin kicked the leg of Lochlan's chair and narrowed a hostile glare. "One day, brother, I hope to see a woman plot your downfall. Then I shall be the one laughing at you."

"Downfall?" Callie asked. "How ominous you make it sound. There is no downfall being plotted. Merely a question being asked."

Sin looked at her drolly. "Aye, and empires have been splintered apart over the mere utterance of a single word."

"But it's not an empire I wish to splinter. It's the ice encasing your heart."

Silence rang in the hall on the heel of those words. Sin sat in stunned disbelief.

Callie blushed as if embarrassed by her confession and tucked her chin to her chest.

Simon quickly got up and led her from the hall so that they could speak.

"Sin," Lochlan said from beside him. "I realize I'm

not a man to be giving advice on this matter, but it seems to me only a fool would let a woman like that slip from his grasp. If I ever found a woman who could look past my shortcomings and still want to be with me, I would move heaven and earth to keep her by my side."

"You're not me, little brother. And I can't let myself be open to her when I know that in a short time she will hate me. Hatred and scorn are mother's milk to me, and yet I can't bear the thought of seeing it in her eyes."

"Then don't betray her."

He looked at Lochlan. How easy his brother made it sound. "All I have ever had in this world is my word and my honor. They are the only things that weren't stripped from my flesh. The only things I have never bartered or sold for my survival. And you would have me forsake them? You ask more of me than I am able to give. Nay, I must do as I promised."

And yet, as he looked to where his wife had vanished with Simon, he hurt from the pain of what his honor would see him do. But it wasn't just his honor that mattered. He knew Henry in a way few men did. If he failed to deliver the Raider, Henry would see this clan obliterated.

Silently, Sin ate his food while his brothers made their excuses and left him alone in the hall.

He had barely finished eating when Callie returned. She looked to the vacated seats. "They left already?"

"I fear my dour mood hastened them off. Now, are you going to tell me what you spoke to Simon about?"

"I have absolutely no intention of answering that."
He shook his head at her. "You are a cheeky lass."

"I am that. Vexing to the point my father oft said that I would try the patience of Job."

She took his hand and pulled him to his feet. "Now we're off to have our day of fun. Come, Sir Ogre, and let me see if I can keep a smile on your face."

Little did she know, her very presence kept a smile in his heart, and that was the biggest feat of all.

Sin saddled horses for them, and once they were mounted, Callie led him to the village of Tier Nalayne, where the bulk of the MacNeely clan lived and worked. It was a pleasant day and the village was rife with activity.

Children ran and played games, rushing up and down the roads between the cottages and shops. Women and men paused along the way to gossip and talk while they went about their daily chores.

Callie had them dismount, leave their horses at the stable and walk about on foot.

It didn't take long before they became the center of hostile attention. Women grabbed their children and scurried away at their approach.

Callie took a deep breath and counted for patience at the way her people greeted her husband. It was a good thing he'd left his armor behind. She could only imagine how much worse they would behave had he come wearing his mail and sword.

The butcher's wife stepped out of her shop, saw them approaching, then ran inside, slammed the door shut and hung a sign on the door saying they were out of meat for the day. Callie glared at the sign, then looked to see Sin's reaction.

There wasn't one. He merely took her clan's disdain in stride as if he expected nothing better. And that made her maddest of all.

She'd known these men and women the whole of her life. How could they be so blind?

"Morna?" she called, seeing her stepmother talking to her best friend Peg outside of the cobbler's shop. Callie took Sin's hand and led him over to her. "How fare you this day?"

Her stepmother beamed a happy smile at them, while Peg inspected the contents of the basket she was holding. "We're fine, aren't we, Peg?"

Peg looked up and raked a sneer over Sin. "I need to be getting back to me chores."

Sin said nothing, nor did his face betray even the slightest offense.

"How are you, milord?" Morna asked.

Callie saw relief flash in Sin's eyes for such a brief time that she wondered if she imagined it. "I am quite well, milady, and you?"

"Oh, posh, no milady here. I'm just simple Morna, especially to the man who helped my Jamie. You know, you're all he talks about."

"And I'm certainly far from noble myself. Call me Sin. As for Jamie, he's a good boy. You've done a fine job with him."

Morna beamed a smile at him. Her eyes glanced over Sin's shoulder, then she looked to Callie. "Let's see if we can bash a few stubborn skulls and make the others see what we do."

Before Callie could ask Morna what she meant, Morna grabbed Angus as the old man walked past. His long gray hair was tangled and his beard was so full that no one knew what he really looked like. Still, he was one of the most respected men in the clan and if you could get Angus to like you, the rest would follow suit.

"Angus, my love," Morna said cheerfully, "have you met Callie's new husband?"

The old man curled his lip as he took in Sin's English clothes. "I've no desire to be meeting a—"

Morna cut his words off by clearing her throat. "Don't you think you should judge a man by his deeds and not by his birth?"

"I know the deeds of his kind."

Morna sighed as Angus hobbled off. "Don't take it to heart," she said to Sin, "They're good people, really."

"Believe me, I don't even hear it. I fear Callie is the only one to be hurt by such comments."

He might say that, but Callie didn't believe it. How could it not hurt him?

Callie glanced to see a group of eight men, led by Fraser, headed toward them. Oh, this wasn't good. By their swaggers, she could tell they meant harm.

Fraser glared at her. His sneer twisted his reddish blond beard. "Why did you bring him here?"

"I wanted to show him the village."

"Why?"

"Because we live here and I thought he might like to see it."

Fraser's eyes were dark and menacing. "You might live here. He is visiting. At least he'd best be."

Sin scoffed as if amused by Fraser's words. "Let me guess. If I don't leave soon, you'll make me wish I had gone home. Or better yet, you'll make me wish I'd never been born, or some other worthless cliché meant to frighten me."

Fraser opened his mouth to speak.

Sin spoke before he had a chance to. "I know already that you don't want me here. You've no use for me or my kind. You don't even want to be bothered having to see me in your midst." Sin cut a hostile glare at the group of men that made several of them take a step back. "Fine, then. Hand me the Raider and I shall gladly go."

"The only thing we'll be handing you is your head."

"Ooo," Sin breathed. "Scary. Have you ever thought of making up children's tales? You might actually succeed in frightening a two-year-old."

Fraser gave Sin a disgusted glare. "I really don't like you."

"The feeling is quite mutual."

Fraser took a step toward Sin, who didn't move at all. Callie held her breath, waiting for them to fight. The two of them reminded her of rams about to lock horns and she had no idea how to diffuse this situation.

Not that Fraser would even let her. The man really had no sense, to be pushing her husband, and she had to admire Sin's control. Any other man who possessed half of Sin's fighting skills would already have Fraser on the ground whimpering.

When Fraser spoke next, his tone was disrespectful and cold. "You think you can come in here and tell us how to live. Look down your English noses at us." He looked to Callie. "Take our women while we do nothing. Well, if you have any sense at all, then you'd be headed home by nightfall."

Sin's smile was evil. "What can I say? I have no sense."

Fraser swung at him.

Sin ducked, caught Fraser's arm and held him in place with a fierce grip. "Listen to me," Sin said in Gaelic. "I will speak slowly so that you can understand me. I have no wish to embarrass you in front of your friends and family by hurting you. So go home and take your men with you."

He released Fraser.

Fraser staggered back as he raked a malevolent glare over Sin's body. "You and I are going to have this out."

Sin cast a frustrated look at Callie. "How mad at me would you be if I hit him really hard? Just once."

She glowed at the realization that his respect for her was the only thing that had kept him from pulverizing Fraser. Whether he admitted it out loud or not, her husband did have feelings for her. In that moment, she could kiss him.

" 'Tis Fun Day," she said simply. "So, if it will give you pleasure, I might be swayed to forgive you."

Sin smiled at that.

Until a scream rent the air.

Women and men started grabbing at children and running for cover. Callie froze as she saw a crazed bull running down the village street, attacking anything and everything that got in its way.

Before she could move again, Sin grabbed her up in his arms and tossed her to the low-hanging roof of a nearby cottage. She scrambled up the roof, making room for him to join her.

He didn't.

Fraser grabbed Morna and did the same with her, then ran for a little boy who'd fallen in the street. He reached the boy just seconds before the bull and managed to get him to a rooftop, but before Fraser could get out of the way, the bull caught him about the leg and gored him with a toss of its great head.

Callie cringed at the way the bull attacked. There was no hope for poor Fraser. He was dead.

Or so she thought, until she saw Sin seize a huge wooden laundry swatter and plaid kirtle where one of the women had dropped her laundry. While the bull toyed with Fraser, Sin smacked the bull across his flanks and clucked his tongue at the beast.

The bull whirled around and eyed him angrily.

"That's it," Sin said, taunting the animal. He wrapped the kirtle around the swatter to make a banner of sorts that would entice the beast. "Run after the idiot who has no sword."

He waved the banner before the bull, which now stood still as it watched the motion Sin made. It stamped twice, put its head down and charged.

Sin spun about and ran for the woods as fast as he could.

"Nay!" Callie shouted as her husband and the bull disappeared. She scrambled from the rooftop, down to where a group of people surrounded Fraser.

With the danger past, people flooded the streets.

"That was the bravest thing I've ever seen," old Angus said as he and several others helped Fraser to his feet and inspected his injured leg.

"We have to go help him," Callie said.

Fraser's brother, Gerald, grabbed a bow from his waiting wagon. "English or not, I owe him for my brother's life."

Six others came forward to help. When Callie started off with them, they refused to let her join them.

Angus stopped her. "He didn't risk his life to see you harmed, lass. Now stay here and let the men handle it."

Though it went against her nature to stand by and do nothing, she didn't argue. It would only cause them to delay their rescue when they needed to be finding Sin as quickly as possible.

Consumed by terror, Callie watched as the men left the village, and she prayed for her resourceful husband to have found some way to outmaneuver the bull.

Time seemed to move on the back of a snail as she waited with the women. Fraser's leg had been sewn and bandaged. Still no sign of the men.

Callie prayed and prayed, hoping he was all right.

At long last, she heard a cheering roar from the people of the village. Turning around, she saw the group of men coming toward them.

And in their midst . . .

Nay. It couldn't be.

Callie frowned, then blinked, trying to see if her eyes were deceiving her.

Angus was the first to reach the village. "I'll beat the first one of you who laughs," he said in warning. "No mon who fights like that for our women and children will be mocked. You hear me?"

"We wouldn't dream of it, Angus MacDougal," Peg said.

Choking on her laugher and filled with tremendous relief that he was unhurt, Callie ran to her husband and wrapped her arms around him. Her heart pounded at the feel of his strong arms holding her close. Och, how she loved this wonderful man. She kissed his cheek, then pulled away to look him over one more time and make sure he really was unharmed.

Again, she had to purse her lips to keep from smiling.

In truth, she had no idea how the village refrained from laughing at the sight of her proud husband. He only had one boot on and his breeches were shredded. The kirtle he'd wrapped around the swatter was now wrapped around his body in a poor, ill-fitting state. He was covered in mud and looked like some half-formed fey beastie.

Sin looked at her with humor dancing in his midnight eyes. "Go ahead and laugh, dove. I promise I won't be offended." He draped an arm over her shoulders, drawing her close to him again, and looked around at the people gathered to welcome him back. "By the way, methinks I owe someone a new dress."

Several snickers broke out and were silenced as Angus turned a feral glare to the crowd.

"Where's the bull?" Callie asked.

"Tied to a tree, eating my boot. I'm just glad my leg is no longer in it."

That succeeded in making everyone laugh.

Angus shook his head as he drew near. "Lad, how did you manage it?"

"I run fast when chased by large bulls."

Several of the men clapped him on the back and Peg came forward with a tankard of ale.

"Where are your clothes?" Callie asked, noting he wore very little underneath his "borrowed" kirtle. Very little except for that warm, tawny flesh she found so delectable.

"The brambles caught him," Angus answered. "That's how we found him. There's shreds of English clothing from hither to yon."

Callie felt weak at the news of how close her husband had come to being seriously injured. "Are you truly unharmed?"

"A bit scratched and bruised, but nothing other than my ego is seriously damaged." Sin grinned playfully. "See now why I always travel with a sword? One never knows when a raging bull is likely to come storming down the street."

They all laughed.

"God love you, lad," Angus said, patting him on the back. "You've got a good sense of humor. Not many men could laugh in the face of such an event." Angus pushed him gently toward her. "Callie, take your mon home and see to his wounds."

"I will, Angus. Thank you."

Callie took her husband's arm. She turned him around to see one of the young lads leading their horses to them.

Sin helped her mount, then swung himself up onto his own horse.

As they left the village, she couldn't suppress the happiness inside her. "I think you won them over."

"That was never my intent."

And that was what she loved most about him. Even though her clansmen had mocked and shunned him, he had still put his life in jeopardy to save them all.

Most men wouldn't have cared one way or another about her people. But he hadn't even thought twice about risking his life for them. "You're a good man, Sin MacAllister."

He reined to a stop and turned angry, tormented eyes to her. "Never call me that."

Callie's heart clenched at what she saw on his handsome face. The raw emotions that swirled in those dark eyes. "Forgive me. It was a slip of the tongue that will never happen again."

The fire in his eyes died as she led him back to the castle.

It wasn't until they had reached the castle and entered the great hall that Callie remembered what she had asked Simon to do . . .

Out of the gathered group, she didn't know who was more stunned. Poor Sin, still wearing his one boot and dressed in a kirtle, or his brothers and Simon, who stood with Jamie, Aster, and to her surprise, Dermot.

Jamie stepped forward hesitantly. He threw his shoulders back and spoke like a grown-up. "Caledonia, I know you said we were to make him feel at home. So I'll pull one shoe off, but no one's going to make me wear a dress."

Laughter resounded through the hall. But no one laughed harder than Sin, who scooped Jamie up in his arms and tickled him. "I don't know, lad. As pretty as you are, you might look at home in a kirtle."

"I'm not pretty. I'm fierce."

Callie grabbed her brother from Sin and gave him a hug of her own. "As fierce as a gentle cub. And as precious as a rose in the dead of winter." She kissed his cheek and set him on his feet.

Grimacing, he wiped his face and dashed off to stand behind Dermot.

Lochlan shook his head. "Should we ask?"

"I had a run-in with a bull."

Simon laughed. "From where I'm standing, it looks like the bull won."

Sin smiled. "Nay, you should see the bull. He's dressed in swaddling." Sin looked about the hall, which had been decorated with bright color serge drapes and wrapped gifts that were spread out on the main table. "What's all this?"

"We're celebrating your birthday," Simon said.

Sin frowned.

"Callie's idea," Lochlan said.

He looked to his wife, who was sidestepping away from him. Catching her hand, he pulled her back. "Care to explain?"

"Aster, would you please have the pastries and cakes brought in while I attend my husband's change of clothes?"

"Aye, love."

"If you'll excuse us," she said to the men before leading Sin up the stairs.

He followed her up the narrow stairs. "Are you not going to answer my question?"

"I didn't wish to do it in front of the others."

"Why?"

She opened the door to their room and let him enter first. Then she closed the door and crossed the room to stand beside him. She wanted to pull him into her arms, but something in his demeanor told her he wouldn't welcome that. "Lochlan told me no one knew when you were born. Is it true?"

His eyes blank, he moved away from her to pull his armor out of the trunk by the window. "Aye."

Callie didn't let him get away. She crossed the room to join him at the window and as soon as he straightened, she took his chin in her hand and smiled up at him. "Then today shall mark the day of your rebirth."

He looked baffled by her words. "My rebirth?"

She nodded as she fingered his whiskered cheek, then traced the line of his jaw to his silken hair. "You're no longer alone, Sin. You now have a home and a wife who wants you. Spurn me if you must, but you will always be welcome here. And if you've no wish to be a MacAllister or earl or anything else, that is fine. But from this day forward you are a MacNeely."

His dark eyes narrowed. "I told you, I've no wish to be owned by you or anything else."

Callie's stomach drew tight in frustration. How she wished she could make him understand what it was she was offering him.

"And I am not trying to own you or even claim you. That is not the nature of what I offer and it breaks my heart that you can't understand it. Maybe one day you will. If you have to go, go. I won't hold you here. I will stay behind, and every day you are gone I will miss you. Every hour, I will think of you and wonder where you are and be worried that something might happen to you."

Sin stood in silence as her words cut through him. He'd never been more than just the most passing of thoughts to anyone. Not even his brothers. What she offered . . .

If it wasn't love, it was a damned good substitute.

"I hope and pray that I already have your child in

me. And I hope he grows to be just as fine a man as his father."

Sin ground his teeth at her words. The pain, the ache, the need inside him roared up and screamed through his soul. He couldn't stand the agony of it. It was overwhelming and shattering.

"Do not say such things to me," he growled.

"Why?"

"Because I can't stand to hear it." He felt tears prick his eyes, but he quickly banished them. Against his will, he reached out and cupped her cheek in his hand. "I don't know how to love, Callie. I don't know how to be the man you need."

"You are the man I need."

He turned away from her with a curse. Inside his emotions were tangled. He was afraid to trust in her. It was easy for her to say she would stand by him now, but once he had proof of her brother's crimes she would feel that way no longer.

Neither one of his parents had ever stood by him. His brothers might, yet they had never been put to the test.

He had been hurt so many times. Betrayed over and over by everyone in his life. His brothers each carried the same guilt Draven did over the fact that when he had been sacrificed for them, they each had felt a twinge of relief.

He didn't blame them for it, it was more than understandable, but having been the sacrificial lamb so many times, he refused to believe she wouldn't turn on him as well.

Her clan meant everything to her and her brothers even more.

Nay, her words were a lie. Not in her heart, for he knew she meant them right now. But to believe in them . . .

He'd been many things in his life. A thief, an assassin, a starving beggar, a knight and an earl. He had never been a fool. And it was one role he wouldn't play now.

But when he looked at her, it was hard to remember that. Hard to think of things other than just losing himself in the comfort she offered.

It's not meant to be.

Nay. He closed his heart. He would do as he must, and when he was through here he would return to England. Alone.

It was the way of it. He couldn't fight destiny.

Chapter 15

Callie watched as Sin dressed, his muscles rippling with every move he made. He was stunning and yet as unreachable as the sky above them. How she wished she could think of some way to breach the distance between them.

" 'Tis amazing how well you can lace your armor without assistance. I thought knights usually had a squire to help them."

Sin paused, then returned to lacing his hauberk. "I've never had a squire."

"Truly?" she asked, surprised by his confession. He was always so patient and calm with Jamie that she couldn't imagine why he detested being around children as much as he did. "Why not?"

He shrugged.

Before she could stop herself, she moved forward and poked him in the ribs.

Frowning, he rubbed his hand over the place where she had poked him. "What was that for?"

"You've got that serious face again. Remember what I said I would do to you should you get it?"

"You said tickle me, not poke me."

She smiled impishly. "In that case . . ." She rushed him.

Sin stumbled back as she tickled him even through his armor. He laughed, trying to catch her hands to stop her, but she moved even faster than he did. His spur caught in the rug on the floor and sent him crashing to the ground, with Callie on top of him.

Still laughing, he rolled over and pinned her to the floor beneath him. "You are the Mistress of Madness, aren't you?"

"Aye, and I am maddest of all for you."

His eyes were gentle and kind as he stared down at her with a hot look that made her breathless and weak. Leaning down, he rubbed noses with her, then he dipped his lips to kiss her.

Callie sighed at the passion she tasted. Och, but he felt good on top of her, even with the weight of him in his armor crushing her. He nibbled and teased her lips as his tongue swept against hers.

She buried her hands in his silken hair and held him close, delighting in the feel of him. The warm, masculine scent of him. *Don't leave me . . .*

The silent plea burned through her and she wished she could bind him to her. Wished she knew the words or actions that would make him want to stay with her as much as she wanted to stay with him.

If only it could be.

Sin closed his eyes and inhaled the sweet lavender scent of her. Felt her breasts pressing against him even through his heavy armor. He wanted inside her so badly that he shook from it.

He would give anything to have her. Anything to run away from what Henry wanted him to do.

She saw only the best inside him and it scared him to think of the day her opinion of him would change.

Sooner or later the fresh bud of love always changed into something else. If a man was lucky, it blossomed into a lasting friendship, but many more times it became hatred. He was new to her now. Yet should he stay, and she learn more about him, she would see his faults with clarity and she would grow to despise him.

It was a chance he couldn't take. For in his heart, he knew she alone could destroy him. She held the power in her eyes to do him more damage than any enemy or army.

She alone held his wary, shriveled heart.

"They will be waiting for us below," he whispered, moving to rise from her.

"They say waiting is good for a soul. It builds character."

Sin smiled at that. "Aye, but you went to such effort on my behalf that it would be remiss of me not to enjoy it."

She snickered at that. "Blaming me, are you? Now, there's a fine thing. Very well, then, we shall go, but tonight after we sup, you are mine." She raked a hungry look over him that sent even more heat to his groin. "All mine."

Sin hissed at her seductive face as he pulled her to her feet. "When you speak like that, milady, you send chills down my spine."

"Stay in this room with me, and I shall send more than that down your spine."

His body reacted instantly to her words, growing hotter and harder than he'd ever been before. Against his will, he glanced to the bed and imagined the look of her naked and beneath him. "You are an evil temptress."

She took his hand and kissed his knuckles. She ran her tongue over his flesh, sending waves of lust burning through him before she nipped his skin with her teeth. Then she pulled him toward the door. There was an evocative swish to her hips that made his body sizzle even more.

"Anytime milord is tempted, just let me know."

Grinding his teeth to stave his desire, he very reluctantly let her lead him from the room.

They headed back downstairs. But instead of the family they had left, the hall was packed full of clan members who stood about talking until their voices were united into a loud, resounding drone. People stood in groups, laughing and bantering. Dogs ran loose between legs as people ate and drank, while five men had taken up pipes and drums to play in one corner.

Callie froze at the sight, half scared of why they were there. But as soon as the crowd saw Sin, a cheerful cry of greeting echoed in the room.

"You didn't tell us you'd saved the town, lad," Aster said, stepping forward to clap him on the back.

Sin bristled and she quickly noted just how uneasy he was with all the attention. "I didn't really."

"And he's modest, too," Peg said.

"Why didn't you tell us you were a Highlander?" Angus asked. "And a MacAllister, no less. We should have known our Callie wouldn't—"

"Angus," Callie said, cutting the man off before Sin grew any more agitated. "What are all of you doing here?"

Morna came forward, leading a herd of servants bearing baked goods and treats from the village. "After the two of you left, the village decided it was time for a wedding celebration."

Sin looked bewildered by the people's newfound attitudes.

Morna smiled up at Sin. "Then, after we got here, Aster told us this is the anniversary of your birth, so now we have a double celebration."

Morna went off to direct the servants.

Smiling, Callie approached her husband, who was looking almost sheepishly at the ceiling. "Is something amiss?"

"Aye, I am wondering at what point the roof will collapse down upon us and kill us all."

She frowned at his doomed prophecy. "I beg your pardon?"

Still, he continued to inspect the walls and ceiling. "Nothing good comes without a steep price. I'm merely afraid of what limb I shall have to sacrifice for this moment."

She shook her head at him. "Ever the pessimist."

"Relax," Braden said, handing him a mug of ale. "I would say you've paid the price and this is the reward."

Sin didn't believe it for a minute. Something bad

was going to happen. It always did. Every time in his life when he had thought himself safe or even at peace, something horrible had disrupted it.

He watched as several of the villagers cleared a space in the center of the hall where people could dance to the music the five men played. Food and drink flowed freely while everyone made merry with the day.

He watched as woman after woman came up and talked to his wife and, oddly enough, spoke to him as well.

Oh, this was evil. Truly, truly demonic.

He half expected the devil himself to crash through the wall and swoop Callie up and run away with her.

"You have the look of a deer caught by a poacher," Simon said as he came to rest by his side.

"I feel more like the deer who knows the poacher is near and can't sight him."

Morna joined them and offered Sin a small cake. " 'Tis tradition for the groom to eat it."

Sin took it from her hand. "Thank you, milady."

She blushed and ambled off.

Simon leaned over. "That smells delicious."

Sin smiled. "You and your stomach, Simon. I swear, one day your gluttony shall be the death of you."

Callie came up and took him by the hand. "Come, my Lord Ogre, I want a dance with you."

Sin handed the cake over to Simon and followed his lady.

Callie was amazed at how well Sin danced. In all honesty, she'd expected him to protest or tell her he didn't know how, but that was far from the case. The man was a wondrous dancer. "I thought you said you never danced."

"I haven't before, but I've watched others enough to know." As she twirled around behind him, she raised up on her toes and placed a sweet kiss to his cheek.

The look on his face made her laugh as a cheer went up through the crowd.

"You are an amazing woman," he breathed.

"Not hardly, my lord, but I'm glad you think so."

When the song ended, they left the floor. Morna handed Callie her bride's cake.

Callie turned to him. "We're supposed to eat them together. Did you eat yours already?"

He indicated Simon with his thumb. "I gave it to Simon, but I'm sure it's gone already."

"It's supposed to be good luck to eat them together."

Morna clucked her tongue at Sin. "It's supposed to guarantee fertility. A child for every poppy seed the two of you consume."

He passed a wicked smile to Callie, not believing the superstition in the least. Still, he wouldn't insult the woman who had been kind to him. "Well, in that case, I'd best go claim it, then." He winked at his wife.

Sin crossed the hall, and it was only then he saw Simon looking a little pale. "Is something wrong?"

Sweat beaded on Simon's forehead. "I can't breathe."

Sin heard Jamie yell that one of the hounds was ill. The dog limped to the center of the hall and collapsed.

Sin's heart stilled. "Simon, did you feed anything to one of the hounds?"

"The cake," he said, his voice ragged. "It didn't taste good, so I gave some to the dog."

"Poison." Sin narrowed his eyes on Callie. "Fetch me a purgative."

He grabbed Simon's arm and wrapped it around his shoulder, then headed for the stairs. "We have to get you upstairs before any more of the poison gets through your body."

Simon stumbled so much that finally Sin picked him up and carried him like a babe.

To Sin's amazement, Simon didn't argue. That more than anything told him the severity of his friend's illness.

By the time they reached his room, Simon was trembling and sweating sheets of perspiration.

Callie quickly joined them. She gave Sin a cup of her potion and held a bucket.

Sin forced the putrid-smelling liquid down Simon and waited until his friend had emptied the contents of his stomach into her container.

All the while Sin raged inside that someone had stooped so low to kill him. And that poor Simon had been innocently caught in the plot.

Callie tended Simon as best she could. He still looked pale and weak, and she prayed they had gotten the poison out of his system in time for it to do no lasting damage. "Who could have done this?"

Sin narrowed his eyes. "Obviously one of your rebels."

"But why Simon?" she asked, not understanding why anyone would want to harm a man so kind.

"He ate the cake intended for me, Callie."

Her heart shrank at the thought. Nay, it couldn't be. After today she had thought her clan was warming up to her husband. Great saints, he had saved

Fraser's life. Why would anyone hurt Sin after what he'd done earlier?

"Who?"

Sin didn't answer. "Stay here and watch over him. I will send word to his brother."

She nodded, but in her eyes he could see the doubt she held. The pain. God have mercy on her, but by her face he could tell she couldn't grasp the horror of what someone had done.

Unfortunately, he could.

Angry and needing vengeance, Sin left the room and headed below.

Once he reached the hall, he saw that the party had dispersed. Only a few people remained in the hall. His brothers, Aster and Angus.

"How's the lad?" Aster asked.

"We don't know yet."

The looks on his brothers' faces were of hell's wrath. "They meant to get you, didn't they?" Lochlan asked.

"I would assume so."

Ewan popped his knuckles. "Then I say 'tis time we conked a few heads. What say you, brothers? Ready to beat the devil?"

"Not yet," Sin said. "I have something I need to do first." He looked to Aster. "Have you seen Morna around? I have a quick question for her."

"She was headed to the kitchen last I saw."

"My thanks." Sin went after her. By the time he reached the kitchen, she was making ready to leave.

She looked up, startled, as he came through the door.

In that instant, Sin knew. The nervous way she looked about, her instant unease.

"Where is he?" Sin asked.

"Who?"

"Dermot."

Her face grew even paler. Her hands trembled all the more. "Why would you be asking that?"

"Morna," he said, laying his hand gently on her arm to reassure her, "this is serious. It was bad enough when he had me shot with the arrow, but now an innocent man may die because he wants to play hero to his people."

She shrugged his touch off. "My son would never do anything like this." Her body told him otherwise.

"I swear to you, I just want to talk to him. I'm not going to harm him." For the moment at least.

Tears spilled down her cheeks. "I don't know where he is. He took off running the minute you carried your friend upstairs. But he didn't do it. I know he didn't."

Sin took a deep breath as the confirmation of his suspicions resonated through him. There was no longer any doubt. "He gave you the cakes, didn't he?"

"He didn't do it," she sobbed. "He's a good lad. He loves his sister. He would never seek to do her harm."

Sin drew the woman into his arms and held her quietly as she sobbed against him. "Shhh," he whispered against her head. "I just want to talk to the lad."

Regaining some of her composure, she pulled back. "I really don't know where he went."

Damn.

Sin released her and offered her a smile. "Wipe your eyes, Morna. All will be well, you'll see."

She nodded.

Sin left and headed back toward the hall. He found Aster in the narrow hallway, wringing his hands.

"It's Dermot you're after, isn't it?" the old man asked nervously.

A chill went down his spine as he watched the Highlander shift about. "You knew he was in charge of the rebels?"

Aster scoffed. "I suspected he was one of the rebels, but if you think he's got the ability to lead, there you'd be mistaken."

Sin didn't think so. He'd seen the way the others responded and looked at the boy. "He's the eldest son of the last laird. It would only make sense."

"Aye, but when Neil died, 'twas Callie they wanted as leader."

Sin arched a brow as he recalled Callie's words on the matter. "Truly?"

Aster nodded. "She's the king's blood kin and has a good head on her shoulders. Everyone in the clan agreed that even though she was a woman and barely a score-and-four years, she would be a good leader for the clan."

"Then why isn't she?"

"She wouldn't do it. She was afraid it would insult Dermot and me. She thanked everyone at the meeting and then graciously stepped down."

"And they voted you in."

"Aye."

Now everything made sense to him. Dermot's innate hatred of him and the envious stares the lad would cast at his sister and uncle when he thought no one was watching. "It must have set ill with Dermot to see his sister and then his uncle voted in while he, the legitimate son of the laird, was not."

"Aye, but he was only ten-and-three at the time. He couldn't have really hoped for it."

Sin knew better. A boy at that age held an arrogance that was surpassed only by youthful foolishness. "How did Dermot react to the news?"

"He was mad, of course. Said if he'd been born of noble blood, they wouldn't have hesitated to vote him in. He stormed out, but once he calmed down, he agreed that it was fitting I should lead."

Sin clenched his teeth. There was none so blind as a devoted parent or uncle with a child in pain. They couldn't accept the fact that the boy they loved could be capable of perpetrating such mayhem. But at Dermot's current age, Sin had been the very essence of brutal destruction.

"How long after that did the raiding start?"

"Maybe six weeks."

"And it has continued since?"

Aster nodded.

"Have they ebbed and flowed any?"

"Just while Callie was in London and since she's been back. But that doesn't mean it was Dermot. No one in the clan would want to see the lass hurt."

Sin listened and weighed the old man's words carefully. But what Aster failed to realize was that Dermot would have attacked him just based on the fact that Callie had married the enemy. Dermot would want him out of the way as soon as possible. Especially given the way the MacNeely people had treated Sin today. If they accepted Sin, then they would accept the

English, and in Dermot's mind such a thing would have to be stopped at all costs.

Even if it hurt Callie.

Nay, unlike Aster and Morna, Sin held no doubt of the boy's guilt. Their words only solidified it.

"Have you any idea where Dermot might have gone to hide?"

Aster thought it over. "Aye."

"Where?"

He tilted his chin stubbornly and eyed Sin in a way that let him know the old man would never willingly betray his nephew. "Let me go and see if I can speak to him. If you go, he's liable to run even farther."

That was true enough. "Then find him and bring him home."

Aster hesitated. "What are you going to do to the lad if I do?"

Sin took a deep breath as he considered it. In the end, he told the old man the truth. "I don't know yet. I want to speak to him before I decide."

Fury smoldered in Aster's blue eyes. "I can't let you harm him, nor send him to live with those English of yours. You'll only have him over my dead body."

Sin took the edge out of his voice and tried to reason with him. "Aster, this isn't a game we're playing. Henry is ready to make war on your clan. And Dermot doesn't seem willing to stop until that happens. Do you truly want to see your entire clan destroyed because of the actions of one hotheaded boy?"

"I know he's not the leader," Aster insisted with blind devotion. "I will go talk to him and find out who put him up to this. Whoever it is, we will see him punished."

"And if I'm right?"

The old man's eyes turned dull. "You're wrong, lad. You have to be."

Callie sat with a bowl of cool water and a cloth, bathing Simon's forehead. She found it strange that she cared so much for this Englishman, and yet she did. He and Sin's brothers had come to be family to her in a very short time.

But what amazed her most was how much her husband meant to her. How much the thought of living without him hurt her inside. It was almost enough to cripple her.

The door opened.

Looking up, she saw Sin hesitating in the threshold with one hand on the doorknob and the other on the wooden frame. Och, but he was the finest-looking man she'd ever beheld. Even when he had grief and worry lining his brow.

"How is he?" he asked quietly, stepping inside the room and shutting the door behind him.

"He's sleeping. I think he'll be all right, though. What of you?"

Sin drew near, his gaze on his friend. "I wish I had eaten the cake instead."

She knew how much he meant that. She could see the sincerity on his face and it cut her deeply. "Did you send word to Draven?"

He nodded. "Dermot has run off and Aster has gone to find him."

Callie's chest tightened at the news. "I should have confirmed your suspicions that Dermot was one of the rebels."

"My lady, never apologize to me because you sought to protect someone you love. I'd expect no less of you."

"But my silence could have killed you and Simon."

Sin reached out and touched her hair. He ran his fingers through the silken strands ever so gently. He ached with yearning. Her light green eyes were filled with the same fear and uncertainty that ate at him.

Hold me, Callie. It was a silent plea that tore through his soul.

He'd known painful desires all his life. For food, for shelter, for love.

But what he felt for her made a mockery of every one of them. Morbidly, he wondered if she would ever protect him the way she had protected her brother.

Would she care if he were dead? She'd told him as much, but he couldn't quite accept the reality of it.

In his heart was the fear that she would leave him soon. That the last few days were all some imagined dream and that he would awaken alone in his castle with no one but servants who feared his very presence. He couldn't imagine a day without her gentle teasing. A day without her laughter.

He didn't even want to try.

"Would you two go on and kiss already?"

Callie laughed and turned to face Simon. "What?"

Simon opened his eyes and pinned them both with a bored stare. "I'm not dead and I wasn't really asleep. I feel like the devil used me for tilting practice, but still I'm quite sure I shall live. That is, if someone will stop trying to tie my intestines into a knot.

"Being as I am in pain, the last thing I want is to watch the two of you all lovey-dovey over there. My stomach is quite queasy enough. Sin, tell the woman you love her, for Peter's sake. Callie, do the same, and let me lie here in my sweet misery all alone."

Sin stroked his jaw with his thumb as he eyed his friend irritably. "Little brother, at the moment I should like to tie your intestines into a knot myself."

Simon was completely unperturbed. "Have at it, then, just make the pain stop."

"Can I get you anything?" Callie asked Simon.

"Nay, just promise me the next time I see a cake, you'll slap me before I take a bite of it." He rolled over. "Now, may I preserve what little dignity I have left?"

Sin smiled. "Look to the bright side, Si. You didn't empty your stomach on a guest."

"So say you. Now leave."

Callie led Sin toward the door, then paused and looked back at Simon. "If you need anything, call."

Simon rolled over and gave her a peeved glare.

"We're going," she said, taking Sin's hand and pulling him from the room.

Sin thought he had a reprieve from Simon's tirade until Callie cornered him in the hallway outside Simon's room. She pegged him with a penetrating stare that let him know he was in serious trouble. "What did he mean by that?"

"By what?"

"That you love me. Do you?"

Sin swallowed. He thought he did, but who was he to know the difference? So he answered her honestly. "I don't even know the meaning of that word."

She looked as though she couldn't decide if she should kick him or strangle him. "Stubborn man. But at least you're not like the others of your kind, quick to declare your heart and then ever quick to reclaim it. At least this way, should you ever say the words, I shall know you mean them."

He stared at her in awe of her inner strength. "You're not mad at me?"

"I am merely mad for you, Sin. One day, I hope you'll feel the same for me."

Stunned, he watched as she walked off.

"Oh, I am a fool," he whispered under his breath. She had offered him so much of herself and he had offered her so little.

And for what?

Fear?

Stupidity?

You've been alone all your life. You know you can survive solitude. You know you can survive conditions that would make hell seem paradise.

So why was he so afraid now?

And so what if he ended up like Ewan? He already lived that way—lost in his solitary company, with no friends save a tankard of ale.

"Callie."

He hadn't realized he'd spoken her name aloud until she turned to face him. "Aye?"

He stared at her in the hallway, her red hair curling

around her shoulders. She wore the dark blue, green and yellow plaid of her father, her black kirtle hugging her lush figure.

He'd never beheld anyone or anything more beguiling or precious.

"Can you teach me what love is?"

Callie couldn't breathe as the quiet words reached out to her. There was so much pain and heartfelt yearning behind them that it brought tears to her eyes. He was so vulnerable standing there. He stood proud and tall before her and yet she sensed just how easily she could hurt him if she rejected him. Not that she ever would.

Laughing and crying, she ran to him and threw her arms around his shoulders. "Aye, my love. I would be delighted to."

Sin hadn't realized until that moment just how afraid he'd been of her rejection. Just how much of his heart he'd left exposed to her.

His wounded heart soaring, he scooped her up in his arms and kissed her. The taste of her lips drove him to madness. The feel of her body so pliant and warm against his . . .

He had to have her. Now. This instant. He couldn't stand another moment of being without her.

With determined strides, he carried her to their room and laid her gently on the bed.

Her cheeks turned bright pink. " 'Tis the middle of the day."

"I know."

"What if someone comes looking for us?"

He bolted the door.

Callie laughed, until he turned around and she saw the raw hunger in his eyes. The look singed her.

He moved slowly, languidly toward the bed, peeling off his clothes as he came, until he was naked before her. She trembled at the fierce sight of him. The sleek rippling of his muscles as he joined her on the bed.

"I want you, Caledonia," he breathed, unlacing the neck of her kirtle. "I want to taste every inch of your body. Slowly, until I've devoured you."

She shivered at his demanding tone and the feel of his hot hand cupping her breast.

"I want your heart, Sin," she said, running her hand through his hair.

He pushed her dress down her body and removed her clothes until she was fully exposed to him. "It's battered and useless, but what remains of it is all yours, milady."

No one had ever spoken more beautiful words to her. His eyes hooded and dark, he stared at her bare body as if he relished every piece of it.

He ran his hand over her skin, gently testing the texture of her. Callie arched her back, her body on fire for more of him. He pulled her leg up to rest against his chest and kissed her knee, while his hands ran up and down her thigh, sending chills all over her. He locked gazes with her as he tilted her leg toward him, exposing her to his questing fingers.

She moaned as he touched her core.

"I love the way you look when I do that," he whispered, nipping her bent knee.

His fingers continued to torment her while he shifted his body to lie between her legs.

Callie looked down at him as he nudged her legs farther apart so that he could stare at the most private place of her body. Heat scalded her cheeks. Surely this was indecent, and yet it made her entire body burn with erotic pleasure.

He brought his other hand up, and slid it down her wet cleft, then he gently separated her nether folds and placed his mouth upon her.

Callie threw her head back and moaned as pleasure ripped through her. Never had she felt such unbridled pleasure or heat.

Sin growled at the taste of her. He'd never tasted a woman before, and yet he doubted if any could compete to the rare treasure he'd found. Closing his eyes, he savored her. He felt her body quivering to every lick he delivered, felt her thigh muscles involuntarily contract as he took his time pleasuring her.

She buried her hands in his hair, pressing him closer to her as she lifted her hips in invitation.

She looked wild and beautiful in her abandon.

Callie shivered and burned from the sensation of his mouth tormenting her. She'd never experienced anything like this at all. It seemed she was all conflicted emotions. Weak and strong, hot and shivery.

And still he gave her pleasure. She'd never dreamed anything would feel like this. And when he slid two fingers inside her, she really feared she would die from the ecstasy of it.

The feeling of his hands and mouth on her was more than she could stand. Her head swirling, she felt her body rip apart into spasms of pure bliss.

Sin growled again as he watched her face while she

came for him. Aye, he loved the sight of her that way. The feel of her body clutching his.

And he wanted her in a way that bordered on desperate. Licking and nibbling his way up her body, he lay down behind her.

"What are you doing?" she asked, her voice breathless.

"I want to try something different." It was something he had heard of from other men and had seen a few times from men and women who hadn't been particularly bashful about who saw them flagrante delicto.

Kissing her on the shoulder, he rolled her over until she was on her knees.

Callie frowned at him, but trusted him completely. She knew he would never hurt her.

He came up behind her, wrapped his arms around her, and, holding her back against his chest, he ran his hands all over her body. She sighed contentedly at the warm feel of him. His hot, pulsing shaft rested against her hip as he gently ran his tongue down her neck.

"Oh, Sin," she moaned, her body on fire from his touch.

"I will never get enough of you, Caledonia," he said raggedly in her ear.

He ran his hands down her arms until he captured her hands in his. Then he gently pushed her forward until her hands rested on the carved headboard. He laid a tender kiss on her shoulder and spread her legs wide.

Callie bit her lip nervously, not sure what he intended. He pulled back from her and braced his hands on her hips. Two seconds later, he drove himself inside her, up to the hilt. She cried out at the pleasure of his body so hard and deep inside hers.

Hissing in pleasure, she felt herself go weak from it. Saints, how she loved this man. Loved sharing her body with him and knowing he was hers. All hers.

He buried his face in her neck as he moved against her. Hot and slow. In and out he slid, making her quiver. She loved the way he felt inside and behind her, the way his lips and tongue teased her flesh.

Acting on instinct, she matched his strokes until he paused and held himself still.

"That's it, my love," he whispered to her. "Show me what feels good to you."

Sin ground his teeth as pleasure ripped through him while she rode him slow and easy. She pushed herself away from the headboard until she was leaning back against him while she writhed in his arms. She reached over her head, pulling him closer to her as she claimed his lips with hers.

He gladly obliged, while he ran his hands over her taut breasts and down her soft belly until he reached the moist, tangled curls.

Their tongues danced in time to her strokes as he separated the tender folds of her body and slid his fingers against her.

Callie groaned at the feel of him. This was so incredible. She'd never dreamed such a thing existed. His touch branded her. Made her ache and yet gave her comfort.

And when she came again, she held his head close to hers and screamed out from the fierceness of it.

Sin laughed softly at her hold on him. He could

barely breathe, but he didn't mind in the least. He waited until the last spasm had left her body before he took control again. Leaning her forward, he thrust himself faster into her warmth. Aye, she was heaven to him.

And when he found his own release a moment later, he held her close and whispered her name.

Entwined and fully spent, they collapsed on the bed.

Sin lay there, holding her back to his chest, his mind wandering. He'd never had an afternoon like this. Never experienced the comfort of loving arms.

He wrapped his arms around her and listened as she quickly dozed off.

Smiling, he leaned over her to watch the tranquillity of her features while her breath tickled the flesh of his arms. If he could, he would stay here forever. Lost in this peaceful paradise that was her.

Closing his eyes, he did what he hadn't done since he was a small boy. He prayed. He prayed for the politics of Henry and her brother not to come between them. Prayed for some miracle that would see them with a future together.

And as he lay there, behind the lids of his eyes he did another thing he'd not done since early childhood. He hoped. He saw in his mind the children he would love to have. Little boys and girls with their mother's warmth and spirit.

He wanted this dream. With every piece and part of him, he ached for it.

He had to have it.

And yet even as the peaceful thoughts lulled him, in the back of his mind he feared that hope. Because the realist in him knew better. Dermot was out there, right now, plotting the downfall of his own clan, and if Aster couldn't put a stop to it tonight, then one way or the other, come morning, Sin would.

He only hoped that when he did, his wife could forgive him.

Chapter 16

That night, neither Aster nor Dermot came home. Callie and Morna paced the floors of the great hall, while Sin and his brothers sat at the table, drinking ale and saying little. Simon's health had improved, but he was still upstairs in his bed.

Sin watched the women as long as he could, but a prickling in his gut told him something was seriously wrong.

"Morna," he said gently. "I know you have no trust of me. But I really think you ought to tell me where your son might be hiding. I want to go find both of them."

She shared a nervous look with Callie. The doubt in her eyes was tangible.

Callie patted her arm. "I trust him, Morna."

Still, the woman looked skeptical, and Sin couldn't blame her. It was her mother's love for her sons that he adored most about Morna.

Sin sought to reassure her. "I will take Lochlan with me. He's a good Highland laird and you know you can trust him."

Morna hesitated a minute more before she finally spoke. "While my parents lived, they had an old crofter's hut up in the north hills. It's dilapidated and aged, but I'm relatively sure he'd be there now."

Sin rose to his feet. "Lochlan, Braden, we ride. Ewan, stay here and wait for the men. If Dermot returns, make sure he stays put."

Ewan nodded earnestly while they made for the door.

Callie followed the small group outside and watched as they mounted. Her heart was heavy with fear and worry. It was typical of Dermot to be out and about at all hours, but Aster . . .

She hoped he was all right.

"Please be careful," she said to them.

Lochlan and Braden rode ahead, while Sin kneed his horse to the steps where she stood. She could see the dark desire in his eyes as he watched her. "I will return them to you, my lady."

"I know you will. I've never doubted you."

He closed his eyes as if he savored her words. He moved his horse closer, then reached up and pulled her into his arms.

Callie moaned as he covered her lips with his and gave her a fierce kiss. His tongue stroked hers while she clung to him, needing to feel his reassurance.

He pulled back and brushed his hand over her swollen lips. "Watch over Morna until my return."

"I will."

His eyes hungry and tormented, he set her back on the stoop, then kicked his horse forward.

Callie watched him ride out of the bailey, her heart heavy. She had seen something in his eyes. Something dark and evil that scared her.

But she refused to doubt him. He loved her as much as she loved him. She was sure of it. And one day, she hoped he would realize it, too.

Sin, Lochlan and Braden rode for two hours before they reached the hut. As quickly as possible, they dismounted and searched the dark cottage.

It was empty.

"Someone was here," Lochlan said, his hand on the hearth. "It's still warm."

"Where would they be?" Braden asked.

Sin sighed. "There's no telling."

Disgusted and weary, Sin led them to the horses, then back in the direction of the MacNeely castle. They hadn't gone far when they saw a tremendous blaze in the valley far below on the opposite side of the hill.

"Any idea what's over there?" Sin asked Lochlan.

Lochlan shook his head. "None whatsoever, but it looks like a bad fire. Like an entire village is going up."

They raced toward the fire as fast as they could.

As soon as they were close enough to see what was going on, Sin reined his horse to a stop. It was unbelievable. Bodies, both Scots and English, were lying everywhere.

This was no village. This was a battlefield.

"What the devil is this?" Lochlan asked, dismounting his ride.

Sin couldn't speak. He'd seen things much worse than this in his life as a soldier. But what horrified him was the faces he knew so well on both sides of the conflict.

What he couldn't figure out was how the Englishmen had gotten here without his knowing it.

"They're royal guards and knights," Sin said, sliding from the saddle. His heart pounding, he looked to Braden and Lochlan. "Henry is here."

"The king?" Braden asked.

He nodded.

Lochlan actually went pale at the news. "What do you think happened to cause this?"

Sin closed his eyes as he fought the rage swirling inside him. Unfortunately, he had a really good idea what had transpired this night.

"I would say Dermot led a sortie against the king. I can't imagine why he would be so damned stupid. Nor do I know why Henry is here in Scotland right . . ." Sin paused as he recalled the notice from Oxley. The king had been riding to Scotland to survey the damage of the MacNeely rebels. Damn!

And Dermot had been there in the crowd to hear that announcement.

"Henry will want blood for this," Braden said.

"I know." And Sin did. Henry would never forgive a massacre like this. He would want to make an example out of everyone who had participated in it.

Lochlan came forward. "Why don't we stand guard over the bodies while you return to get help so that we can either get these men home or—"

"Nay," Sin interrupted. "If any more of Henry's forces return, they will kill you without question. All they will see are the English bodies and your plaid. We have to go back together and let me send word to Henry."

When Callie heard the horses approach, she thought it was her husband returning. She ran to the door in relief, then stumbled back as she saw Dermot carrying Aster's limp body in his youthful arms.

She crossed herself. "What is this, Dermot?"

His cheeks were covered in blood, dirt and tears and his eyes were those of an ancient who had seen the devil and left his soul with him. "I killed him," Dermot wailed. "I killed them all."

Morna's scream echoed as she rushed to her son.

Dermot sank to his knees in the foyer and held Aster in his arms. He rocked his uncle back and forth as if willing him to wake up and live again. "I dinna mean it. Oh, God, I dinna want you to die, Aster, you old fool."

Morna wailed and wrapped her arms around Dermot while he sat there rocking Aster in his arms. Jamie came running down the stairs to see what had happened, but Callie whirled and sent him to his room with Ewan. She didn't want the lad to see this.

She herself didn't want to see this, and the last thing Jamie needed was the memory of his brother and uncle wrapped together and covered in blood.

Tears welled in her eyes, but she held them back. She had to understand this event that was completely beyond her comprehension.

She knelt on the floor by Dermot's side. "Dermot, tell me what happened."

He was sobbing now.

Callie took his face in her hands and forced him to look at her. "You must tell me what happened."

"I just wanted to capture Henry." His words came out in short staccato.

Her heart shrank. "*Henry . . . king of England?*"

He nodded.

"What were you thinking?"

Dermot wailed. "Fraser told me he was come to settle this matter once and for all. That the king would have all of us on a gibbet. I thought if we captured him like he did you, we could settle this by forcing him to sign a charter leaving Scotland to the Scots."

His shoulders shook from the weight of his grief and guilt. "The English are supposed to be cowards. Da always said one Scot could beat ten of them, and they've always run from us in the past. Never once did they turn and fight."

Callie's tears fell as she felt for her brother's youthful arrogance. This was a harsh way to grow up and she would sell her soul if she could erase this night and give him back his innocence.

"Before you attacked settlers, Dermot. Not knights trained and sworn to protect their king."

"They fought like demons. They were everywhere at once. Behind us, in front of us. We couldn't move for them."

She brushed his muddy and blood-soaked hair back from his face as he continued his tale. "Aster tried to stop the fighting. He was trying to get me home, and . . ." He squeezed his eyes shut as if reliving it. "The cowardly bastards stabbed him in the back while he was reaching for me."

Callie closed her eyes as her heart splintered.

The door to the hall opened. She looked up, half expecting to see the English king in the doorway, demanding Dermot's head.

It wasn't.

Sin stood in the entranceway with his brothers. By the look on his face, she knew he'd already found out about the attack.

Sin stood frozen by the scene before him. Dermot cradled Aster's body while his mother held onto his shoulders and wept. Callie sat by his side with the weight of grief and fear dark in her large eyes. The tears on her cheeks weakened his anger.

The sound of Dermot's and Morna's weeping cut through him.

"It was an accident," Callie said, rising to her feet. "He dinna mean for any of it to happen."

Sin looked at her blankly, shielding his own grief from her. "I need to speak with Dermot. Alone."

Nodding, she pulled Morna away while the older woman protested.

"Me wee bairn needs me," she wept, reaching for Dermot.

Sin cast a grateful look to Callie, then he took Dermot's arm and hauled him to the small council room near the stairs.

None too gently, he sat the boy down in a chair, then went to slam the door closed.

"Wipe your face," Sin said, his voice harsh. "If

you're man enough to lead an army into battle, then you're man enough to sit there and not weep like a woman over it."

Dermot wiped his ragged and torn tunic sleeve across his face, the gesture so childlike that Sin realized just what he was dealing with. At ten-and-six, he had been battle-hardened and empty. Death had meant nothing to him.

But the boy before him had never known such. He'd been pampered and coddled by all of his family and clan. The little raids they had perpetrated had been meant to frighten the English and had amounted to nothing more than sport and property damage.

Tonight had been a hard birth for Dermot.

Dermot sniffed back his tears and drew a ragged breath.

Sin softened his tone as he spoke. "Now tell me what happened."

To his credit, Dermot pulled himself together and faced him like a man. "We went to capture Henry to use as a hostage."

"Your brilliant plan?"

Dermot nodded. "We knew he was headed to Oxley and we'd been waiting in the valley, knowing he'd have to come through there to reach it. So we thought we would extend him our hospitality."

"How did the fighting start?"

The boy's lips quivered. "We stopped them and asked them to turn Henry over. They laughed at me, and the next thing I knew, the English attacked us."

It was on the tip of his tongue to ask him how he

could be so stupid as to think they would just hand over their king, but Sin withheld his caustic sarcasm.

Dermot drew another deep breath. "I tried to tell the others to run, but they wouldn't listen. They kept yelling to kill the king. I got scared and . . ."

"Ran?"

He nodded. "I met Aster in the woods. He thought he could stop the others. He thought they would listen." Tears seeped quietly from his eyes. "You bastards, you killed him."

"Nay," Sin said gently, "fate killed him. It wasn't you, nor I, nor anyone else. You haven't been in battle to know the mind-set that takes over a soldier. The bloodlust, fear and self-preservation that knot your gut and make you do unspeakable things."

Unfortunately, the boy knew it now.

Dermot looked up at him with a maturity that surprised him. "What am I to do now? I'm dead, aren't I?"

Sin drew a deep breath as he considered the matter. God help him, but he saw no other resolution. "Do you want me to lie to you?"

Dermot shook his head. "How do you stand living with the knowledge of the men you have killed?"

"I honestly don't know. I try not to think about it, but when I do, I try to rationalize it. I tell myself that had I not killed them, they would have killed me. As for the others . . . Again, I had no choice. Had I not done it, my life would have ended by a means that would make even an executioner have nightmares."

Sin moved to sit on the edge of the desk and he eyed the boy with compassion. "The cloak of leadership is a hard one to wear. But once donned, you can't just shrug it off casually."

"Meaning?"

"You have to bear the consequences of your decisions. Those men believed in you and followed you because they thought you were worthy of leading them. If you choose to run away from this and hide, it will be a slap to every man who was with you tonight. To every man who thought you were worth the cost of his life."

Dermot sat quietly for a long time, thinking on those words. "I wish I could do this day over."

"I know, lad. Many are the times I've had the same thought."

He met Sin's gaze. "If you'll let me change my clothes and wash my face, I'll go quietly to your king."

Sin stood there in silence. In his mind, he could see the way Morna had held on to Dermot. The way Dermot had looked when Sin had first sat him down in that chair.

In the span of the last few minutes, the boy had just become a man.

"Go clean up."

Dermot nodded and left.

Sin followed and paused as he caught sight of a servant taking Aster's body upstairs for burial preparation. His wife stood in the foyer, leaning against Lochlan. But as soon as she saw him, she ran to him for comfort.

Sin held tightly to her and felt her shaking in his arms. She didn't speak, but he knew her thoughts. In one night, over one act of foolishness, she'd lost her brother and her uncle.

He only prayed she didn't lose her clan as well.

"Braden," he said softly to his brother, "I need to get a message to Henry. Will you dress in some of my clothes and deliver it?"

"Aye."

Sin inclined his head in thanks. Callie lifted her head and it was the look in her eyes that scorched him. She was terrified and grief-stricken.

"You're going to give Dermot to them." It was a whispered statement.

"Henry will demand someone be given to him. He can't let such actions go without punishment. This was an attempt on his life and many men were killed over it. If he does nothing, he will be seen as weak and ineffectual. Two things a king who is fighting for his throne can't afford."

"I know." She trembled even more, but her tears were gone. "I need to speak to Dermot."

Reluctantly, Sin watched her go, then went to write his missive to Henry while Braden dressed as an English knight.

With every word he wrote to Henry, Sin knew in his heart he was going to lose his wife. She might say she understood, but she was choosing between brother and husband. A husband she barely knew and a brother she had loved for almost a score of years. True, not all siblings loved one another, but she and Dermot did. Much like he and his own brothers. Even though distance and time had separated them, they had always cared for each other.

Nay. In time, she would grow to hate him for this.

Growling, he tore up his note and quickly wrote another. In his heart, he knew what needed to be done. It was the only way to see her happy.

Chapter 17

It amazed Callie that Sin didn't send her brother straight to the king.

But in the morning, she knew why. Henry, his guard, and all the Englishmen who had inhabited Oxley came to rest outside her castle. Her people gathered in the bailey, terrified of what the English army wanted.

Sin had ordered the gates closed and manned, and had left her so he could don his armor. Her heart hammering, she did her best to keep everyone calm.

But inside, she was shaking and terrified.

She stood on the stoop of the castle, with Braden, Lochlan, Dermot and Ewan by her side. Simon, looking a bit pale and weak, joined them. "Henry is out there, eh?"

Callie nodded. "Aye and wanting MacNeely blood." Her gaze went to Dermot, who stood proud beside her. She saw the fear in his eyes as he held tight to Jamie's hand.

The door to the castle opened and everyone present fell to silence. Callie turned to see what had them transfixed.

Her heart stopped.

Standing in the doorway was her husband. And he was dressed in her father's dark blue, green and yellow plaid.

The magnitude of that gesture tore through her. *I will not be owned.* How many times had he said that to her?

Tears welled in her eyes at the sight. In that instant, Sin had declared his allegiance to her in a way that shook her soul deeply. The man who wanted nothing to claim him, and nothing to own, wore her colors.

She'd never loved him more.

Their gazes locked, but it was the emptiness of his that scared her even more than the fact that Henry was waiting outside to kill her brother.

Sin was hiding his feelings from her.

"I am ready to go," Dermot announced bravely.

Sin inclined his head to him. "Let me speak to Henry first."

"You think you can talk him into sparing Dermot?" Morna asked, her tone thick with hope.

"I shall see what I can do."

Sin moved to Callie and cupped her cheek in his warm hand. "Wish me luck."

"I do, Sin. You know I do."

He dipped his head and kissed her lightly on the lips, then walked down the steps and through the crowd. Callie didn't move again until she saw him leave her castle by the small postern gate.

She ran to the wall and up the wooden stairs to the

parapets with Simon, her brothers and the MacAllisters behind her. Her heart hammering, she watched her husband approach his king.

Silence held the air and not even the wind itself dared to stir the tenseness of this morning.

Sin took a deep breath as he surveyed the English knights around him. The few he knew frowned at his garb, but said nothing as he made his way slowly toward Henry, who regarded him curiously.

"Henry Plantagenet, King of England, I, Sin MacAllister of the Clan MacNeely, greet you."

Henry looked less than pleased. "Are you trying to amuse us or anger us with your clothes?"

"Neither, Sire. I am here to set right what happened last night."

Henry slid from the back of his horse and approached him so that they could speak without being overheard. "Then you know about it?"

"Aye. Unfortunately, I found out too late to stop it."

Henry nodded as he led him farther away from the crowd. Two of Henry's personal guards fell in behind them, but kept a discreet distance. "Then you know we've come for the Raider. Hand him over."

"I can't do that."

Henry stopped dead in his tracks and arched a censoring brow. "Is our hearing failing or did you say what we think you said?"

Sin stiffened his spine, prepared to bear the full brunt of Henry's anger. "The MacNeely is dead. He was killed in the fighting last night. Those who remain have learned their lesson. Believe me. There will never be another raid by the MacNeelys against you."

"Who is the new MacNeely laird?" Henry asked curiously.

"They have yet to vote, but I can assure you, the new laird will want nothing but peace from you."

Henry narrowed his eyes suspiciously. "And the Raider? Was he killed as well last night?"

Sin stood in silence. *Lie, damn you, lie.* If he told Henry the Raider was dead, then the matter would be dropped. Instantly. But he had never lied to Henry before.

You could have her forever. No one would ever know.

But it would be built on a lie.

What kind of future would they have if he knew he had deceived the very person who had given him his freedom?

Nay, he couldn't do that. He refused to. All he'd ever had in this world was his honor, and no one would take that from him.

"The Raider is finished," Sin said simply.

"But is he dead?"

Sin shook his head slowly.

"Then we want him. Now."

Sin closed his eyes at the words he'd known Henry would speak. Facing his king without fear or remorse, he said slowly, "Then you'll have to come through me."

Henry scoffed and glared. "Are you mad?"

"Nay, Sire. But I am in earnest."

Henry gaped in disbelief. "You would die in his place?"

"If need be."

"And if he raids after your death, you will have sacrificed yourself for naught."

"He will not raid again. I know it."

Rage darkened Henry's face. It was a look Sin knew all too well.

Sin summoned the last of their friendship as he spoke to his king. "I will sign a full confession of treason claiming that I was the one who raided you from the very beginning. My enemies at court will gladly believe it and you will have your Raider for public execution. All I ask is for your word of honor that you will not retaliate against the MacNeelys once I'm gone."

"If I refuse?"

"You will lose face and I will fight you with every ounce of my ability."

Henry's eyes showed his respect at those words. They both knew Sin had no equal in battle. Not even Henry.

"Very well, then, we proclaim you the Raider."

"Do I have your word, Henry? You will leave the MacNeelys in peace?"

"Aye, old friend. I give you my word that so long as they refrain from further attacking my people, I will leave them in peace."

Sin nodded. Henry might be a lot of things, but he, too, was a man of honor.

"Guards," Henry ordered, "take him."

Sin didn't protest as they seized his arms and led him away.

His only regret was that he didn't dare turn and look up at his wife. He was afraid that if he did, he wouldn't be able to go through with this. He wanted her more than he wanted anything else in the world.

But in his beleaguered heart, he knew this was what had to be.

Callie watched in terror as the royal guards grabbed her husband and tied his hands behind his back. "What are they doing?"

"They're taking Sin," Simon whispered.

Fear tore through her. "What does this mean?"

Simon refused to meet her gaze. She saw the fear and pain in his eyes as he watched them put Sin on a horse while the king remounted his steed. "It means he refused to give Henry Dermot's name."

"Nay," she breathed, her heart shattering. "Why would he do such a thing?"

"I have no idea."

"Because he's a bloody damned fool," Lochlan snarled. "He's planning to die in your brother's stead."

Callie couldn't breathe as those words assailed her.

"Wait!" Callie shouted down to the Englishmen below.

She saw Henry kick his horse forward. "What say you?"

"Why do you take my husband?"

Henry arched a regal brow. "He has proclaimed himself to be the Raider and as such he is to be executed for his attempt on our life."

His words ripped her heart into pieces. Nay, this couldn't be real. It had to be some horrible nightmare. And yet she knew it wasn't.

She glared at King Henry. "Sin didn't do it and well you know it."

"He says he did."

"He lies to protect . . ." Her voice faded as she caught herself before she betrayed her brother.

Henry leaned forward in his saddle, very interested in her words. "Tell us, my lady, whom does he protect?" Then he said the cruelest thing of all. "Caledonia, if you have any love in your heart for your husband, then give us the name we need to save his life."

She stiffened her spine as she looked to where Sin sat on his horse with his spine rigid, his shoulders proud and determined. She would never betray Dermot, nor did she intend to see Sin suffer for a crime he hadn't committed. "I want my husband released. Now."

Henry smirked at her. "Then offer us another to die in his stead."

She looked to Simon, whose face had gone pale. "What can I do?" she asked frantically.

"Nothing. Henry must have a scapegoat. It's either your brother or your husband, milady. There's no way around it."

Uttering a fetid curse, Ewan grabbed Dermot and moved to toss him over the wall.

Lochlan and Braden grabbed their brother and pulled the squirming Dermot from his hands, then stood between the two of them.

"Nay!" Ewan roared, reaching for Dermot, who was now cowering behind Braden's back. "I won't see Sin killed for a stupid lad who has no more sense than a leek pea."

Lochlan grabbed his brother and hauled him back. "Calm yourself, Ewan. None of us wants to see Sin dead."

Tears fell down Callie's cheeks as she watched the king withdraw from her castle and give the order for them to leave.

Oh, Lord, nay! The protest choked her as she watched them leading her husband away. To die.

All his life, Sin had been sacrificed to save others. He'd lost his innocence, his childhood, his freedom, his very soul, and now he would lose his life.

And for what?

"Oh, Sin," she breathed.

Callie turned around on the parapet and looked to the people who stood along the walls with her. The people gathered in the bailey below. These were her people now that Aster was gone.

She would be leader. There was no one else to take the seat of power over the MacNeely clan.

What is your first act of duty?

It was her father's voice she heard in her head. Her father's philosophy that came back to her with an alarming clarity.

Safe by my strength. Twas the motto of her clan. The motto she and Dermot had been raised with.

For the first time in her life, she truly understood those words.

No one threatened a MacNeely. She would die before she saw her Sin sacrificed in protection of her brother.

Her heart fired by an inner strength and certainty she didn't understand, she pulled back from the wall.

"I have a plan," she announced to the men. "Lochlan, I need a favor."

"It appears your wife has abandoned you already," Henry said as he rode beside Sin.

Sin refused to let Henry know how much those words hurt him. He would never admit to anyone, not even himself, that what he had really wanted was for her to stop him.

Right until the moment the castle had faded from his sight, a part of him had longed to hear Callie cry out that she loved him too much to see him die. That she would do anything to see him safe.

It was a fool's dream and well he knew it.

"She does what she must to protect her people, much like someone else I know."

Henry snorted. "We never thought we'd see *you* self-sacrificing for a putrid Scot. Nor bearing their mark. Tell us, Sin, what brought about this change in you?"

Sin didn't answer. He couldn't.

What had brought about this change? The gentle smile of a winsome maid who had reached deep inside his dead heart and restarted it.

Closing his eyes, he summoned an image of her face and held it dear.

What he did, he did for her. Now she would be able to have the peace that meant so much to her. Dermot would never again dare to raise MacNeely arms against England, and Callie would have her people safe and whole.

There would be no more bloodshed.

Henry let out a slow breath, and when he spoke, it

was without the cold formality of a king. "Sin, don't make me do this. You are the only man I truly don't want to kill. Give me something to save your life."

"I can't do it, Henry."

"Can't or won't?"

"Won't."

"Damn you!"

Sin laughed at that and repeated the king's words back to him. "If I am damned, it is surely for more than this small matter."

Henry's jaw flexed. "Very well. We shall take you back to London, where we will make quite an example of you. Our only hope is that when your innards are being scraped from inside you while you're still alive to feel it, you will still think this sacrifice a noble one."

Henry kicked his horse forward and left Sin alone with his thoughts.

They rode through the day, only breaking for a small repast at noon. As expected, no one bothered to offer food to Sin. There was no need to waste supplies on a dead man.

Ostracized by all, he was left alone until they made their camp that evening.

Sin spent the night lying on the cold ground out in the open, chained to a log. He should be cold and uncomfortable, but thoughts of his wife stayed in his heart.

He'd always assumed he would die in battle. Felled by an enemy sword or arrow. He'd never dared to dream that it would be love that killed him.

He'd known love for such a short time that it

hardly seemed right it would be the death of him, and yet he could think of no better ending.

He couldn't stand by and let Callie's brother be taken and killed, nor could he have killed Dermot himself.

His days as an assassin were over. He'd left that part of himself in England, and his heart he had left with his wife.

Now there was nothing left of him. He was an empty shell that existed only to remember Callie's gentle face.

Closing his eyes, he took comfort in the knowledge that though he wouldn't live out his life with Callie, at least he'd been fortunate enough to have her for a small span of time.

Dying was inevitable, but until the day she had turned that breathtaking smile on him, he had never really lived.

In the morning, Henry gathered up his troops and they began the long march that would take them home. With every league they passed, Sin felt the distance from his wife profoundly in his heart. How he wished they could have had one more day together. One more night when he might hold her close and love her.

Why had he fought against her? It seemed so foolish now, and if he could only have the time back, he would spend it in her arms, holding her close and loving her with the whole of his body. His heart.

Aye, to feel her lips one more time . . .

A strange sound from the woods alerted them.

"What was that?" one of the guards asked.

It had sounded like some sort of hoarse bird. Sin looked up to see a movement in the trees. Knights made ready as the royal guard encircled Henry.

From the foliage, they heard the sound of a single horse approaching. The air around them was rife with tension as the knights prepared themselves for battle.

The horse drew closer.

Closer.

Then, from the dense green forest before them emerged a large black stallion and a rider who wore ill-fitting black armor that was covered by a solid black surcoat.

But what caught his attention most was the banner the rider bore that flapped in the breeze.

It was the same dark green color found in the plaids his brothers wore and in the center was an oak trunk with a heart and four swords piercing and uniting the two with the words STRENGTH IN FORTITUDE embroidered across it.

It was a banner he'd not seen since his childhood, only then it had borne four gold swords: one for Braden, Kieran, Lochlan and Ewan. Now the second-born sword was done in black, representing Kieran's death.

His heart pounded at the sight and in an instant he knew the small-framed form on the back of his horse.

It was Caledonia—the pride of her people, wearing his armor and brandishing the MacAllisters' banner.

She reined to a stop just outside the small copse of trees and removed her ill-fitting helm. Tucking it under her arm, she leveled a scowl on Henry that would have made any shrew envious.

"Greetings," she said proudly in an exact duplication of Sin's words when he had gone out to meet his king, "Henry Plantagenet, King of England. I am Caledonia, wife of Sin MacAllister, leader of the Clan MacNeely, and I have come to reclaim my husband from your custody."

The knights laughed at her. But Sin didn't. His love for her washed over him, and if he could, he would run to her and show her just how much he did love her at this moment.

Callie arched a queenly brow as Henry, too, laughed. "What is the meaning of this?" the king asked.

The tendrils of her coppery hair rustled with the breeze. "The meaning of this? It's actually simple. Either you release my husband to me or none of you will make it back to England intact."

Henry scoffed arrogantly at her threat. "And what can a simple girl do?"

Callie smiled coldly. "I was told, by my father, of St. Mary of Aragon who single-handedly brought down an entire Saracen army with nothing more than her faith in God. He also spoke of an ancient Celtic queen named Boudicca who brought Rome to her knees and burned London to the ground. He oft said that a woman was far more deadly as an enemy than a man, because men lead with their heads and women with their hearts. You can argue and win against another's head, but never against her heart."

Henry feigned a yawn as if her words bored him. "We've no time for this, woman. Now leave us."

"Perhaps I am not making my position clear." She gave a sharp whistle. The very forest around them came alive as man after man moved to stand in a circle around them.

A smile broke across Sin's face as he recognized the men.

There had to be seven score Highlanders of both the MacNeely and the MacAllister clans who stood ready to defend him.

Never in his life had he hoped to see one man stand by him—let alone an entire army of them.

He smiled as he saw his brothers standing with Dermot to the left of Callie.

A youth of ten-and-five ran to Callie, who handed him her banner. "As you can see, you are quite outnumbered. If you don't release my husband, then you will leave me no choice save to make your eldest son a very happy man this evening when he learns he is now king in your stead."

Henry's face went red in anger as he blustered at her audacity. It wasn't often anyone got the better of him, and Sin knew no woman had ever flummoxed him before. Not even Eleanor.

"You are willing to declare war for *him*?" Henry asked indignantly.

She didn't hesitate with her response. "I am. Are you?"

Sin closed his eyes as he heard the most precious words of his life. She who believed in nothing but peace was willing to fight for him. He could die happily knowing that.

Still, he couldn't let her do this. Henry would not rest until he buried her and her clan. A king's reputation was all he had, and if Henry lost face . . .

"Callie," Sin said, waiting until her gaze met his. "Thank you, but you can't do this. You can't start a war over me. I'm not worth the cost."

"You are worth everything to me."

He couldn't breathe as he heard those precious words. Dear saints, how he wanted to hold her and kiss those ripe lips that tasted of heaven. "For those feelings you hold, I thank God. But you must think through this. Look at the faces around you. They are your family."

"As are you."

Sin turned to see Fraser standing with his sword ready a few feet away from him. When the man spoke, Sin was stunned by his words. "You are a MacNeely and no one takes one of us without taking us all."

"Aye!" the roar of the clan was deafening.

"And you're a MacAllister," Lochlan added. "Born, bred and raised."

Tears welled in Sin's eyes. He'd never expected anything like this. Never.

"We will not be held hostage," Henry roared, then called for his men to stand ready.

The tension of the moment stretched out.

All of a sudden, Ewan shoved Dermot forward.

The boy stumbled, then regained his feet. He glared at Ewan, who was looking about innocently as if trying to find whoever had pushed him.

Straightening his clothes, Dermot walked slowly toward Henry.

"Dermot," Callie shouted, "get back here."

"Nay, sister," he said without looking back. He

kept his gaze locked on Henry as if afraid to look anywhere else lest he lose his courage. " 'Tis time I quit hiding behind others and took responsibility for myself."

Dermot stopped before Henry. "I am the Raider you seek. It was I who led my men against you."

By the look on Henry's face, Sin knew his thoughts. It was quite a blow to learn he had been thwarted all this time by a half-grown child. "You're just a boy."

Dermot nodded. "And a foolish one at that. Still, I can't allow an innocent man to die for me."

Henry was flabbergasted. "Are we to honestly believe a child led an army?"

Sin loudly cleared his throat.

Henry shifted in his saddle as he recalled all the battles Sin had fought and won in his name while less than two years older than Dermot.

Henry glanced at Sin, then returned his attention to Dermot. "Well, that explains why Sin wouldn't name you. He never could stand for a boy to suffer." Henry gestured toward Sin's direction. "Release the earl."

"Sire," Sin said as one of the guards cut the ropes on his wrists, "you know I can't let you kill him."

Henry bristled as if greatly offended by those words. "We are not so callous a king nor man that we would stoop to slay a child. Dear God, imagine the embarrassment if word ever got out that a mere child perpetrated such." Henry glanced around to his score of guards. "If any of you breathe a word of this, we shall have your tongues."

The guards gulped audibly.

Henry drew himself up and looked back at Dermot. "But he cannot be left to roam the countryside freely."

"What are you proposing?" Callie asked, moving closer to her brother.

"That he remain under royal custody until he is a score-and-five in age."

Both Callie's and Dermot's faces blanched.

"Simon?" Sin called, knowing of only one way he would agree to Henry's terms. He rubbed the circulation back into his hands as he walked slowly toward his wife.

What he really wanted to do was run, but even though the crowd was less tense than before, the men around him were still wary and ready to battle, and he didn't want anyone to mistake his intentions. "Think you Draven would welcome a new squire into his home?"

A slow smile spread across Simon's face. "Aye, he would."

Sin nodded in acknowledgment, then turned to face Henry. "Is that agreeable to you, Sire?"

"Aye," Henry said, his eyes filled with relief. "I believe Lord Draven would be quite capable of whipping the boy into shape. And you, Lady Laird, do you find that acceptable?"

Callie smiled. "I do indeed, Majesty."

"Draven?" Dermot asked. "Who is this man?"

Sin stopped in front of his wife and cupped her face in his hands as he stared into those lush green eyes. "He's brother to Simon and a friend of mine." He stroked her cheeks with his thumbs as he dropped his gaze to her lips.

Callie trembled at the look on Sin's face. His eyes were filled with such love and gratitude for her.

She'd been terrified every moment of his capture that they wouldn't get to him in time or that Henry would force them to battle.

Now that he stood before her, she felt as if she were the luckiest woman ever born.

She stood up on her tiptoes and leaned toward him.

He took her invitation. Crushing her to him, he kissed her hard and passionately.

A deafening cheer sounded from those gathered.

Callie surrendered her weight to her husband as joy burst through her. He was safe and they had their peace.

Sin savored the taste and feel of her lips. He didn't care if time stopped at this moment. All that mattered was the love he felt for his wife.

And the fact that at long last, he had a home and a people who accepted him.

His brothers and Simon gathered around as he reluctantly pulled back from Callie's lips.

Henry dismounted and moved toward them. His eyes amused, he measured Callie with his gaze. "You are a brazen woman, Lairdess. Think you we were rash in marrying you to such a pigheaded man?"

"Nay, Sire. For that I thank you."

Henry turned to Dermot and shook his head. "The Raider, eh? We see potential in you, boy. Come and let us tell you a story about a man called Malek in Ölüm."

Sin cringed as he watched Henry and Dermot walk off. So, it appeared his friend had found another generation to warp in his image. He would have to have a long talk with Henry.

But first he had a more important need to see to.

Ewan grabbed him from behind and picked him up in a ferocious hug. "Thank God you're alive. I thought I'd have to be tearing me some English hides and skinning me one young Scots buck."

For once Sin didn't protest his brother's bearish affection. "Aye, I saw the hand you gave poor Dermot. He's lucky you didn't break his leg."

"Me?" Ewan gasped. "I'm innocent."

Lochlan and Braden removed Ewan from him.

"Sin MacAllister?" Lochlan said. "I wasn't sure if I should laugh or curse when I heard you announce that." His eyes grew serious. "It's been a long time coming, my *braither*. Welcome home."

His brothers drew back to give him a moment with his wife.

Sin pulled her close and just reveled in the feel of her in his arms. "Thank you, Callie," he breathed.

"There's no need to thank me. You didn't really think I would let the king kill the man I love, did you?"

He took her hand in his and stared at the ring he had given her. His heart pounding at her words, he held it to his heart. "I love you, Callie ingen Neil, Lairdess of the MacNeelys and wife of a man who is so unworthy of you that he swears he will spend the rest of his life trying to show you just how much you mean to him."

She smiled at that. "There's no need to try, Sin. All I have to do is look into your eyes and I know." She kissed him deeply, then pulled him toward his horse. "Now come, husband, and let me take you home."

Sin closed his eyes at her words. For the first time in his life, he truly had a home.

Epilogue

Christmastide
A few months later

The great hall was warm in spite of the freezing snow outside and it was packed with Mac-Neelys who had come for the annual Christmas celebration Callie had warned him about. Music filled the hall as people sang, and Jamie ran about the hall with the rest of the clan's children.

Sin sat at the lord's table beside his wife, holding her hand as he stared at the merriment around him. He'd never expected to have a Christmas like this.

Even Dermot was there with Simon. Because of the season, Draven had procured permission from Henry to let the boy visit with them in Scotland so long as he remained under Simon's constant supervision. Draven would have come as well, but neither he nor Emily had wanted to risk exposing their infant son to the harsh climate of the Scottish Highlands. But in the spring, they would bring Dermot and their new babe for another visit.

"Should we send someone out to look for your brothers?" Callie asked.

Sin shook his head. "I am sure they are fine. No doubt the weather has slowed them a bit, but I expect them to join us at any time."

Callie watched her husband watch her people. He'd become so relaxed these months past. Gone was the harsh, guarded man, and in his place was someone she learned to love more with every passing day.

She covered their joined hands with her other and just reveled in the feel of his strength in her palm.

The doors opened, ushering in a torrent of swirling snow and six bundled figures. By the height of three of them, she knew it must be her brothers-in-law.

Before she could rise to greet them, one of the shorter visitors threw back her cowl and revealed a beautiful older woman with striking black hair. Callie would have thought nothing of it had she not felt her husband go tense.

She looked to see hatred in his eyes as he stared at the small woman. Instantly she knew who this woman was. Aisleen.

Why would his stepmother come here?

The men removed their cloaks and Callie recognized Braden's wife, Maggie, and their infant daughter, Ada, who was snuggled in her mother's arms, as well as Kieran's son, Connor.

All of them stayed in the foyer, tense, as Aisleen moved forward.

Sin couldn't breathe or move as he watched his

stepmother approach. His head rang with all the insults she'd ever dealt him.

Aisleen looked first to Callie and offered her a smile, then she turned her gaze to Sin and the smile faded.

They sat in total stillness as they held each other's full attention. For the first time in his life, he saw something other than hatred in her eyes. Strangely enough, he saw guilt and remorse.

Aisleen drew a ragged breath. "Well," she said quietly. "This is even more awkward than I had thought it would be. So let me say my piece and then you can have the satisfaction of seeing me thrown out of your hall."

Her words stunned him so much that he couldn't have responded to them had he wanted to.

"I was very wrong in the way I treated you, lad. I won't even try to make excuses for it. But I was a very young lass and heartbroken. More than that, I was a fool to blame a child for something not his fault."

She gave him a tender look that surprised and stunned him. "I know you don't believe this, but many a night I have lain awake wishing I could have done things differently where you were concerned."

"You owe me nothing, my lady," Sin said.

"Aye, but I do. When you were burned and staying with us, I wanted to tell you then how I felt, but every time I tried, I turned coward." She placed the wrapped gift in her hands on the table before them. "Merry Christmas to you both, and congratulations on your marriage." She smiled at Callie. "I hope you'll be giving him all the love I should have."

Then she turned and headed for the door.

Sin watched her walk away, his feelings tangled and confused. His wife reached for the present and opened it.

"Sin?"

He looked from his stepmother to the MacAllister banner in his wife's hands and his heart lurched.

Instead of four swords, it now held five. And in Callie's hand was the small note card that was embellished with Aisleen's crisp, clear script: *For Sin MacAllister.*

He looked to his brothers and Maggie, who watched him expectantly as their mother crossed the room.

"Aisleen," he said before he could stop himself.

She stopped and turned back to face him.

Sin left the table and went to stand before her. "I learned a long time ago to forget my past. Granted, there have been times when that was easier said than done, but I am not one to dwell on old hurts. You are welcome in my hall, my lady."

Tears filled her eyes as she stared at him. "You'll never know how much I wish I had shared your compassion. I am sure many are the times you'd wished I had said those words to you."

Sin said nothing. He had no idea what to say.

Then she did the most unexpected thing of all. Aisleen reached out and hugged him.

Sin stood frozen in shock.

She patted his back, then released him. Looking up at him, she wrinkled her nose and did something no one ever had before. . . .

She reached up and straightened his hair and

clothes like a mother worried about her son's appearance. "There," she said, patting his arm. "I didn't mean to muss you up."

Sin laughed as his brothers, wife and Maggie joined them. Servants brought drinks for the family and they adjourned back to the table, where they dined in pleasant company and love.

Hours later, when everyone was fed and well sated, the servants distributed the gifts.

Sin gratefully took the one from Callie. It wasn't very large and when he opened it, he frowned.

"I must have Ada's by mistake," he said, noting the tiny white baby shoes.

He started to hand them to Maggie, but Callie stopped him. "Now, I know what a generous man you are, Sin MacAllister, but don't be giving those away when we'll be needing them come summer."

His jaw went slack as his mind made sense of her words. "You're with child?"

Biting her lip, she nodded.

Sin shouted in joy as he pulled her into his lap, then quickly apologized for it. "I didn't hurt you or the baby, did I?"

She laughed at him. "Nay, love. I'm sure if he's anything like his father, he's quite indestructible."

Lochlan stood with a cup of wine in his hand. "To Callie and Sin. May this be the first of many little treasures to come."

Sin drank to the toast, then handed his cup to his wife and watched as she drank from it. "You know, my lady, they say drinking wine from a man's cup is a good way to find yourself carrying his child."

She kissed him gently on the lips. "I'm afraid we're too late for that."

"Oh, for God's sake," Simon said, placing his hand over Jamie's eyes. "Would you two please adjourn upstairs? Every time I turn around I find the two of you locked together, and I just got my stomach settled."

Sin laughed at that. "Och now, we can't be having Simon's stomach upset while there's food to be had, now, can we?"

Callie shook her head, but her smile interrupted the serious gesture.

"Very well then, good night, my family. Sleep well and we shall see you in the morning." Sin stood, then swung her up in his arms and carried her toward the stairs.

Behind him, he could hear his brothers wagering.

"Five marks they don't appear until late morning," Ewan said.

"Ten for noon," Lochlan joined.

"She's pregnant," Braden said. "I'll wager ten for early morning."

A soft, feminine laugh rang out. "Men," Maggie said. "Aisleen, what say you? My money is on late afternoon."

"Aye. Most definitely."